Bitter Truth

Bitter Truth

A Bitter Roots Mystery

C.J. Carmichael

Bitter Truth

Tule Publishing First Printing, February 2018

The Tule Publishing Group, LLC

First Publication by Tule Publishing Group 2018

ISBN: 978-1-948342-48-3

Chapter One

BY MIDNIGHT IT would be done. Irrevocable. There was no reason to feel guilt.

The old woman had lived a long life on the land she loved, and she was leaving behind two sons and three grandchildren to carry on her legacy. If she'd been a different sort of woman she could have relaxed and enjoyed her golden years. But Lacy Stillman was a strong, interfering, opinionated person. And so she had to go.

Tuesday, November 21

ZAK WALLER WAS at the coffee machine when the call came in to the Lost Trail, Montana, Sheriff's Office. He'd been about to offer a refill to Deputy Nadine Black, mainly to see if she'd stop communing with her laptop and actually look at him—something she'd avoided doing since she showed up at work two hours ago.

Zak abandoned his mug and leapt over a box of evidence from their last big case to grab the phone. "You've reached 911, what's your emergency?" He grabbed his notepad and pen, ready for whatever was to come.

Deputy Black was also priming for action. In her case this involved checking her gun and slipping it into her holster.

The man on the line said, "Not sure it's an emergency. I didn't know who else to call."

Zak had heard that voice before but no address or name had popped up on the display. Probably the caller was using a cell phone.

"Your name?"

"Oh, right. Eugene Stillman. I'm at my mother's house."

Zak had no trouble placing the caller then. The Stillmans owned the largest ranch in the county, and Eugene's mother, Lacy Stillman, was the wealthiest woman around. Eugene was her eldest son.

"Mom didn't show up at the barn this morning. She's never late. I knew something was wrong, but I figured…I figured she'd caught a bug. I never guessed…"

His voice sounded like it was grinding through gravel until it finally choked to a stop. Zak waited for the tough, old rancher to get control. For men like Eugene it was weak to show emotion.

"I found Mom in her bed. Dead."

"You check her breathing? Her pulse?"

"She's already cold. Must have had a heart attack. I didn't know whether to call 911 or Doc Pittman."

"You did the right thing, Eugene. I'm sorry for your loss. Are you alone at the house?"

"Yeah. I need to tell my wife and my brother. But I thought I should report the death first."

"Definitely. We'll handle things from our end now. Call your family and get someone to come over and keep you company while you wait for the paramedics to arrive."

"What's the story?" Nadine Black towered over his desk, vibrating with anticipation of a juicy emergency. The fitness she'd gained in her years of competing in barrel racing still showed in every muscle of her body.

"Lacy Stillman had a heart attack in bed last night." A part of him was still absorbing the news. Just yesterday she'd invited him for a beer after her annual checkup with Doc Pittman. It wasn't like they were drinking buddies or anything. He just happened to cross her path at the right time. She felt like celebrating, she said.

And now she was dead.

Nadine deflated, dropped back on her heels. "I take it this Lacy Stillman was old?"

"If you call ninety-one old."

Nadine acknowledged the humor with an almost-smile. "Even if ninety is the new eighty, it's still old."

Encouraged by the moment of rapport, Zak considered asking her about last night, why she hadn't shown up at the Dew Drop as planned. But she was already back at her desk.

He eyed the stiff set of her shoulders a few seconds longer, then dialed Doc Pittman, the county coroner.

"Sorry to hear that," the doctor said after Zak delivered

the news. "I know Lacy was old, but she was one of those people you expect to live forever."

"That's for sure. I ran into her after her appointment with you yesterday. She was pretty pumped. Said she had a great checkup."

"Lacy had more energy than someone half her age. And no obvious health issues. But there are no guarantees once you reach your nineties. Send the paramedics out to the ranch, Zak. I'll do my exam here at my office."

Zak wanted to argue the point, for reasons that were slowly coalescing in his mind, but he was just the dispatcher. So he did as instructed.

Once the paramedics were on their way, he went for the coffee he was craving now more than ever. He had work to do but thoughts of Lacy wouldn't leave him alone. "I saw her yesterday."

Nadine glanced up from her computer screen. The old radiators clicked and clunked, the sounds loud in the quiet office. Sheriff Ford was in Missoula for the day and Deputy Butterfield was patrolling the Bitterroot Forest Preserve. Not much else was going on. A normal state of affairs in this sleepy corner of Montana.

"You talking about the old woman who died?"

He ignored the marked lack of interest in Nadine's tone. "Lacy was leaving the medical clinic when I was on my way home. She insisted on buying me a beer at the Dew Drop. Said she wanted to celebrate."

Lacy had been dressed like a rodeo queen with her hand-tooled boots and fitted shearling coat. Petite and sprightly, with alert, bright eyes and an I-love-life smile. No one would guess Lacy was in her nineties. She still led cattle drives every spring and fall and volunteered for the 4-H club.

"Lacy told me she got a clean bill of health and a vitamin K shot for good measure. She figured she was going to live another decade for sure."

Nadine gave him the sort of condescending look he used to get daily from his older brothers. "There are no guarantees when you're ninety-one."

Which is what the doctor had said. "It's kind of sad, is all."

She waved her hand. "You're too soft-hearted for this job."

Really? A few weeks ago she'd given him hell for not applying for a deputy position. Now she questioned whether he could handle the dispatcher role—a job previously held by Rose Newman, whose main skill, as far as Zak could tell, had been crocheting doilies for every wooden surface in the office.

On Zak's first day on the job, the sheriff had tossed those doilies. "Hope you don't crochet, Waller."

Zak had smiled at what he assumed was a joke. That was before he realized the sheriff had zero sense of humor.

Unlike Lacy who had an excellent one. Her eyes had sparkled with mischief when she told him her sons were going to be thrilled the doc had green-lighted her continued active involvement on the ranch.

The irony was obvious. It was no secret around town that Lacy's old-fashioned ideas about ranching drove both Eugene and Clayton crazy.

Then there was the more recent disagreement about selling off a small portion of land to a real estate developer, which Zak had only learned about last night.

"The timing of her death sure is convenient for her sons."

"Yeah?" Nadine glanced from him back to her computer, a not-too-subtle hint that she had work to do. But she played along. "How so?"

"I overheard a couple out-of-towners talking about the Lazy S at the Dew Drop last night."

Nadine dropped her gaze when he mentioned the pub.

Huh. She wasn't even going to offer an excuse for blowing him off. "These guys were talking about a meeting they had with the Stillman family that morning—*yesterday* morning—trying to convince them to sell off a fifty-acre parcel of land along the river. Apparently the sons were all for it, but Lacy vetoed the deal."

Nadine straightened, her gaze a little keener than it had been before. "What do they want the land for?"

"A big operation out of California wants to invest in a luxury resort. They'd promote skiing in the winter and fly-fishing in the summer."

"How much land do the Stillmans own?"

"About eighty thousand acres."

Nadine whistled. "Who the hell owns that much land? They'd hardly miss fifty acres."

"You wouldn't think. But it would be a matter of principle with Lacy. Land is everything to old-time ranchers like her. Besides the decision to sell a bit of land could be a slippery slope, making it easier to divest a few more acres the next time an offer presented itself."

"You're not seriously suggesting her sons somehow managed to give her a heart attack so they could do this deal?"

Was he? Zak didn't know the answer himself. But... "When the richest woman in the county dies a day after she blocked her family from making a cool million or two...don't you think questions should be asked?"

Nadine regarded him for a long moment, then slowly shook her head. "Sheriff Ford will never okay opening an investigation."

Just last month the boss had practically crushed Nadine for taking too much initiative. She was learning to keep her place.

"No, he won't open an investigation." Especially since Eugene and Clayton were generous supporters of his campaign and election time was around the corner.

If Zak wanted to clear his conscience where Lacy Stillman's death was concerned, he was going to have to find the answers himself.

×

JUSTIN PITTMAN GLANCED in his rearview mirror. Geneva, his four-year-old adopted daughter, was in her booster seat, idly playing with a Rubik's Cube his father had given her at their last Sunday dinner.

"Dad, are we going to do Thanksgiving this year?"

"We'll have a turkey dinner with Grandpa. Is that what you mean?"

"And pumpkin pie? And trimmings?"

"Would you like that?"

"I think so. I've never had pumpkin pie. But I like trimmings. Can they be pink? Can we put them all over the dining room?"

Justin laughed. Thank God for this little girl in his life. Not many things could have made him laugh after the news he'd just been given.

"You can do all the trimming you want, honey."

"We never did Thanksgiving with Mommy and Paul."

Almost two weeks had passed since Willow, his wife and Geneva's mother, had left them, to return to her jet-setting life with Paul, Geneva's biological father.

Justin worried about the effect being abandoned by her mother would have on Geneva. He did his best to explain and reassure but it was impossible to guess what was going on inside his daughter's head.

She simply didn't talk about her mom.

But the last few days she was doing more smiling and chatting. Hopefully his father was correct about children being amazingly resilient.

"Grandpa and I always celebrate Thanksgiving," he said in answer to Geneva's question. Most often friends invited them out for the holiday. Last year they'd spent it with the Mastersons who always put on a big spread for the entire staff of Raven Farms, their family's Christmas tree operation.

This year, though, Justin wanted to celebrate in his own home. It was time to build Pittman traditions for Geneva.

Though God only knew how long he'd be around to maintain them.

On the drive to Missoula this morning he'd been worried, but at least he had hope.

Then it had been his turn to step into the doctor's office. A kindly nurse offered to keep an eye on Geneva, who had a bag of toys and a snack to keep her occupied.

As soon as Justin saw the oncologist's compressed lips, his hope had been stripped away. Listening to the results of his test, and the treatment options left to him, had felt like facing a corrupt judge as he capriciously ruled against him.

Not fair, dammit, not fair. They told him the cancer was gone. He'd beaten it. How could it be back, so soon?

People need me. My father. My young daughter. I can't be sick. I can't...die.

Justin had sat, still and quiet, as his thoughts and emotions stormed inside of him. He guessed his eyes must have looked blank because the doctor put a hand on his shoulder and repeated all the key points.

Eventually the words sunk in.

There was a real chance that by the time next Thanksgiving rolled around Justin wouldn't be here anymore.

A bunch of things had to go right to prevent that from happening.

A stem-cell donor had to be found. The transplant had to be successful. He had to be spared any of the life-threatening complications that claimed a scary percentage of patients with his form of lymphoma.

Justin wanted to live for his own sake. He wanted to travel. Maybe one day find true love.

Even more he needed to live for Geneva—verbally, and possibly physically, abused by her father, abandoned by her mother. He was all she had now. If something happened to him, where would she go? She loved her grandpa, but it wasn't fair to expect a busy doctor nearing retirement to become the guardian of a little girl.

"Daddy, do you want to marry Debbie-Ann?"

"What?" Geneva ought to be a baseball player—she was great at throwing curves. What had made her think of her caregiver at Little Cow Pokes?

"Ashley doesn't have a daddy. My mommy is gone. If you and Ashley's mom got married then we could be a real family."

"Well." Since he couldn't think of a response, he countered, “Is that something you would like?”

“It was Ashley’s idea. She said we could be sisters.”

He hoped Debbie-Ann hadn’t planted the idea. He didn’t need those sorts of complications in his life. Especially now.

“Sometimes having a good friend is almost as fun as having a sister. And I can’t marry anyone—I’m still married to your mom.”

“Oh.” Geneva puckered her lips as she digested all that.

His phone rang then, a call from his father. The car’s Bluetooth picked it up. “Hi, Dad. Geneva and I are on our way back from a shopping trip to Missoula.” This was true, as they had stopped at the mall after his doctor’s appointment.

His dad said hello to Geneva, then his tone deepened and lowered. “I wanted to let you know Lacy Stillman passed on last night. Eugene found her in her bed this morning.”

“Oh no.” It was odd how upsetting the news felt. Lacy had been ninety-one, which was pretty damn old. But she was one of the most life-loving women he knew. Only a few weeks ago she’d driven through town in search of homes for an unexpected batch of puppies, which was how he had come to adopt Dora. “Was it a heart attack?”

“I’m just about to do my examination, but I expect so. The family is making arrangements for a celebration of life on Wednesday.”

“Tomorrow? That’s fast.”

"I guess they didn't want the public event looming over them during the holidays. The plan is to have a family-only graveside ceremony on Sunday."

"I know she was old, but I'm sorry. Lacy was one of my favorite clients." Never a dull moment with Lacy. She'd been forever changing her will when one of her sons did something to annoy her. No doubt Eugene and Clayton would be anxious to hear the details of that will now, since Lacy had been strict about keeping it secret.

After the call he was silently processing the news when his daughter piped up.

"Is the lady who gave us Dora dead?"

Justin flashed another glance at the rearview mirror. Geneva was only four but she didn't miss a trick. "I'm afraid so. She was very old."

He hoped Geneva wouldn't stew over the news. Even though she'd never met Lacy, sometimes just the idea of death could be upsetting.

"Can we have pizza for dinner?"

Some of the day's heaviness lifted at the simple request. In the weeks and months ahead there would be difficult conversations with those he loved, tough decisions, operations, pain and worry.

But tonight he could have pizza with his daughter.

"You bet we can."

He gave the voice command to dial Lolo's Pizza and caught himself before he asked for "the usual." Now that

Willow was gone, no one was going to eat the sundried tomato and artichoke pizza that had been her favorite. "One small cheese and one medium supreme, please."

"Sure, Justin, your order will be up in fifteen minutes."

"Perfect. Thanks."

He was driving by Raven Christmas Tree Farm now, acres and acres of perfect trees, growing in perfect rows. He caught a glimpse of the family's log home and wondered how Tiffany, just a few years younger than him, was adjusting to living with her aunt and mother after so many years on her own in Seattle.

It couldn't be easy, especially given the family's tragic history.

And then he was back in the town limits, driving by the street where Willow had grown up. She hadn't been in contact since she left, so he had no idea where she was, or what she was doing.

Probably she and Paul were out of the country, traveling in some exotic locale. The fact that Justin and Willow were still legally married probably didn't bother either of them.

With hindsight Justin had no doubt Willow had come back to Lost Trail—and to him—looking for a responsible parent so she could ditch her daughter. He couldn't judge her too harshly, though, since his reasons for going into the marriage hadn't been particularly noble either.

Having undergone radiation treatments that could affect his chances of ever fathering a child, he'd seen this as an opportunity to have a daughter—and to make his own dad a grandfather. The fact that Geneva wasn't Justin's biological child didn't matter. He loved her as much as if she were. And his father did, too.

No, he could never regret adopting Geneva.

He just prayed he would be around long enough to raise her.

WHEN TIFF MASTERSON'S ex-boyfriend's name popped up on her cell phone, she hesitated before opening the message. Six months had passed since his name had appeared in her notifications. Six months since she'd cheated on him. Six months since he'd said he never wanted to see her again.

Why was he reaching out now?

Did he have more anger to get off his chest? She wasn't sure she could cope with that.

Did he want to get back together? She wasn't sure she could cope with that, either.

She pushed aside the stack of invoices and glanced out the window of her father's study. Her dad had been dead for sixteen years and she still thought of this room as his. Just last week she had moved some of the farm records from the office in the barn to the house. Now she was glad she had.

Not only was the weather cold, but the bleak November landscape was not inspiring either. Brown grass and bare trees and a low, muted sun. Once the leaves were all gone and before the snow arrived had to be the ugliest time of year on their Christmas tree farm. It was hard not to miss the warmth of the West Coast and the evergreen appeal of Seattle.

Her finger hovered over the miniature photo of Craig's face. Maybe it would be wiser to un-friend him and cut this final tie. Before she could decide, the landline rang. Knowing her aunt was visiting friends in Hamilton and her mom rarely answered the phone, Tiff dashed to the kitchen.

A row of white linen napkins—folded into fancy fans—were on the table, ready for the Thanksgiving feast. Her mother was carefully printing names onto cardboard place holders. She gave Tiff a vague smile as the phone rang for the third time.

"Want me to get that?" Tiff asked, trying not to feel annoyed.

"If you want."

Her mother had taken a calligraphy course a long time ago but today she was struggling with each letter. It hurt to watch and Tiff turned with relief to the phone. "Hello."

"Is that you, Tiff? How are you, honey?"

"I'm good, thanks." Sybil Tombe was the town librarian and one of her mother's oldest and dearest friends. Actually, thanks to her mother's prolonged depression, Sybil was her mother's *only* friend now.

Tiff missed her brother and father, too. But what was

happening to her mother had gone beyond mourning.

When she was eighteen Tiff couldn't wait to leave home. Now that she was thirty she worried she had been too selfish. Clearly her mother had mental health issues. Tiff owed it to both her mother and her aunt to try and help.

"I wanted to let your mom know Lacy Stillman died in her sleep last night," Sybil said.

News of death, even of someone very old, was always disconcerting. "I'm sorry to hear that." Lacy was an institution in this town. She and Tiff's grandmother Holmes were once good friends. According to Aunt Marsha the two matriarchs concocted a scheme to get one of the Stillman boys to marry one of the Holmes girls.

It hadn't worked. Rosemary, Tiff's mother and the youngest of the Holmes daughters, married Irving Masterson, a man she met in college, while Marsha never married at all.

"The celebration of life is already scheduled for tomorrow. And there'll be a potluck at Lacy's ranch house afterward."

"Thanks for letting me know. I'll make sure Mom gets there."

There was a hesitation. And then: "Your mom looked worn out after Riley Concurran's service. Maybe you should skip the church and take your mom to pay her respects later in the evening."

Tiff glanced at her mother who was lining up the folded

napkins at the center of the long, hickory dining table. It was true that Riley Concurran's death—ruled homicide in the end—had taken a lot out of her mother. Riley had been one of the farm's temporary workers, a recent hire whose tragic past led her to an unfair and untimely end.

"Maybe you're right. We'll see you tomorrow evening."

After the call ended, Tiff went to the dining room to help her mother. "Do you want me to set out the plates and cutlery?"

"No, dear. I'll do it."

"I can pull them out of the cabinet at least." The blue-trimmed Wedgewood plates were as familiar to her as the color of her mother's eyes. She set a stack of them on the corner of the table where it would be easy for her mom to reach them.

"Did you hear me talking to Sybil? Lacy Stillman died last night."

Her mother's hands stilled and for a moment she was like a statue, shrinking into herself. "More death. I hate it."

"Lacy was very old. And it sounds like she didn't suffer."

"No. It's always the ones left behind who do that."

Chapter Two

Wednesday, November 22

ZAK DROVE HIS old truck through a log entry gate. Hanging from the overhead beam was the ranch brand: a circle with a sideways "S." Artistically speaking the S could represent the west fork of the Bitterroot River, which wound through the property. It also looked like a snake.

Pretty much all the land before him, stretching to the Bitterroot Mountains, belonged to the Stillmans. Kind of awe-inspiring to a guy who didn't even own his own home yet. One day soon he would, though. Every month he saved more than half his paycheck. After three years at the sheriff's office he had enough for a good down payment. All he needed was to find the right place.

On the passenger seat of his truck was a plastic-wrapped plate of freshly baked chocolate chip cookies. Tradition in this part of the world was to bring gifts of food when making bereavement calls. And since his work had kept him from the celebration of life, that's what Zak was doing.

If he happened to reach a deeper understanding of the circumstances under which Lacy Stillman had died…well, that would be a bonus, but nothing he'd ever admit to his boss or colleagues.

If he told anyone he didn't feel right about Lacy's death, they'd laugh him out of town. That didn't change his need to find answers. He was used to thinking differently from other people, especially his parents and older brothers, who fortunately no longer lived in Lost Trail, or Montana for that matter.

Zak steered his Ford around a curve in the graveled road, then to the top of a rise. On impulse, he pulled over and shifted into Park. From this vantage point he could see all three of the main ranch houses. Each sat on about an acre of land with ponderosa pine and quaking aspens between them. The original ranch house, the one in the middle, was where Lacy Stillman had lived, alone since the death of her husband. Built of log, timber and rock, it was a modestly sized, L-shaped home with a small front porch and a vegetable patch to one side.

The house to the right looked like one of those fancy lodge-styled homes advertised in slick magazines. The materials used were the same as Lacy's, but the windows were massive and the roof sloped at a deep pitch to allow for a generous second story. The views would be fabulous from up there.

Lacy's younger son Clayton lived in this impressive house along with his glamorous wife Vanessa and daughter Nikki. Nikki had been two grades behind Zak in school, a plain-looking girl who was involved in 4-H and loved horses.

The third house was a ranch-styled bungalow. The various shades of gray and tan in the cedar-shake roof suggested a lot of patching had happened recently. The paint on the white picket fence surrounding a dried-up garden was badly flaked and he could tell from here some of the windows had lost their seal. This less-than-immaculate home was Eugene and Em's and the only one Zak had previously visited. Their son Tom was two years older than Zak, but Luke was the same age.

Luke, as well as his brother, had been one of the cool kids when they were growing up. He and Zak hadn't hung out together on weekends, but they'd become friends when they both joined the track and field team. Since graduation they saw each other rarely, but Luke always invited Zak to the family's awesome New Year's Eve parties.

From those occasions Zak knew the inside of the house, a lot like the exterior, showed signs of neglect. No one in Luke's family seemed to care much about decorating or housekeeping. For the party the main rooms were usually presentable but last year Zak had spotted a fluffy layer of dust on the bookshelves in the office next to the bathroom.

Three houses. Three very different families.

Zak pulled back onto the road and began the descent into the valley. He passed another signed gateway and his tires rumbled over the metal cattle guard meant to keep livestock on the correct side of the fence. He parked at the end of a line-up of vehicles, behind Dr. Pittman's sedan. He grabbed the plate of cookies, and then made his way to the front entry.

The sun had set in the minutes he'd taken to survey the property and through the uncurtained windows he could see the place was packed. The murmur of multiple conversations, occasional bursts of laughter, and the aroma of chili and corn bread all leached from Lacy Stillman's home.

His mouth watered. The grilled chicken breast and spinach salad he'd eaten for dinner had nothing on this. Since he was training to run another marathon this spring, he had to watch his weight. But he had a feeling tonight he would give in to temptation.

The front door was ajar so he didn't bother knocking. No one would hear him anyway. Right away he spotted Luke, hanging out near the entrance with his older brother, Tom, and younger cousin, Nikki. They had beers in hand and were talking over one another in heated debate.

Tom and Luke were medium height, narrow-hipped men, with skin still dark from the hot summer just past. Tom had a huskier build, and a good twenty pounds on his brother.

Nikki, Lacy's only granddaughter, wasn't dressed up for the occasion. She was in jeans and her brown hair hung in a braid over one shoulder.

Nikki was the first to spot him and stop talking. When she smiled, the guys turned to see what had silenced her.

"Hey, Zak." Luke stepped forward, clasped his shoulder and shook his hand. "Nice of you to stop by."

"Yeah, well, thought I'd pay my respects. Your grandmother was an institution in this town."

"In the family, too." Tom's handshake was firmer than his brother's.

His words to Zak sounded a little bitter, or was he reading too much into them?

"Is that for us?" Nikki nodded at the plate.

"Yeah. Just some cookies." He handed them over.

"They're still warm. And they smell fabulous. I'm glad you didn't bring another casserole. I'll put them on the dessert table for you."

"Thanks." Zak turned back to the brothers. "Sorry I missed the church service. I was working."

"No problem," Luke said.

He probably wasn't missed. Zak was used to blending into the background. It had been a survival habit in a household where his dad could turn from jovial to furious in a second. His older brothers had literally rolled with the punches until they were old enough to fight back.

Zak had preferred to make himself scarce.

"I bet the church was packed?"

"Standing room only," Tom said. "Grams would have been smiling."

"It went okay. I am not looking forward to the family burial on Sunday, though."

"Oh, Luke, are you going to cry?" Tom winked at Zak. "Luke and Nikki were Grandma's favorites. Bet they both get more in the will than me."

"Shut up, Tom. Who cares what's in the stupid will? Sometimes it seems like that's all anyone in this family talks about."

"Chill, man. Zak, help yourself to a brewski. They're in the kitchen."

The front door opened again, admitting Zak's old school friend Tiff Masterson and her mother, Rosemary, and Aunt Marsha. Zak caught Tiff's eye and gestured that they would talk later. Then he left the Stillman brothers to welcome their new guests.

In the kitchen Tom and Luke's mother, Em, offered him a beer. She looked uncomfortable in a black dress that strained around her middle and gaped awkwardly at the neck. She was also shifting from one foot to the other, a lot. Zak guessed her modest high heels were to blame.

"Sorry for your family's loss, Em," he said. Judging from her puffy eyes and the tissue peeking out from the edge of one long sleeve, she was in genuine mourning.

Em looked at him, bewildered.

"I'm Zak Waller. A friend of Luke's."

"Oh, yes, you're my son's track and field friend. Did you know Luke started running again?"

"No, I hadn't heard."

"Lacy considered running a strange hobby for a rancher's

son, but she indulged him. Luke could never do wrong in his grandmother's eyes."

"I imagine it's helpful to stay fit when you work on a ranch."

Em's lips tightened. "It's so hard to imagine this place without Lacy. Over the years she's stepped away from most of the hands-on work. But she still made it out to the barns every morning. Led the cattle drives. Made all the key decisions."

"No doubt it'll be an adjustment." According to Luke, his mom's philosophy on ranching was a lot closer to Lacy's than her husband Eugene's was. In most ranching decisions Luke would side with his mother, and Tom with their dad.

Not that it mattered when Lacy was alive, since she made the final call. But now that she was gone it *would* matter. A lot.

"I had a beer with Lacy when she was in town last week. She mentioned how lucky she felt to live and work so close to her family. I'm sure you'll miss her very much, but at least you know she had a good, long life."

"We will miss her. Definitely. And she did have a good life, particularly after her husband died."

The comment struck Zak as odd. "How long ago was that?"

"It's been sixteen years since Jack died in a ranching accident. A long time. But Lacy sure wasn't ready to join him. Her father didn't die until he was ninety-eight and her mother lived to be one hundred and one."

Interesting. Eugene and Clayton had probably expected to live under their mother's thumb for another ten years.

Behind him Marsha Holmes was waiting for her turn to talk to Em, so Zak stepped aside, joining the line-up at the buffet table. Besides chili and corn bread there were assorted salads, pickles, freshly baked buns, and a variety of sliced meats and cheeses.

He took some of the chili and corn bread then moved out of the way. While he was spooning back some of the spicy chili, an old friend of his father's came over to commiserate about the shutting down of Zak's father's hardware store.

"Sign of the times, when our small-town businesses fail," the man said. "Now we have to drive all the way to Hamilton when something breaks down."

It was a shame, Zak agreed, though he did not miss one thing about working at the old family business. Or the family that had owned it, either.

Once he was finished eating, Zak paid his respects to both Eugene and Clayton. They were standing in the far corner of the living room, Clayton a few feet in front of his brother, and seeming more in the spotlight.

The brothers were so similar in appearance they could have been twins. Clayton, however, besides being more outgoing, was also better dressed. In his suit, shirt and tie he looked more like a banker than a rancher.

"Zak Waller." Clayton clasped Zak's hand between both of his warm, callused palms. "Sure do miss your dad's hardware store in town. Any thoughts of starting up a business of your own one day?"

"No, sir. Going to stick to working for the sheriff's office."

He wasn't sure Clayton heard his answer. He was already shaking the hand of another visitor. Zak stepped further into the corner where Eugene was taking long gulps from a tall crystal glass containing a deep amber liquid—and no ice.

Eugene wore a western-styled blazer and black jeans. His bolo tie was on crooked. It didn't seem appropriate to point this out, however.

"Sorry for your loss, Eugene. Our town won't be the same without your mother."

Eugene said a gruff thank-you then took another drink from his glass.

Obviously not in a chatting mood.

Well. He'd done his duty, made his rounds. There was still Clayton's wife Vanessa, holding court at the other end of the room, next to the dessert table. Like her husband, she was dressed and groomed impeccably. She certainly looked more at ease in her black dress and heels than Em. But Zak was sure she wouldn't have a clue who he was so he gave her a pass.

Zak set down his empty beer and went in search of a toilet. "There's only one bathroom," Luke told him. "Down the hall and first door on the left."

The door was locked and Zak had to wait for a turn. Once he was inside, he took a quick look around then opened the medicine cabinet above the sink.

The contents were sparse and dull. Toothpaste, deodorant and a few small vials of makeup on one shelf. Below that was a box of Band-Aids, a tube of ointment for dry hands, and a bottle of cod liver oil tablets.

The medicine cabinet of a healthy person. He wasn't finding any answers here.

JUSTIN BROUGHT FLOWERS to the Stillmans' house the night of the potluck. Eugene and Clayton would have appreciated a bottle of bourbon more, but he wasn't sure their wives would deem that gift appropriate. Nikki greeted him at the door and took the flowers, and then Tom invited him into the kitchen for a drink and some food.

Justin wasn't much older than Lacy's grandchildren—who ranged in age from mid-twenties to thirty-one—but they seemed so much younger to him.

So far not one of them had gone to college or married let alone had children. Lacy had complained about that a lot during their regular meetings to discuss her will and other ranch business.

He'd told her things were different for this generation.

Millennials weren't in a rush to do the whole marriage and children thing.

"Well who's going to run the Lazy S fifty years from now?" Lacy had demanded. "That's what I care about."

It was a valid question, one Justin wished she had an answer to before she'd gone to her grave. He still couldn't quite believe she was gone. He kept expecting to feel her hand on his arm, thanking him for coming, or hear her voice offering him a drink.

But it was her daughter-in-law, Em, pouring libations this evening. She had a crowd around her at the moment, so Justin veered toward the family room where he found his father in conversation with Zak by the fireplace.

Watching from a distance he noted his dad's gray complexion and the dark bags under his eyes. For years his father hadn't changed. Lately he'd begun showing his age. Justin wondered if he ever thought about retirement—or wished his son had studied medicine so he could take his place.

But if he did, he never spoke those thoughts aloud.

Justin dreaded the effect the news about his cancer was going to have on his dad. Unfortunately there was no way to spare him this time. His dad would have to be told, and soon. As would Geneva. And his clients. And his friends.

The prospect was utterly depressing.

"Hey, Dad. Zak." He rested his left hand on his father's shoulder and reached out to shake Zak's hand with his right. "Looks like you're having a serious conversation."

Zak Waller was an enigma to Justin. He was too bright for his administrative job as dispatcher, yet seemed in no hurry to apply to be a deputy. Justin knew his father liked Zak. In fact he credited him with solving the Riley Concurran homicide case a few weeks ago.

"We were talking about Lacy," Justin's father said. "Zak said it was nice that she died without suffering, and it's true, a heart attack is a faster way to go than, say, cancer."

Cancer. The word hit him like a punch to the heart and Justin froze, a look of indifference to his face like a tight mask, so his expression wouldn't give him away.

"Did she die in her sleep?" Zak asked.

"I'm pretty certain she did. One odd thing though. She was still dressed in her regular clothes, even though she was under the covers. I'm guessing she felt too unwell to change into her nightgown when she went to bed."

Zak frowned. "She wasn't sick when I had a beer with her after her checkup with you. She seemed very healthy then."

"That's true. She was. But you can never tell when a person gets to be that old."

Justin studied the painting over the fireplace. It was a beautiful oil of a rancher on his horse, next to a herd of longhorned cattle. You never can tell when a person is young, either, he wanted to say.

"I wonder how the family will cope now that she's gone?" Zak said.

"Lacy had her own ideas about ranching. I'm sure Clayton and Eugene will want to modernize," Justin's father said.

"I'd bet money on it," Justin agreed. Maybe Lacy's family truly was grieving her loss, in their own way. But both Clayton and Eugene had called him within an hour of Lacy's death to ask about the will. He had suggested waiting until after the holiday weekend before the official reading.

But they balked at postponing the reading until Monday, so now they were meeting the day after the holiday. And perhaps it was appropriate that Lacy's will would be read on Black Friday.

"This is quite the house." Zak ran his hand along the mantel of the massive castle rock fireplace that was the main feature of the room. His gaze traveled up the wall to the Charlie Russell painting. "Is that an original?"

"Sure is." Lacy had made special provision for it in her will, leaving it to her granddaughter Nikki, so Justin was aware of its substantial value.

On either side of the painting were some exposed holes. Zak pointed to them. "I wonder what happened there? Did someone misjudge the size of the painting?"

"The painting has only been in that spot for about ten years. Before that a huge moose head was mounted on the wall. Right, Dad?"

"Yup. Lacy pulled it down after Jack died. She had no issue with hunting but hated displaying trophies of dead animals. She took her time searching for the perfect piece of art to replace it. And she sure did find it, though I guess it wasn't large enough to cover all the holes."

THE PINPRICK OF disbelief Zak felt when he'd first heard about Lacy's death had expanded after hearing Doc Pittman's comments about the death scene. Why would Lacy go to bed with her clothes on? She'd been perfectly fine when they parted ways at the Dew Drop around five-thirty on Monday. Why, a few hours later, was she feeling so badly she'd slipped under the covers with her clothes on?

The room was packed. No one would notice if he slipped away for a bit. Pretending he was off to the toilet again, he returned to the hallway. This time he surveyed the three closed doors beyond the bathroom. Their exteriors gave nothing away.

With a mental floor plan in his head, he tried the door at the end of the hallway first, and his instincts proved correct. He stepped into the master bedroom, leaving the door ajar. The overhead lights were on a dimmer switch and he used the lowest setting.

The room was tidy, except for the bed. The quilt was pulled over the pillows haphazardly and hung unevenly over the edges of the four-poster oak frame. He guessed Eugene had straightened the bedding after the paramedics removed his mother's body and no one had been back in the room since.

Across from the bed was an oak bureau in a matching golden stain. On display were some framed photographs, most of them horses.

No wedding photo, Zak noted. That was unusual. In his experience most married people, even if they'd been widowed, displayed their wedding portraits in the bedroom.

A flannel nightgown was laid out neatly on the far corner of the bed. Lacy seemed like the type to put her nightclothes away in the morning, so she must have been in the process of changing for bed when she'd been overcome with…what?

How had she felt in the minutes—or hours—leading up to her death? Most people felt some sort of pain or dizziness according to his research. Wouldn't that lead a person to phone for help rather than go to bed fully dressed?

He turned back to the bed, noting a table with an old-fashioned alarm clock. Lacy would have slept on that side of the bed. He lifted the bedding. Seemed to him he could still see the imprint of her body in the mattress. He wondered if she'd always slept on this side of the bed, even after her husband died.

He raised the covers higher and that was when he noticed a small bandage. It was a different brand than the package in the bathroom. From the pocket of his chinos he pulled out a pair of gloves and a vial. Carefully he transferred the bandage to the vial. In so doing he noticed a speck of blood on the gauze.

As he capped the vial, he heard a soft creak behind him, then a waft of warm air hit his skin. Adrenaline charged through his body at the certain knowledge he was no longer alone.

He turned, half expecting to find one of Lacy's sons with a gun pointed at his head.

Instead he saw Tiff...laughing at him.

"Hello, Sherlock. You planning to go all CSI every time someone dies in Lost Trail? Even if they're ninety-one years old?"

Chapter Three

TIFF WATCHED ZAK calmly slip the vial into his pocket. He then pulled off his disposable gloves and shoved them in the pocket too.

"I'm aware this looks ridiculous," he said.

"Are you practicing for when you're finally a bona fide deputy?" Zak had impressed her—a lot—when he had diplomatically manipulated the sheriff into figuring out who killed Riley Concurran a few weeks ago.

But what was he doing now?

"Don't tell me you suspect Lacy Stillman was murdered?"

Zak gave her a look like the ones she used to get from her father when she interrupted him at work.

"There isn't now, and never will be, an investigation into Lacy's death. I'm just curious about a few things." He glanced behind her at the door she hadn't quite closed. "We need to get out of here."

"No kidding." She ventured into the hall and immediately locked eyes with one of the town's wildest gossips, Gertie Humphrey.

Gertie stepped back from the bathroom she'd been about to enter. Her gray eyebrows rose high, then higher.

Tiff stopped so abruptly Zak bumped into her. Spinning around fast, she grabbed his face with both hands and kissed him.

Zak's body and lips were as responsive as a block of concrete.

And then he loosened up. Warmed up.

The pretend kiss turned into the real thing. Zak could curl a girl's toes. Interesting to know. Gently she eased back until a quarter inch of air separated them. "Is she still there?" she whispered.

"Gertie's gone. Does that mean you're not going to kiss me anymore?"

She slapped his shoulder lightly. "At least we gave her an excuse for the two of us being in Lacy's bedroom."

"Yes. Fast thinking. Well done."

Tiff narrowed her eyes. "You better not be thinking you liked that, Zak Waller."

"You want me to think you're a bad kisser?"

"Get real."

He laughed and then placed his hand behind her elbow and guided her to the family room. "Want a drink?"

"Maybe. Let me check on Mom first." Tiff scanned the room and found her mother at the far end of the buffet. Alone, holding a plate containing a single slice of corn bread, she looked lost.

"I don't think she's comfortable here," Zak commented.

That was an understatement, and such a shame considering her mother was surrounded by people she'd known her entire life. How had her mother become the outsider? Was that what happened when you lost a son, a husband?

Why hadn't the opposite happened? Why hadn't the community rallied around her instead of treating her like a leper?

Tiff thought she knew the answer.

There was a time limit on grief, and the amount of effort people were prepared to offer someone in mourning. Rosemary was about fourteen years past that limit.

Tiff herself was guilty of being impatient and frustrated with her mother. She was also hurt. Yes her mother had lost a husband and a son. But she still had a daughter. Didn't that count?

Zak followed Tiff as she made her way to her mother's side. A moment later Sybil, dressed in black but with a pink scarf holding back her sandy-colored curls—came up to them with a cheerful smile.

"I hoped I would see you here, Rosemary. Isn't this weather dreary? When I die, I'd like it to be in the spring when the trees are budding." Sybil removed the unwanted plate from Rosemary's hands and then gave her a hug.

The relief on Tiff's mother's face was instant. After the hug, she kept one hand on Sybil's arm, as if she needed the contact to keep her balance.

Relieved that her mother was being taken care of, Tiff decided she had time for a beer. "Zak and I are heading to the kitchen for a drink. Can I get you guys anything?"

Both women shook their heads no.

She and Zak wound their way through the crowd to the kitchen. Em Stillman was sitting at the kitchen table she'd presided over earlier. She'd kicked off her heels and loosened the belt of her dress. Her son Luke was sitting beside her, holding her hands, murmuring something.

Zak grabbed two light beers and handed Tiff one. His gaze turned to Em, and Tiff saw his expression soften with compassion. Giving them space, he gestured for Tiff to follow and they moved on to the living room.

As they brushed by Tom and a group of his friends, including a very pretty young woman with straight blonde hair who was clinging to his arm, Tiff noticed her aunt Marsha in an intense conversation with Dr. Pittman. There was too much background chatter to hear what they were saying, but it was obviously a personal conversation, judging by how close they were standing and how focused they were on one another.

She'd often wondered if there was something romantic going on between her aunt and Justin's father. Her aunt had worked as a nurse in Dr. Pittman's clinic for decades. She'd never married and Doc Pittman's wife had died when Justin was a small boy. So it would hardly be a surprise if they'd fallen in love. But if they had, why keep the relationship a secret?

By the far windows a table had been set up with assorted desserts. Vanessa Stillman, cake knife in hand, was chatting with several of the local ranchers who were gathered around her like paparazzi. All you had to do was look at her hands, milky smooth with long, polished nails, to know she was different from any other rancher's wife in the county.

Tiff was going to give the desserts a pass until she noticed Zak's signature chocolate chip cookies. Quickly she detoured and grabbed two off the plate. Neither Vanessa nor her admirers paid her the slightest mind.

She handed one to Zak. "I haven't had one of these since you used to bring them in for snack time in grade school."

"I copied Mom's recipe before they moved. Pretty much the only cookies I know how to bake."

"The addition of crumbled Skor bars is a brilliant touch." She took a bite of hers, savoring each hit of butter and sugar and chocolate deliciousness.

From here she had a view into the dining room and Sybil, bless her, was still loyally by Rosemary's side.

Physically the two women were very different. Her tall, willowy mother was a natural beauty next to the round-faced and rotund Sybil. But Tiff would have given anything if her mother's eyes held the same sparkle as her friend's.

As if reading her mind, Sybil looked at her then. She raised her eyebrows, then took Rosemary by the arm and began walking in their direction.

Tiff and Zak met them halfway. "Ready to go home, Mom?"

The pinched lines around her mother's eyes and mouth smoothed into relief. "Yes, that's a good idea."

"We'll grab Aunt Marsha on our way out. She and Doc Pittman are right by the door. How about you, Sybil?" Tiff asked. "Do you need a ride?"

"The library stays open late on Wednesday so I just got here. I haven't paid my respects to Eugene or Clayton, yet." Sybil hesitated then added, "It's so sad to see Lacy go, isn't it? She was pretty much the last of her generation."

Tiff's mother tipped her head to one side. "Cora Christensen's still alive…isn't she?"

Sybil frowned at the mention of the woman who for so many years ran and taught at Dewbury Academy. The private school had been closed for sixteen years, but people still had strong feelings about Cora. Those who had been her pet students tended to love her. The rest hated her guts.

Clearly Sybil had been in the latter camp.

"Yes, Cora's still with us…more's the pity. But she wouldn't show up here. Lacy couldn't stand her."

"Oh, that's right. I'd forgotten. Such a shame, all that business."

"All what business?" Tiff looked from her mother to Sybil.

"It's just old gossip," Sybil said. "And this probably isn't the right time or place to entertain it."

Rosemary nodded, but the confused look had returned to her eyes. Tiff suspected she'd lost track of what they were talking about.

Which was a shame, because Tiff really wanted to know why Lacy, who had been too old to be one of Cora's students, had disliked her so much.

And she could tell by Zak's expression that he did too.

TIFF HAD OFFERED to drive her aunt and mother to the ranch earlier, an offer she regretted once she was behind the wheel with her aunt next to her and her mother in the back. The darkness was so absolute in the country.

Tiffany focused on the road as her aunt began to chat, sharing some of the trivial gossip she'd picked up at the party. Apparently Vanessa was annoyed her daughter hadn't worn a dress for the funeral or done something nice with her hair.

"It's funny Vanessa and Nikki are so different." Tiff kept her speed down, alert for signs of wildlife. She'd been told the accident that took her father's life had been caused when he'd swerved to avoid a mule deer on the road. Others speculated her father's depression after her brother's death had been a contributing factor.

"Nikki is a lot more like her grandmother than her mom," Marsha agreed. "I never understood why Vanessa married Clayton in the first place. She wasn't meant to be a rancher's wife."

"Did Vanessa grow up around Lost Trail?" Tiff asked.

"No. Clayton met her when he went to college in Missoula. He must have promised her the moon and stars to get her to marry him. He didn't count on his mother controlling the purse strings so tightly, though. From what I hear Vanessa's spending habits are out of control. She and Jennifer Sparks have a trip booked to a health spa in California next week. You can bet it isn't cheap."

"Now that Lacy's died maybe they'll cancel it."

"I expect the opposite to happen. Now that Lacy isn't here to object, Vanessa will spend more than ever. But listen to me. I shouldn't be gossiping." Marsha sighed heavily. "It's just sad to see how things have changed from when we were young. Your mother and I used to spend a lot of weekends on the Lazy S...Eugene and Clayton taught us to ride. Remember that, Rosemary?"

From the back came a non-committal murmur. Tiff couldn't tell if her mother had even been following the conversation.

As soon as they were home, Marsha urged Rosemary to get ready for bed. "I'll bring you up your herbal tea and pills."

Tiff wasn't ready to go to bed yet, so she decided to watch TV. She set herself up on the sofa in the family room, pulling a blanket over her chilly feet. She made a note to buy thicker socks now that she was back in Montana. She needed other things too. A warmer coat, more sweaters, good boots.

After half an hour on Netflix, Tiff still felt restless.

She needed fresh air.

In the hall Tiff snatched her navy down sweater from a peg, then let herself out the back door. The cold air pinched her nostrils, tightened the skin on her face, stung her eyes. She glanced toward the guest cabin—Kenny's cabin now—and noticed a pale blue light in the windows. He must be watching television. She was tempted to knock on his door and see if he was up for a late nightcap.

But something held her back. It wasn't just the message from Craig. Since she'd met the new farm manager a strong attraction had been pulling her toward him, while an equal and opposite force warned her to be careful.

She started to walk, heading toward the barn. After she tripped on a stone she couldn't see she remembered the flashlight app on her phone. She switched it on, then played the light over the path. Decades ago her father had cleared a two-mile circuit through a stately grove of Douglas firs so they could take families for hayrides during Christmas tree season. She'd walk that.

At first she enjoyed the sense of calm and quiet, but then a branch snapped. Tiny feet scurried over dried leaves. A huge mouse…or rat?…ran across the path, just inches from her boots, reminding her there were larger creatures who prowled the forests at night. Coyotes and wolves, maybe even bear and cougar.

She decided to go back inside where it was safe and warm.

She was hurrying, almost running toward the house when she heard a door close, and then a tired bark from the family's old dog Spade.

"Tiff? You out there?"

It was Kenny. She turned and shone her torch toward the guest house. He was zipping up his jacket as he walked, Spade trotting beside him. As soon as the old dog noticed her, he raced for Tiff, nuzzling her legs when he finally caught up.

Since the dog started having accidents in the house her mom and aunt had relegated him to the guest house with Kenny, who had more patience for that sort of thing. It was a decision Tiff wished she could over-rule. She crouched to give Spade a quick scratch, only stopping when Kenny caught up to her.

As she studied Kenny's wildly tousled hair and scruffy face, she was reminded of Heathcliff, a fictional hero she'd fantasized about in her youth. Kenny had a similar untamed air about him, but so far he'd been a perfect gentleman in all their encounters.

"Not sure you should be out here walking alone."

She did feel safer now that he was here. "I was fine."

Even as she said that a howl started up from the foothills, the primitive calling of the coyotes that sounded so ghostly in the stillness of the night, especially when you were outside and vulnerable.

"On second thought..."

Kenny's laugh was low and husky. "Yeah, that was perfectly timed. Want to walk? Or head inside for a Dark and Stormy?"

The ginger and bourbon drink was a favorite of theirs, and Tiff was tempted. A few evenings now they'd shared a nightcap together. Each time she expected him to kiss her. For the kiss to go someplace more.

But the kiss hadn't happened yet.

Maybe it never would. She'd created a mess out of her life in Seattle by acting on impulse. She didn't want to do the same here. A relationship with Kenny would cause complications, not the least because he was the new manager of her family's farm.

She played her flashlight toward the woods. "Let's walk."

After the briefest hesitation he said, "Sure," and she couldn't tell if he was disappointed or relieved. Maybe, like her, he was both.

Chapter Four

Thursday, November 23

SEVEN A.M. CAME much too early for Tiff. She grabbed for her phone in the still-dark room and jabbed at the button to make the alarm stop. She stretched, savoring the warmth of her bed, simultaneously dreading all the work ahead.

When her father and brother were alive, holidays were filled with laughter and fun. Now she just hoped to get through the day.

She grabbed her robe from the chair next to her bed, then turned on her lamp. Her gaze fell on the poster of a border collie puppy tacked onto the little-girl pink wall of her bedroom. God, she really needed to redecorate.

With a loud sigh, she slipped on the robe. Thanksgiving dinner at Raven Christmas Tree Farm was traditionally served at two o'clock in the afternoon, so the workers would have the evening free to spend with family.

The gargantuan turkey her aunt had purchased from a local organic farmer needed to be in the oven by eight and Tiff figured it was on her to make certain this happened.

But she could smell fragrant onion, sage and thyme on her way down the stairs, and when she stepped into the kitchen, her mother was already stuffing the bird. Dressed in her faded jeans and old sweater, hair pulled up in a high ponytail, she looked at least ten years younger than her age.

"You're awake."

"Of course I'm awake. It's Thanksgiving."

Tiff veered toward the coffee machine. Though her mother was a tea drinker, she'd put on a large pot. "Thank God you put on the coffee. You're a life saver."

On the stove sat a huge batch of corn bread and sausage stuffing, which her mom was scooping out by the handful and pushing inside the turkey cavity.

"You know the family saying," her mother began.

Tiff did. "The staff works hard for us all year long. The least we can do to show our appreciation is work hard for them one day out of three hundred and sixty-five."

"Exactly."

It was good to know that some family traditions still had the power to pull her mother out of her funk. If only this could be the beginning of a trend. But Tiff had seen too many of her mother's highs and lows to allow herself to hope.

What she could do, though, was enjoy each good day when it came their way.

"I wish I remembered Grandma and Grandpa more clearly."

They'd both passed on when Tiff was still in grade school, before Casey and her father died. It was good they'd been spared those tragedies. But maybe if her mother's parents were still alive, her mother wouldn't have been so devastated by her losses.

"They were serious, hardworking people. And they both loved this farm dearly. Dad was so relieved when your father agreed to work here after we were married. Dad had been afraid that with two daughters—and Marsha set on a nursing career—there'd be no one to take over the farm when he was gone."

"And now there's only me."

"I didn't mean to put any pressure on you, Tiffany. Your father and I agreed before we had children that we weren't going to make them feel obliged to carry on the family business."

Rosemary added a final scoop of stuffing to the bird, then nodded toward a small ball of twine on the counter.

"Please cut me off a couple feet of that so I can truss this bird. My hands are too sticky."

Tiff cut the twine and passed it over. It was so lovely to be chatting to her mom like this.

"What else can I do to help?"

"The schedule is by the sink. It's pretty much the same as last year except we're having corn fritters instead of corn pudding."

"That's a pretty drastic breach of tradition, Mom."

When her mother laughed, Tiff's heart felt lighter, too. Once, her mother had laughed all the time. Now it was a rare sound, one to be cherished.

"I've put you in charge of peeling and mashing potatoes, preparing the appetizer tray and making sure we have plenty of wine, beer and soft drinks in the beverage fridge. I'd also like you to serve drinks once people start arriving."

Tiff picked up the painstakingly printed schedule. According to this, Tiffany, her aunt Marsha and her mother would have a job to do for every minute of the day until the guests left, from arranging the cornucopia centerpiece to carving the turkey and bringing the platter to the table.

Tiff took her last gulp of coffee just as her aunt joined them in yoga pants and a long T-shirt. Marsha's hair was in a ponytail as well, highlighting the delicate bone structure she shared with her sister.

But that was where the resemblance between the two women ended. Marsha was dark-haired, Rosemary blonde. And while their features were similar, Rosemary's were more delicate and her eye color a more intense blue.

"Good morning, everyone." Marsha stopped in the center of the room, taking in every detail. "Impressive, Rosemary. You've already made the stuffing."

"Yes. The bird is ready for the oven. Tiffany, please put it in for me. I need to wash my hands." Arms bent up at the elbows, Rosemary made her way to the sink.

"Have you had any breakfast?" Marsha asked, looking

concerned.

"A glass of orange juice."

"You need more than that. How about I make you a cup of tea and some toast?"

"I can do it."

"Let me. You've got to pace yourself. It's going to be a long, busy day."

And it was. Even with the three of them working non-stop, it took until one-thirty to get through the schedule, leaving only the carving of the turkey, which wouldn't happen until serving time. Tiffany barely had time to change into a dress and put on a bit of makeup before the first guest arrived.

Bob Jenkins was the full-time foreman at Raven Farms. He'd been with them for over a decade and so the family knew his wife Janet and their teenaged sons well. Bob was a man of few words, his wife was the opposite, while the teens were at that socially awkward stage where they couldn't speak and look at a person at the same time. Tiff wondered if Bob had bribed or threatened them to convince them to attend. For sure it was one or the other. They both looked quietly miserable.

Kenny arrived next, with a bouquet of white roses for the hostess. He'd tidied up his beard, and was wearing dark jeans and a buttoned, cotton shirt. It was the most effort Tiff had seen him make with his appearance since Riley's funeral.

And yet no amount of spit and polish could take the wild

out of the man. Maybe it was his years as a backcountry ski guide, or maybe it was the sparkle in his brown eyes and the wicked tilt of his grin.

As he presented the roses to Rosemary, Tiff happened to glance at her aunt and noticed a curious expression, as if she was displeased…or maybe hurt? It had to be difficult for Aunt Marsha. She did so much for all of them, yet Rosemary was still considered the hostess of Raven Farms.

Once he'd finished saying hello to her mother and aunt, Tiff handed Kenny a beer. "The flowers were a nice touch. Mom loves roses."

"Maybe I should have bought something for Marsha as well. She's the one I usually deal with when it comes to work. How is it that your mom ended up with the farm and not Marsha?"

"Old-fashioned thinking. Maybe if my aunt had gotten married, it would have been different. But since she was single and had her nursing career, my grandparents decided to leave the house and farm to my parents."

"So was Marsha cut out of the will?"

"She inherited other things. Money, investments, jewelry. I don't know the particulars. Hopefully she felt it was fair."

"She can't be too resentful, or she wouldn't be here."

"She's amazing. After my dad's death she sold her own house so she could live with my mom and help her raise me and run the farm. I've seen the books and so have you. She doesn't even draw a salary for all the work she does."

Kenny seemed about to say something, but there was a knock from the front door and Tiff hurried to open it. Jacob, one of their regular seasonal workers, had arrived with his wife, and right behind him was Robin, a young man whose fresh, round face made him seem too young to be working full-time, though Kenny assured her he was nineteen.

Last to arrive was Rusty Thurston. Rusty was also a seasonal worker, and Tiff always struggled not to stare at the large tattoo at the side of his neck.

Last time she'd spoken to Rusty she'd wondered if he'd had a crush on Riley, prior to her death. But if he had, he'd gotten over it quickly. He'd brought a date with him today: Gwen Lange, a young woman well known to Tiff and her family.

Gwen, in her mid-twenties, worked as the full-time receptionist at the medi-clinic. Tiff could tell by her aunt Marsha's raised eyebrows, that she hadn't known Gwen was dating Rusty.

"Hey, everyone." Gwen's tone was casual. "Hey, Marsha. Bet you're surprised to see me." She wrapped her hands around Rusty's arm and leaned in to him. "Rusty just invited me last night. Hope it isn't a problem."

"Of course it isn't. It's so nice to see you." Marsha's tone was smooth, too smooth. And the smile that followed was far from genuine.

Interpreting a discreet nod from her mother, Tiff went to

squeeze an extra place setting around the table. She was curious about Gwen. While an unexpected guest was a bit awkward, Marsha had seemed more annoyed than inconvenienced.

But why? Didn't she and Gwen get along?

While Marsha spoke often, and fondly, about Doc Pittman, Tiff couldn't recall her ever discussing Gwen, except when she'd first been hired. Marsha hadn't seemed overly impressed with her then, citing a lack of alternate candidates as the main reason Dr. Pittman was taking her on.

Once she had the new place setting ready, Tiff went to the kitchen where Kenny had taken over her bartending duties. He'd already served beer, sodas and wine to all the new arrivals, so she took the plate of appetizers and made the rounds.

Bob's teenagers were keen on the bison meatballs, while Janet and Gwen both gravitated to the mushroom tartlets. Used to seeing Gwen in the clinic environment, it was an adjustment to see her with a ring on one side of her nose.

Noticing Tiff's gaze, Gwen put a hand un-self-consciously to the ring. "I don't wear this to work. Doc Pittman doesn't approve."

It wasn't the only thing different about Gwen's appearance. Her eye makeup was darker and thicker, and her low-cut top and short skirt revealed a sleazier side to her personality. Rusty seemed to appreciate the look. Even when he was talking to the other guests, his gaze kept drifting back to his date.

Kenny approached her from behind, whispering in her ear. "Young love. Isn't it sweet?"

A warm zing of attraction made her want to lean back in to him. Instead she whirled around putting the tray between them. "Meatball? Tartlet?"

"Definitely the tartlet."

She had to laugh.

Then her aunt announced it was time to sit at the table. Everyone shuffled around the table trying to find the place setting with their name beside it. Tiff offered to carve the turkey, but was relieved when Kenny took the knife out of her hands.

"Okay if I carve?"

When she'd first moved back home Kenny's helpfulness around the farm had felt like over-stepping to her. Now she'd grown to like it. She relinquished the knife with a grateful smile.

If tables could groan, Tiff had no doubt this one would have once all the veggies were emptied from the warming ovens and salads from the fridge. Two huge platters of turkey—one with the white meat the other with the dark—were the final, crowning touches.

Rosemary sat at her usual end of the table closest to the kitchen, while Marsha took the spot once reserved for Tiff's father, and her grandfather before him. Marsha said grace then offered a toast to poor Riley Concurran, who would have been present, had her life not ended so prematurely.

During the toast Tiff noticed the day was taking a toll on her mother. While Rosemary had changed into a sweater dress that flattered her elegant figure, her face was a tired, much-older version of the one Tiff had seen that morning. Most worrying of all, her beautiful eyes had the foggy, absent look Tiff dreaded.

Her glass was filled with soda water, so Tiff couldn't blame the effect on alcohol.

Sadly, after all her hard work, her mom didn't seem to enjoy the beautiful dinner she'd created. Every time Tiff glanced her way, her gaze was fixed on her plate, or she was staring vacantly over the heads of her guests. Those seated next to her—Bob Jenkins to her left and his wife Janet to her right—gave up attempting to include her in their conversation.

Every dish, from the pecan-topped sweet potatoes, to the creamy gravy, and the crunchy Waldorf salad, was perfect.

When it came time for dessert, no one, no matter how full they were, could resist having at least one slice of Rosemary's pies. Most people had two, and a few had three.

The apple and huckleberry pies had been baked from the freezer. The pumpkin was baked fresh yesterday. Thankfully her mom had had the foresight to prepare three of each.

With the serving of coffee and brandy, Marsha took a moment to thank the employees of Raven Farms. "You all work hard, through tough weather from blizzards to windstorms, but I hope you take pride in knowing each and every tree we harvest is going to provide Christmas magic to the family who purchases it. We'll be paying out our usual bonuses on Christmas Eve, but today you're all welcome to take your pick of the trees home for your own families to enjoy."

A similar speech was given every year. It might have sounded rote to an outsider, but Tiff knew her family meant the words sincerely. At Raven Farms providing Christmas magic to families was their ultimate goal. Tiff remembered her father saying that if growing trees ever started to feel like producing widgets, he'd be out of the business in a flash.

Once dinner was over, Rosemary, Marsha and Tiff ushered everyone to the living room. No one was allowed to carry a single dish into the kitchen, let alone participate in the washing up. Rusty and Gwen held hands as they settled on the love seat facing the window. During dinner they'd exchanged a lot of amorous looks and smiles. Tiff suspected they couldn't wait to get out of there, and sure enough, they were first to announce they were leaving, a mere ten minutes later.

Bob and Janet and the twins were next to go, but the others seemed to be enjoying the last of the 2010 vintage Sangiovese. At Marsha's request, Tiff put a match to the logs and kindling stacked in the fireplace. Soon a cheerful, crackling fire was warming the room.

Marsha opened another bottle of wine, then sat next to Jacob Bradshaw's wife, who apparently went to the same yoga classes as Marsha. Meanwhile Tiff's mother sat straight-backed in the chair next to them. Tiff could tell her mother longed to start clearing the table, though her good manners wouldn't let her.

Kenny refilled Tiff's glass. "This is really good wine."

"Marsha buys all our wines from her favorite shop in Missoula. She has excellent taste."

"I'll say." Kenny returned the bottle to the sideboard, then lifted his glass to hers. "Happy Thanksgiving. We've got a lot of trees to move before Christmas. The weeks are going to fly by."

"Are you going to visit your parents for the Christmas break?" He'd told her before he was estranged from his family. But maybe he had friends he'd want to visit.

"Nope. The plan is to stay right here." The long look he gave her seemed to imply lots of possibilities.

Tiff's chest was tight with a giddy sense of anticipation. So much was unsaid between them. But she'd noticed him looking her way a lot during the meal.

"How long have Rusty and Gwen been dating?"

His gaze broke away and he leaned back on his heels. "Not long…a week, maybe."

"They look crazy about each other."

"They do, don't they? Did it seem to you that Marsha was annoyed when she saw Gwen?"

Tiff had picked up on the same vibe. "Yes. Did you notice Marsha pull Gwen aside before dinner? Maybe there's a problem at the clinic."

"I happened to overhear a few words. Sounded like they were talking about Lacy Stillman. Isn't that the woman who died a few days ago?"

"Yes. Did you hear what they were saying?"

"Marsha was accusing Gwen of eavesdropping on some conversation."

"It must have been at the clinic." Zak had mentioned that Lacy had a checkup the day before she died. Tiff made a note to ask her aunt about it later.

But when she did, a few hours later in the kitchen while they were washing up, Aunt Marsha's expression went blank. "I really can't remember what Gwen and I were talking about. I'm sure it was nothing important."

THE DOORBELL RANG just as Justin was pulling his fifteen-pound turkey from the oven. The puppy ran for the door and started to bark.

"Dad!" Justin called out to his father who was helping Geneva string pink crepe paper streamers all over the dining room.

"Got it, Son."

"Race you to the door, Grandpa!" Geneva skidded on her

socked feet as she ran by Justin, missing the hot roasting pan by inches.

"Careful…" Justin set down the pan and shook his hands free of the oven mitts. The bird looked gourmet-magazine perfect. And smelled even better. He followed the sound of commotion to the front door, pausing when he saw Debbie-Ann and her daughter Ashley on the welcome mat.

Debbie-Ann's cheeks were pink from the cold. With a rainbow-colored scarf around her neck and her dark hair in curls, she looked lovely. She proffered a box covered with a towel to his father. "Happy Thanksgiving! Ashley and I baked pies this morning and thought you might like one."

"Thank you, my dear." Justin's father shot a bemused expression back at his son. Justin gave the tiniest of shrugs.

Debbie-Ann sniffed the air. "I'm guessing you were just about to eat. We'll get out of here and let you enjoy your meal."

Justin caught the second look his father shot him. So much for new family traditions. "Would you and Ashley like to stay for dinner? We're about thirty minutes away from serving."

"Grandpa and me trimmed the dining room. It looks really pretty. Come see." Geneva reached for Ashley's arm and started tugging her.

"Hang on, honey. Ashley's still wearing her boots." Debbie-Ann caught Justin's gaze. "I don't want to intrude on your dinner. I've got something waiting at home."

"It isn't turkey, Mom." Ashley mustered every bit of maturity she could into her six-year-old voice. "This smells better."

"Please stay. We have so much food. And you've saved us from the store-bought pie I brought for our dessert."

Justin's father sounded gracious and welcoming, much more so than he had. Justin glanced at his daughter's excited smile and felt immediately shamed. On this of all days he should be teaching his daughter about sharing what they had with others.

"Yes and I could use your help in the kitchen. I've been so busy I haven't had time to open a bottle of wine."

"We can't have that." Smiling, Debbie-Ann helped her daughter out of her boots and jacket, shed her own winter gear, and then followed him to the kitchen. "Where's your corkscrew?"

Less than an hour later they were all at the table and his father was pushing seconds. "More Brussels sprouts, girls? I know they're your favorite."

Both girls groaned and covered their plates with their hands.

His dad winked, then offered the dish to Debbie-Ann.

"I'd love more of everything, but I have to save room for dessert. You're a really fabulous cook, Justin. I've never eaten such moist, delicious turkey before."

"It's the brine. I soak the turkey in salt and herb-infused water a day before I roast it." He'd learned the trick in his college years, on one of the holidays he'd spent with Paul and Willow at the Quinlans' vacation home in Colorado. They'd flown from Missoula on Paul's family's private jet. It was the first time Justin had appreciated just how wealthy the Quinlans were.

"Good thing it's so delicious because we're going to have lots of leftovers." His dad set the casserole dish back on the table. "But I agree with Debbie-Ann. Let's save some room for that pumpkin pie."

"Dishes first," Debbie-Ann said, getting up from the table. "Ashley and Geneva, please collect the cutlery and rinse it for the dishwasher."

Justin was impressed when Ashley jumped out of her seat, clearly used to such requests. After a brief hesitation, Geneva was right in there, too.

Debbie-Ann lifted an eyebrow in invitation to him. "If you put away the leftovers, I'll wash the roasting pan."

"Deal. I hate washing the roasting pan."

"And I'll put on some coffee for the pie." His father settled both hands on the table before slowly pushing up from his chair.

The cleaning was almost as much fun as the eating had been, and Justin couldn't help comparing this to the much quieter Sunday family dinners they'd had when Willow lived here. Willow had been like a butterfly, hovering, not sure where to land. He understood better now why she hadn't made an effort. She'd just been marking time waiting until she could go back to Paul.

Maybe that realization should have wounded him more. But with each day that passed he knew that becoming a father had been the real appeal in marrying Willow.

After pie—which was the best he remembered eating—they played some games of Sorry and Trouble and when Debbie-Ann announced it was time she and Ashley went home Justin was almost as disappointed as his daughter.

"Please stay longer. Can Ashley have a sleepover?"

Justin looked into Geneva's pleading face and wondered how he could disappoint her.

But he didn't have to.

Debbie-Ann grabbed her daughter's coat and held it open. "You girls are a little young for sleepovers. Don't dawdle, Ashley. We're getting up early to go shopping tomorrow, remember?"

Black Friday. Justin's heart sank at the reminder. He wasn't a fan of mob-shopping but he'd rather be doing that tomorrow than facing the Stillmans during the reading of Lacy's will.

Once Debbie-Ann and Ashley left, the house seemed inordinately quiet. Justin gave Geneva a ten-minute warning for bedtime then asked his dad if they could talk after Geneva was asleep.

"It's been a long day, Son. How about we get together for lunch tomorrow after your meeting with the Stillmans?"

His father's shoulders were drooping with fatigue but

Justin couldn't put this off any longer. Tomorrow at lunch Geneva would be around and this was a conversation he didn't want her to hear. She would get a much-edited and age-appropriate version soon enough.

"Please, Dad? It's important."

The concern in his dad's eyes slowly morphed to fear. Justin bit back the impulse to offer false reassurance. Since his mother's death, he and his dad were everything to one another. This was going to be so hard.

"Yes. Of course, I'll stay."

Justin called for his daughter so he could wash her face and help her brush her teeth, but it turned out those normal tasks would have to wait for morning. Geneva had fallen asleep on the sofa. He carried her to her room, turned on the night-light and closed her door.

In the living room he found his dad in the armchair, Dora snoozing at his feet.

His dad looked absolutely terrified. But when he spoke, his voice was calm. "You're sick, aren't you, Son?"

Sick.

The word hung in the air: the unwelcome dinner guest who couldn't tell it was time to leave.

Justin sat on the edge of the sofa closest to his dad. He leaned forward, lacing his fingers together and resting his arms on his thighs. "Yes. It's Hodgkin's lymphoma."

His father slowly shook his head. "It's been a while, hasn't it? The signs were there, I just didn't see them. Didn't want to see them."

"I was diagnosed two years ago. I thought I was lucky. The doctor figured we'd caught the disease early enough and I handled the chemo treatments well."

"That client you said you had in Idaho, the one you kept going on business trips for...?"

Justin brushed a hand over his head. His blond hair was growing back, but it was thin, so he'd kept the trendy buzzed look. "That's when I had my treatments. I'm sorry I didn't tell you. I was hoping this was something I would never have to worry you about."

Most of Justin's friends had poor to average relationships with their fathers. Paul and his father, for instance, couldn't be in the same room for more than an hour without arguing. The link Justin had with his own dad was rare, and came primarily from the fact that since Justin was six, they'd had only one another.

His father was the reason Justin had turned down an offer from a big firm in Missoula and opened his own law practice in Lost Trail.

His father was a big part of the reason he'd married Willow last July, and adopted Geneva, and given her their family name.

And his father was the reason he'd kept his illness secret, knowing the toll it would take and hoping to spare him from all that.

His decisions, his life, might have been different if his

father had shown any interest in dating or remarrying after Justin's mother died. But even though the perfect woman was available—Marsha Holmes, the attractive nurse who had worked with his father her entire career—his father remained single.

Occasionally Justin would catch a snippet of conversation, a lingering glance between them, that made him wonder. But if something was going on between Marsha and his dad, they were keeping it private.

"Who's your doctor?"

"Zimmermann."

His father nodded. "He's good. What's the prognosis?"

Justin's gaze fell to the dog. He wished he could curl up on the floor beside her. "My best chance is a stem-cell transplant."

His dad was quiet for a long while as the implications sank in. "You need a donor. A sibling would have been your best bet."

His father had told him many times he felt guilty about Justin being an only child. Justin didn't want that wound reopened. "I have about a seventy-five percent chance of finding a donor in the registered pool. Those are good odds."

"Transplants from a matched unrelated donor aren't as successful as those from a relative." His father rubbed both hands down the sides of his face. "Oh my Lord, Son. I'm so very, very sorry..."

"You have nothing to be sorry about. This isn't anyone's

fault. It's just...lousy luck."

"I'll get tested."

"You can. But I'm sure you know that as my father and a contributor of only fifty percent of my DNA, the chances are less than one in two hundred you'll be a match."

His father craned his neck, pulled at the collar of his shirt. "What a mess. What a terrible mess."

Tears were falling now, one after the other down his father's gray, gaunt cheeks. And though he was the sick one, Justin had the disorienting feeling of being the parent. Of wanting to hold and protect and shield.

He put his arm across his dad's back, wishing there were reassuring words to say.

"If only it could be me who was sick. If there's a God in heaven, it would be me." His father choked on a sob, buried his face in his hands.

Justin went to the kitchen to get some water and tissues. His body felt unbalanced, his legs weak. He paused at the kitchen sink, resting his weight against the counter and examining his reflection in the kitchen window. He'd never looked much like his dad. But they had the same expression of misery tonight.

Gathering his courage he went back to the living room and sat on the arm of his father's chair. Gently he blotted the tears, then passed his dad the glass of water.

"I'm sorry to ruin Thanksgiving this way. Maybe I should have waited for a better time."

"There is no good time for news like this." His dad took the tissues and blew his nose. "And you shouldn't have needed to tell me. I'm a poor excuse for a doctor if I couldn't see what was right before my eyes. Your shaved head, all that weight you lost…"

"It doesn't matter. We have to look to the future."

It took a moment for his meaning to sink in. And when it did, a fresh new sorrow etched into the lines on his dad's face.

"Geneva…"

Justin swallowed against the huge boulder in his throat. What was going to happen to his daughter if he didn't make it?

Chapter Five

ZAK TOWELED SWEAT off his face and squared his shoulders. He felt ready to take on the world after his fifteen-mile run on Tamarack Trail. Some people thrived on being with family for the holidays. Zak got off on being alone.

He jogged home to his basement suite. It wasn't much, but it was cheap and soon he'd be moving anyway.

Watson, perched on his favorite windowsill, gave him a commanding meow as he entered. Sure enough, his food bowl was empty. Zak opened a can of premium chicken liver pâté, a special Thanksgiving treat for his pet. He had no idea what he was going to eat for dinner himself—probably another chicken breast and some salad—but he didn't care.

His mom was a good cook and no doubt she was serving turkey and all that went with it tonight at his family's new home in South Dakota. But he'd rather eat toast and peanut butter than deal with the tension that always accompanied a sit-down Waller meal.

There was only one person he would have been happy to spend the holiday with, and she was spending the day with her family in Helena. He only knew that because he'd heard Nadine ask Ford for an extra day of vacation.

She was still putting on the cool and distant attitude with him. Still hadn't said a word about blowing him off the other night.

She'd either decided he wasn't for her, or she was playing games. Either way, he'd be smart to keep his professional distance. Work romances were never a good idea anyway.

He poured himself a tall glass of chocolate milk—his favorite recovery food after a long run. The sweet, cool beverage went down in seconds. He needed a shower, but wanted to wait until his metabolism returned to normal. To pass time he checked his phone.

Earlier he'd texted Luke Stillman asking if he wanted to join him on a run. Looked like Luke had responded.

FAMILY STUFF HERE. THANKSGIVING AND ALL. MAYBE ON SUNDAY AT ELEVEN?

SURE, Zak typed back. *C U THEN.*

No sooner had he hit 'send' than his phone started to ring with the theme song from *The Hunger Games.* His mother.

He resisted the urge to hit 'Decline.'

"Hey, Mom. Happy Thanksgiving."

"Same to you, Zak. We just finished eating. Had all your favorites. Turkey, stuffing, gravy, pumpkin pie."

"Bet it was great."

"The whole family was here, except for you. Me, your

dad, and all your brothers—even Matt."

"Sorry I missed it." White lies didn't count. "Matt still enjoying the army?"

Matt, the closest to Zak in age, was also the most aggressive of the brothers. He'd been Zak's biggest tormenter growing up. Like their father, he could switch from being incredibly charming to scary and aggressive at the slightest provocation. Zak hoped his brother's military training would instill some much needed self-discipline and control.

"He's an ordnance officer now, stationed in Florida. Which is a hell of a lot farther from South Dakota than Montana."

Zak ignored the dig. "How was harvest this year?"

His parents and two older brothers were trying to make a go of his deceased grandfather's grain farm.

Zak had been under a lot of pressure to join them, especially from his mother.

But he'd resisted.

"It was good. Well, decent. Curtis took a job in October as an agriculture inspector. Regular hours and good pay. I told you he has a girlfriend…?"

"Yeah…Shari?"

"That's right. I wouldn't be surprised if they got engaged this Christmas. You coming home for the holidays?"

Home to him would never be his parents' farm in South Dakota. "Maybe for a few days. It depends on my work schedule. I'm low man on the totem pole here."

"You still haven't made it out here, yet. We've been gone three years."

His mother sounded sad, but it was difficult to figure out if the emotion was genuine. His mother was the one person in his family who puzzled Zak the most. He couldn't understand how she put up with his father—his verbal and occasional physical abuse.

There wasn't a person in their family who hadn't suffered at their father's fists.

Yet his mom acted as if this behavior was normal. And she wasn't above behaving the same way. When provoked, she lashed out at all her sons with whatever was handy. He'd seen her toss everything from a frying pan to a steel-toed work boot at his brothers. She'd done the same to his father too.

Sometimes his dad would just laugh.

Other times he'd explode with rage.

It was the unpredictability that got to Zak the most. He went to the dinner table each night not knowing if it would be all funny stories and teasing, a major brawl, or something between the two extremes.

"It's a long drive. And I only get two weeks holiday a year."

"Your father is calming down as he gets older. He misses you. You were always his favorite."

"Right." He'd started working at the hardware store when he was fourteen. His father had always introduced him to the customers in the same way. *And this small fry is Zak, the runt of the litter.*

But the thing that hurt even more than his father's insults and punches had been his mother's refusal to stand up for him, not even against his older brothers.

It had been a double burden for Zak, being both the youngest and the smallest. As he grew up, his interest in academics rather than football, his preference for running rather than fighting, all of these had marked him as a misfit in his family. When he was born, everyone had been hoping for a girl. So he'd been a disappointment in that way, too.

His gaze swept over his tidy kitchen. Behind all those cabinet doors the contents were neatly arranged, spices in alphabetical order, plastic bowls with matching lids.

If only he could have such complete control over his feelings for his mother. The rest of the family he could do without. But he couldn't quite say that about his mom.

THANKSGIVING NIGHT, AROUND midnight, an autumn storm swept in from the north, testing the old pine trees near the Mastersons' two-story farmhouse. Tiff was watching the shadow of a branch rock wildly back and forth on her bedroom wall when the door to her room gave a cre-ea-ak and began to slowly open.

Terror froze her for an instant. Then sense replaced blind

fear.

She bolted upright and reached for the bedside lamp. "Mom?"

The door opened further, and her mother stepped inside, her dressing gown disheveled, her hair a tangle of gray-streaked blond curls framing a too-pale and too-thin face. She crossed to the bed and put a hand on Tiff's shoulder.

"We have to go."

Her mother's eyes glowed as if she'd been possessed. Tiff pushed past her childlike fear and gently touched her mother's arm, hoping to ground her. "It's the middle of the night."

"Your father called. Casey needs us."

Shivers zigzagged down Tiff's spine.

"No one needs us, Mom." Truer words she'd never spoken. It was Marsha who ran this house, took care of Rosemary and oversaw the operations of the farm.

Marsha was the one who was needed. Not Tiff or her mother.

"You need to listen." Her mother spoke as if Tiff was a child, not a woman of thirty. "Your father was in a car accident. He's okay, but we have to pick Casey up at the hospital."

"No, Mom. Please. Just lie down beside me for a minute. You're shivering." As was Tiff. She was used to her mother being vague and forgetful. Not delusional.

Rosemary clutched her dressing gown over her chest.

"It's so cold."

"We turn the furnace down at night, remember?" Tiff pulled back her covers, making space in the double bed.

Gingerly Rosemary settled, still wearing her dressing gown and slippers. For a moment she lay stiff as a cadaver. Then quietly she repeated, "We have to go."

"No, Mom. It's okay. It's very late. Time to sleep." Tiff placed a hand on the side of her mother's face, remembering the beautiful, vibrant woman she'd once been. The mother who had tucked *her* into bed, who had calmed *her* fears, who had stroked *her* face.

Slowly Rosemary's eyelids fluttered closed. On her last breath before succumbing to fatigue, she whispered, "We have to..."

And then she was asleep.

Tiff watched her mother for a few minutes before turning out the light. She could hear the storm hurling wind and rain at the world outside. By morning the cottonwoods and tamaracks would be stripped of the last of their golden leaves and needles.

An overwhelming sense of loss pressed down on her. How quickly her favorite season had passed during her first autumn home in over ten years. Now she—all of them—had to find the fortitude to make it through another winter.

Tiff closed her eyes, aware of her mother's weight next to her and the uneven sound of her shallow breathing. And yet her mother's voice still echoed off the walls. "Your father's been in an accident. He's okay..."

If only.

Tiff had thought nothing could be as painful as losing her brother. No one had conveyed to her the risks of Casey's operation. So when her parents told her he had died—it hadn't felt real. Days went by. There was a funeral. A huge hole in her life where Casey had been. Anguish replaced the blessed numbness. At night, in bed, she'd wondered if the pain would stop her heart.

It hadn't.

Two months later when the car accident happened, she'd learned her true capacity for grief. Her dad died at the scene. For a few days her mom was in a coma from which no one expected her to recover.

Aunt Marsha had been bruised and traumatized, but she'd fared the best because she'd been in the back seat. She'd been the one to break the news to Tiff, to hold her tight and promise, no matter what, she would always be taken care of.

Was it survivor's guilt that had led Marsha to devote the rest of her life to looking after her sister and niece? Or was it duty? Or love? Marsha must be so tired of spending her days at work helping the sick, then coming home and doing the same for her sister.

Yet she never complained. Never made Tiff feel it was her turn to carry the load.

But it was. Past time actually. Tomorrow she would talk

to her aunt. There had to be more she could do to help.

THE NOISE OF the curtains flapping in the wind woke Justin from a dark dream where he'd been lost in a strange land, without his wallet, or cell phone, or any form of ID. He got out of bed to close the window—he always slept with it open no matter the season. A light dusting of snow had sifted through the screen onto the windowsill, and he brushed the fine, white sand aside with his fingers. Outside snow seemed to be falling horizontally, the wind was so strong.

He pulled on his robe—the cashmere one that had been a gift from Paul over a decade ago. His generous gifts always made Justin uncomfortable, but Willow told him not to be a fool, so he never rejected them.

The wooden floor was cool on his bare feet as he made his way to Geneva's room. She was still and quiet in her bed, eyes closed, one hand curled behind her neck. At her feet was the puppy, also fast asleep. Since Willow left them, Dora had taken to sleeping in the little girl's bed. Justin didn't object.

He sat on the corner of the bed, resisting the urge to stroke the plump softness of Geneva's cheek. From this angle he could see the photo of Willow holding a newborn Geneva in her arms. Willow was looking at her baby, not the camera, and there was a vulnerability about her face Justin had rarely seen in real life.

Did Willow think of them anymore?

Did she miss her daughter, worry if she was doing okay?

He couldn't even guess. Willow had always been an enigma. She wasn't someone who talked about her feelings. When she made decisions she never explained the reasoning behind them.

When they were high school friends and then sweethearts, he had loved and admired Willow's toughness. Her self-sufficiency. It was the history between them, and the friendship, that had been the basis for their marriage.

Her reluctance to speak of Paul, or the relationship he'd had with Geneva, had tested their relationship. From little things Geneva said, misbehaviors such as harshly scolding the dog, he surmised she had suffered at least verbal abuse from her father.

And of course Paul's willingness to rescind his legal rights as Geneva's father so Justin could adopt his child said a lot.

No matter how you looked at it, Geneva's early years had been tumultuous. And now he had to figure out some way to tell her about his cancer. How the hell was he going to do that?

Justin left his daughter's room, and went to his study. From the bottom drawer he pulled out a book he'd borrowed from the library. Written by a child psychologist, it provided guidance on how to talk to children about difficult subjects like divorce and cancer. He found the chapter he'd bookmarked for himself and read it through.

When he finished, he closed the book and tucked it away. The weight of his heart pinned him to his chair. God, he was so tired of this struggle, yet it had barely begun.

Eventually he got up and poured himself a scotch. He thought longingly of his lover in Missoula. They had broken things off when he made the decision to marry Willow.

Justin missed physical intimacy. He missed sex. He missed talking to someone who didn't need him to be strong.

The first swallow of the liquor radiated warmth through the empty cavity of his gut. It helped but was a poor substitute for human companionship. If he could find Willow, get her to give him a divorce…

Then what? His inner voice mocked him. He couldn't go back to his old lover. Or look for somebody new.

Not with the cloud of cancer hanging over his head.

Justin lifted the glass a second time and tossed it back in one gulp.

Friday, November 24

THE FRESH SNOWFALL didn't stop the Stillman brothers from driving into town with their families for their meeting with Justin the morning of Black Friday. He hadn't expected it would.

They arrived as a group promptly at ten. Justin had a full

pot of coffee ready, plus a tray of muffins and fruit he'd ordered from the Snowdrift Café. Both the coffee and the baked goods were finished before he had a chance to hand out the summary document he'd prepared for the meeting.

"Thanks for the snacks," Em said. "Most of us—" she shot a quick disparaging glance at Vanessa "—have been up since five-thirty and chores are never easy after a storm."

"Hopefully this won't take too long." Justin repositioned his water glass so it wasn't sitting directly on the wooden desk. Then he gestured to the summary notes. "As you know before he died in 2001 your father put all the ranch, including land, outbuildings and livestock into a corporate structure. When he died your mother inherited seventy percent of the shares, while his sons—" he glanced up to make eye contact with Eugene and then Clayton "—each inherited fifteen percent, making up the final thirty percent of the company."

"Yeah, yeah, that's ancient history." Eugene was leaning forward, arms resting on his knees. His right leg was jiggling, as if he was suffering from restless leg syndrome.

"In her will your mother has divided her shares in such a way that Clayton, Eugene, Em, Tom, Luke and Nikki will each own an equal percent of the ranch."

Vanessa had been alternately surveying his office and examining her manicure since she arrived. Now her spine straightened and her eyes bore into him. "Em? Em gets an equal share in the ranch, but not me?"

"I'm afraid not."

Vanessa's pretty mouth compressed into a line that made her look hard and mean. "I always knew that bitch didn't like me."

Clayton put a hand on his wife's back. "I have to agree it's hardly fair. When you boil it down, my family ends up with two-sixths of the ranch while Eugene's gets four-sixths."

"I think it's fair," Em said quietly. "I can count on one hand the number of times Vanessa has stepped into the cattle barn. Or ridden one of the horses."

"Your mom didn't want her death to divide the family. While she wanted to treat you fairly as individuals, she hoped you would continue to work as a team."

Eugene waved his hand impatiently. "Let's cut the complaining and get on with this. What about Mom's investments?"

Lacy had sliced and diced the over one million dollars she held in stocks and bonds a dozen different ways over the years she'd been Justin's client. If the family hadn't liked the way she'd divided the land, they sure weren't going to like what was coming next.

"Lacy left a hundred thousand dollars to each of her sons, and twenty thousand to each grandchild." He could see the frowns emerging at the mention of such a relatively insignificant sum. "The remainder is to be donated to Ducks Unlimited to assist their work in conserving wetlands."

"What?" Eugene exploded out of his chair.

He wasn't the only one who looked blindsided. In fact, only Luke and Nikki didn't seem surprised by this news. Justin didn't want to put the young people in the spotlight, but he suspected their grandmother had warned them of her intentions. Lacy had often told him how pleased she was that both Luke and Nikki shared her concerns about land stewardship and conservation.

"We can contest this, right?" Vanessa had a white-knuckled grip on the arms of her chair.

"You can. It won't be easy to overturn the donation to Ducks Unlimited, however, given the high value of the shares you've all inherited."

"Excluding me." Bitterness added ten years to Vanessa's face. "But then I'm only a daughter-in-law. I don't count."

Justin wished his water glass was filled with scotch. He'd known this wouldn't go well. And the worst was yet to come. He held up a hand to still the family bickering. "We have one last curious bequest to deal with."

"We do?" Clayton turned from Justin to his brother. Eugene shrugged, as if to say he was in the dark as well.

Justin stalled for a few moments, straightening papers on his desk. "Next we need to discuss the homestead house and the land it sits on."

"Grandma's house?" Tom's eyes were bright. "I was hoping—"

A sharp glance from his father shut him down.

"In his will," Justin continued, "Jack Stillman left that

house and land to Lacy for the duration of her life only. Upon her death the house and the land it sits on…" He paused. Took a sip of water.

None of them were going to understand this. He hadn't understood it himself until Lacy explained. She'd forbidden him to do the same for her family.

"Get on with it." Eugene spoke again, his leg jiggling double-time now.

"…the house and the land it sits upon goes to Cora Christensen."

Chapter Six

TWO INCHES OF fresh snow had transformed the barren earth into the magical wonderland of winter. With a cup of coffee in hand, Tiffany surveyed the changes from the glass doors leading off the back of the house.

"I hate the cold, but you can't deny fresh snow is pretty."

Her aunt was at the table, eating a slice of leftover pumpkin pie for breakfast. At some point last night Tiff's mom had returned to her own bed, and she was there still, not ready to get up.

"Mom did this weird thing last night. She came to my room and said Casey needed us. She spoke as if he was still alive."

"Oh, honey." Marsha set down her fork.

"I've known her to be forgetful and spaced out. But last night…she was delusional."

"She probably dreamt about your brother."

"Maybe. But she was awake when she said my dad—*who's been dead for sixteen years!*—called and asked her to come to the hospital."

Tiff pressed her cheek against the cold window. She was

getting too worked up. She could see the worry in her aunt's face.

"That must have been upsetting for you."

"It was." Outside the sun shone so brightly, Tiff was beginning to get a headache. She went to the coffeepot for a refill. "Have you ever seen her like that before?"

"No."

Tiff stopped pouring. Turned to look at her aunt. "Never?"

"Oh she's been forgetful and anxious. But she's never spoken as if Casey and Irving are still alive."

So what did that mean? "Is it possible she's overmedicating?"

"Definitely not. I control her pills very carefully."

"What medication is she on, exactly?"

"Just a minute and I'll show you." She disappeared for a moment before returning with a sheet of bubble-wrapped pills, which she passed to Tiff. "After your father's death, your mom was on medication to control her depression and medication to help her sleep at night. Over the years Clark has reduced the dosage to the absolute minimum."

Tiff examined the bubble-wrapped pills. There was just one pill for morning and one for evening. It seemed doubtful that this could be the cause of her mother's delusions.

She handed the pills back to her aunt, then took her coffee to the table. "I moved home to help. So far it seems I'm doing the opposite. Tell me what I can do. Should I take

Mom on more outings? Does she need to see a specialist? Maybe Mom has dementia or Alzheimer's?"

Her aunt reached across the table to pat her hand. "We've seen the specialists, including a very good neurologist in Missoula. All the tests show the same thing. There is no physical cause."

"If these delusions are new, maybe it would be worth seeing the specialists again."

"Possibly." Her aunt hesitated before adding, "But I think it's more likely that your presence in the house is bringing back memories for Rosemary. She's very sensitive to any change in her routine. It's going to take some time for her to adjust."

"There has to be some way I can help her."

"I know you worry about your mom. I worry about *you*. You're young. These should be fun years. Maybe things went sideways for a bit in Seattle, but you could easily find a new job. Maybe even patch things up with Craig."

Tiff's gaze dropped to her cell phone, charging in the dock next to the phone. "Funny you should say that. I had a message from him recently. Totally out of the blue."

"Oh?" Marsha scooped up the remainder of the pie crumbs and finished off her pie. "What did he say?"

"He…sounds like he wants to see me again. He might even be open to renewing our relationship."

"Would you like that?"

"Craig is great." He was cosmopolitan and fun and with

him Tiff had done things a girl from Lost Trail, Montana, could only dream about. They'd gone to museums and art galleries, done the club scene, tried all the trendy restaurants.

She'd loved that Craig knew nothing about her background or family history except for what she chose to tell him. With him she'd been granted a fresh, tragedy-free life.

He was the only child of wealthy parents. The worst hardship he'd had in life was when his trust fund had tanked in 2009.

A part of her had known she couldn't get away with playing "city-girl Tiff" forever. The past was bound to crash in on her, and so it had when Dr. Pittman and Justin, in Seattle for business last winter, invited her out for dinner. They had a fun time, but that night Tiff dreamt about her mother and her dead brother and father.

Her insomnia—always hovering, ready to create havoc with her life—returned with a vengeance and she began screwing up at work, and destroying her relationship with Craig as well. A stupid, late-night drink and hookup with one of her clients had marked the curtain call for that phase of her life.

"If you still love him, or feel you *might* love him again, don't you owe it to yourself to do as he asks, and take that second chance?"

"I used to really like the person I was when I was with Craig. But I'm not sure that was the real me."

Her aunt was quiet, and when she shook her head slowly

Tiff could tell her answer had disappointed her.

"Tiff, your family's tragedies have defined and limited your mother's life. I'd hate to see that happen to you."

✕

JUSTIN HAD GUESSED the Stillmans would take some time digesting the contents of Lacy's will, but two and a half hours into their ninety-minute appointment, they were still asking questions. He tried a few discreet glances at his watch, but no one took the hint.

He wasn't going to make lunch with his father and Geneva.

He'd be lucky to get this family out of here before Cora Christensen showed up for her one o'clock. The old school teacher and administrator would probably arrive early and it was already twelve-thirty.

In the end he had to be direct. "I'm afraid I have another appointment. Why don't you discuss this as a family and let me know if you plan to contest."

Ushering them out of his office was like herding bison—almost impossible and more than a little dangerous. He shook hands with each of them, and inched them closer to the door. To make sure there would be no unpleasant encounters in the stairwell, or outside his building, he followed them to the street and waited as they climbed into their assorted vehicles.

Eugene and Em and their sons were in a ten-year-old Dodge truck, quite a contrast to the top-of-the-line Ford F-450 that Clayton, Vanessa and Nikki climbed into.

Even as they were driving west out of town, Justin spotted Cora approaching from the east. Her ramrod posture and no-nonsense gait were very familiar to him after years of seeing her patrolling the hallways at Dewbury Academy.

He could tell she'd seen him, so he waited.

Back in the day, he'd been one of her favorite students, but he hadn't been oblivious to how she treated the other, less fortunate kids. Cora had been a master manipulator, pitting students against one another, undermining the confidence of weaker children, and all under the guise of being nurturing and caring.

What Lacy had shared about the other woman had only lowered his opinion of the woman.

Cora was like a month-old candy apple. Sickly sweet on the outside but rotten at the core. The metaphor was especially apt for Cora because she cared so much about appearances. Unlike most teachers, she hadn't chosen favorites based on academic brilliance but on a combination of family standing in the community and the student's physical attractiveness.

Which explained why he—the doctor's son, golden-haired, blue-eyed and tall—had caught her favor.

The downside of being one of Cora's pets was that the other kids in the schoolyard tended to hate you. He'd been lucky to have Willow as a champion back then. Fearless and confident, she'd stood up to the kids who wanted to ostracize him. And from her, he too had learned to be brave.

"So good to see you, young man." Cora had groomed herself for the occasion. Her white hair was curled and frozen into place with a spray that was thick enough to gleam in the sunlight. On her lined face were visible touches of blue eye shadow, pink rouge and lipstick, but the colors weren't quite where they should be, as if they'd been applied with a shaky hand, or by someone with poor vision. She wore a brown wool coat with a pale pink scarf at her neck, and sensible rubber-soled boots on her feet.

"Good afternoon, Miss Christensen." He clasped her hand between both of his, striving for a smile that was suitably friendly, while respecting the formal nature of this meeting. "Are you okay taking the stairs, or would you prefer the elevator?"

"I'm not as active as I used to be and the walk was long. Let's take the elevator."

On the way up he asked how her Thanksgiving was.

"Fine. There was a dinner at the church. I went to that. It's what I usually do for holidays, since I have no children. But that's the price I pay for devoting my life to my students."

There was a note of reproach in her voice. Perhaps she wondered why none of her favored students ever invited her to join them for the holidays.

Justin wasn't about to enlighten her.

Once in his office, he offered coffee and she accepted.

"Cream and sugar, please."

He added both, then put some chocolate and vanilla cookies on a plate. The Stillmans had devoured all the freshly baked ones, so he had to take some from a package he'd bought from the Girl Scouts that fall.

To his surprise Miss Christensen took two and ate them in rapid order between gulps of coffee.

He took his seat. Rearranged some papers to give her time to finish. "You must be curious about the purpose for this meeting."

"I expect it has something to do with Lacy's will. Or, more accurately, a provision in her late husband Jack's will."

Justin paused for a second to gauge her expression. She looked…pleased with herself. "You knew about the life tenancy?"

"It's what Jack told me he would do. Of course, I had no guarantee he actually followed through on his promise."

Cora took a sip of her coffee, then set down the mug gently. She would have been appalled to know she had a smudge of chocolate on her upper lip. Justin could have handed her a napkin, but didn't out of a perverse sense of loyalty to Lacy.

"I suppose you're wondering why Jack Stillman would leave me his family house." There was a smugness in Cora's watery blue eyes, an air of superiority that made Justin's dislike veer toward hatred for a moment.

Maybe if he hadn't been so fond of Lacy, he wouldn't be finding this so difficult. But he'd admired Lacy. For all her flaws, she'd been a straight-shooting person. The very opposite of the woman before him.

"It's not my business."

"True. But I don't mind telling you Jack Stillman had a thing for me back in the day. And he was grateful for all that I did for his sons."

Thanks to Lacy, Justin knew there was a hell of a lot more to the story. He reminded himself of his professional obligation.

"That's not my concern. My job is to handle the legalities. Once the will goes through probate, the house and land it sits upon will be yours for as long as you live. Again, this is a life tenancy. Once you're gone, the property will revert to the Lazy S corporation owned by Jack's descendants."

Miss Christensen considered for a moment. "There would be a certain…satisfaction in moving into Lacy's house after all these years. But I am getting older, and driving is an issue. I suppose I could let it out?"

Ah, Jack, how could you be such an asshole?

"Yeah, you could. I believe Lacy's grandson Tom is looking for a place to live with his girlfriend." At the wake Justin had overheard Tom and his girl discussing what they would do to the place if they could move in. "Maybe they would rent it from you." It would be irritating for the family to pay for what should be theirs. But at least they wouldn't have strangers in their midst.

"Where would the fun be in that?" Cora asked.

Distaste curdled in his gut. "I don't know what you mean by that."

"I think you do."

He could guess. She wanted to make life uncomfortable for the Stillmans so she would probably find the most obnoxious tenants possible.

Cora reached over his desk and squeezed his hand. Her skin felt cold, her fingers bony. "You were always one of my favorites."

He knew.

But she would never be one of his.

✕

Saturday, November 25

BY SATURDAY THANKSGIVING was ancient history at Raven Farms. Turkey leftovers had been divided into meal-sized portions and stacked in the freezer. Tiff and her mother had cleaned the main-floor rooms and disposed of the cornucopia. It was time to bring on Christmas.

It had been more than ten years since Tiff had been involved in decorating the house for the holidays. Usually by the time she made it home from Seattle, it was already Christmas Eve and the house and grounds were perfect.

Dragging the boxes from storage and pulling out generations' worth of ornaments brought back some of the happiest memories of her childhood.

At the very back of the boxes she found Casey's old train set. It had been his Santa gift when he was six and every year after that he'd insisted on setting up the train so it ran a circle around the Christmas tree.

Since his death, though, the train had remained in its box.

Tiff opened the lid and gently removed the engine. This was no cheap toy. Her parents had found her brother a beautiful vintage set and added pieces to it every year. Finding out which new car would be in his stocking was always the highlight of Casey's Christmas.

"I'd almost forgotten about that train set."

Her mother had come up from behind her. Feeling guilty, Tiffany returned the locomotive to the box. "Sorry, Mom. I'm probably not supposed to be touching this."

Her brother's room had been enshrined after his death. Tiff could still remember the day her father had removed Casey's jackets from the pegs on the mudroom wall and carried them up to his bedroom closet. Nothing of Casey's had been given away or donated to charity. Maybe it was wasteful, but her mother had said she couldn't stand it if she saw another boy wearing something of her son's.

"We should put the train around the Christmas tree again this year."

"Really?" She couldn't believe her mom had suggested it. "I think…that would be nice. I'd like to have something that reminds me of Casey around. Not that I ever forget him."

"I know you don't. But I agree. I've missed the train. Would you mind setting it up?"

"I'd love to."

Tiff interpreted her mom's change of heart about the tree as a good sign, a sign of healing. Later that day, after they'd strung the lights on the tree and hung all their favorite ornaments, she pulled out the box. Her aunt frowned when she noticed her piecing together the track.

"I'm not sure that's a good idea."

"Mom asked me to."

"Really?" Marsha frowned. Then shrugged. "I just hope it doesn't bring on one of her sad moods."

For a moment Tiff considered putting the train back. But despite her aunt's reservations, she felt certain this was the right thing to do.

Later that night, after the tree was decorated, the mantel and stair handrails strung with greenery, and the wreath hung on the front door, Tiff warmed up turkey leftovers for dinner. They ate in front of the TV.

A Christmas movie was playing, a sweet story with a little romance, a cookie exchange, and a happy ending under a garland of mistletoe. It was just the sort of story Tiff's mom loved, and one of Marsha's favorite actors was playing a lead role, so it was the perfect show for them to watch.

As the final credits scrolled, Tiff couldn't remember the last time she'd felt so relaxed and at peace hanging out at home. Even her mom looked contented.

Then the doorbell rang and, immediately, Rosemary tensed. "Who could that be?"

"No idea." Marsha pushed on the cushions to stand, but Tiff beat her to it.

"I'll go see."

Tiff checked out the window before unlocking the door. Doc Pittman, dressed in a black wool coat, with a scarf twisted around his neck, stood on the front porch. He looked cold. And worried.

Quickly Tiff opened the door. "Hi, Dr. Pittman. Come on in. Sorry to keep you waiting. We were in the family room watching TV."

"I apologize for interrupting. It's just—I've been trying to reach your aunt. She's not answering her phone."

Now that he was inside, Tiff noticed a sheen of moisture over his eyes. Tears. From the cold…or something else?

Then he blinked, and turned his head toward the sound of her aunt's approaching footsteps.

"Hello, Clark."

Somehow her aunt had found the opportunity to put on a quick coat of lipstick.

"I'm sorry you couldn't reach me. We were watching a movie and my phone was up in my room charging. Why didn't you try the landline?"

"I didn't want to bother the entire family. Could we talk privately for a moment?"

"Come into the study." Marsha gestured with her hand for the doctor to precede her.

Tiff hesitated, wondering if she should suggest her aunt use a different room. Just that afternoon Tiff had been catching up on paperwork. She'd left invoices strewn all over the desk. She wasn't even sure she'd closed the Excel spreadsheet on her computer.

But she'd never claimed the office as her personal work space. And her aunt was used to having the run of the house…a privilege she'd certainly earned during all the years Tiffany had been living in Seattle.

So she said nothing, just quietly headed for the kitchen where her mother was washing their empty cocoa mugs. Behind her she could hear her aunt say, "I assume there's a problem at the clinic?"

"Uh…yes. Quite a big problem."

From his manner, Tiff thought the problem was a lot more personal than that. She picked up a towel to dry the mugs. "Mom, have you ever wondered if there's something going on with Aunt Marsha and Dr. Pittman?"

"You mean romantically?"

Tiff nodded.

"I know they have a close friendship. I suppose it's possible. But why would they keep it a secret?"

Exactly. "Has Aunt Marsha ever had a serious boyfriend?"

"In high school she and Eugene Stillman were an item. That ended when she went to nursing college in Missoula."

"That was a long time ago."

Finished with the washing, her mom released the water, then folded the dishcloth neatly. "Honestly, that's the last time I remember her dating someone special. In college she had a lot of fun, but never got serious about just one guy. Once, when I was eighteen, our parents allowed me to go to Missoula and visit her. It was at one of the parties she took me to that I met your father."

"Did she know Dad?"

"I guess she must have since she introduced us."

Her mom winced, the telltale sign of an impending headache.

"You're tired. Let me make you some tea."

Her mother waved her away from the kettle. "You and Marsha coddle me too much. I can do it."

Tiff stepped aside, but it was difficult to watch her mother's shaking hands as she filled the kettle, then the way she set her mouth, as if denying her pain, as she waited for it to boil.

"We like helping you, Mom." Perhaps she shouldn't speak for her aunt. "At least, I do."

"Thank you, honey. It's so lovely having you home. If I was a good mother I'd encourage you to spread your wings and leave Lost Trail, like Marsha thinks you should. You're so beautiful and smart. You could set your sights a lot higher than opening your own accounting business in the wilds of Montana."

"This is my home. And you and Aunt Marsha are my family." She thought of mentioning the message from Craig, but decided to wait until she had a better idea about what she was going to say to him. It was nice to know her mother wanted her here. But she wished she could be certain her presence was helping.

Her aunt Marsha didn't think it was.

Her mother's strange behavior on Thanksgiving evening seemed to confirm that. But then there were moments like this one... It was all so confusing, trying to figure out what was best for her mom and for herself. She ought to consider her aunt as well. Maybe if she didn't feel so tied to looking after her sister and the farm, her relationship with Clark Pittman would be smoother.

The kettle began to whistle and Tiff handed the box of Sleepytime tea to her mother. She heard the door to the study open, then a male voice in the hall.

Though the tone was hushed, it sounded like Dr. Pittman was angry.

Marsha's answering words were muffled, the tone soothing.

Then the front door opened and all was quiet.

"She must be walking him to his car," Tiff surmised.

"I hope she put on a jacket. It's cold out there." Rosemary tried to remove the saturated tea bag from her mug, but her hand was too unsteady. Tiff reached over and did it for her.

"Let me carry this up to your bedroom."

This time her mother didn't argue.

Once her mom was settled in her room, Tiff came back downstairs and found her aunt in the kitchen, refilling the kettle.

"You okay, Aunt Marsha?"

"I'm fine, honey. Just tired."

"Are you sure?"

"Of course." Marsha's voice was too bright. She wouldn't meet Tiff's gaze. "After I take your mom her tea I'm going to bed."

"Mom made her own tea tonight and she's already in bed."

Tiff thought her aunt would be relieved; instead she frowned.

"If you weren't here she would have waited for me."

"But isn't the point of me being here to take some of the pressure off you?"

Her aunt took a deep breath. "It may seem silly to you. But your mom and I have been living on our own for a long time and we have a routine."

"Yes, but—"

"I'm sorry if I'm cranky. Clark never should have come by the house so late."

"It must have been something important."

Her aunt made no reply, merely turned off the kettle.

"Aunt Marsha, are you sure you're okay?"

"Good night, Tiff. I'll see you in the morning."

Sunday, November 26

ZAK WAITED FIFTEEN minutes at the beginning of Tamarack Trail on Sunday morning before Luke Stillman drove up.

"Sorry, man. Things have been crazy at our house. I swear no one's stopped talking since we found out about Grandma's will Friday morning."

Zak was curious about the will, but he was also damned cold. He stamped his feet and swung his arms. "Ready to start? I've got to get moving."

"Sure. Hang on, let me grab my hat." Luke reached into the truck to pull out his black wool cap and gloves.

Less than a minute later they were loping on the snowy path at a slow, warm-up pace. Luke turned on his Garmin watch as they ran. "Hang on. It's not kicking in yet…oh, wait, there it is. Good to go."

Zak waited until they rounded the first switchback and his body warmed up. Already his spirits were lifting. After three days on his own it was good to have company. And something interesting to talk about.

"So. What's the problem with the will?"

"What isn't? Grandma had a few tricks up her sleeve. First she divided the shares in the farm in such a way that all of us—except Vanessa—have an equal share."

"That sounds fair…except for Vanessa, I guess."

"Not really. My dad and uncle expected they'd be running the show."

"Did your grandma tell them that?"

"No. They assumed. As for my aunt Vanessa—she's always hated the ranch. She uses any excuse she can to get away on a girls' holiday or to visit her folks in Portland. But the fact that she was excluded means Uncle Clayton and Nikki only have two shares, to my family's four."

"So you're saying your family could outvote your uncle Clayton's family on key decisions about the farm's future?"

"Yeah. It's possible. But the real issue dividing us right now is what to do about an offer we have to sell fifty acres of our nicest riverfront land."

Zak decided against telling his friend he already knew this. "Who's in favor?"

"My dad and brother and Uncle Clayton. They all want the cash—and trust me, it's a lot of money. We're talking two point five million."

"The rest of you don't want to sell?"

"My mom, Nikki and me, we see things differently, more like Grandma did. We view ourselves more like stewards of the land than owners. It's up to us to protect it as much as possible and pass it on to the next generation without causing too much damage. We're ranchers, sure. But most of our land is wild and we want to keep it that way."

"I like the way you think."

"Thanks. But there's going to be some real hard feelings if we don't bow to the others and let this sale go through." Luke exhaled heavily, releasing a cloud of vapor. "That's not even the strangest thing about the will."

Zak's heart rate ratcheted up faster than his pace demanded. "Oh?"

"Turns out Grandpa left the house to Grandma only for as long as she was alive. After that it goes to—you're not going to believe this—Cora Christensen."

Zak skidded to a stop. "Our old teacher?" He studied Luke's face to see if he was joking. "Why the hell would he do that?"

"That's what everyone in my family is asking. Dad says he remembers hearing rumors at school that his father sure was friendly with the principal. But hell. None of us can believe Grandpa Jack actually had an affair."

"And why would he pick Miss Christensen?"

Luke shrugged. "She's old to us. But Dad says when she was younger she was pretty. And she used to dote on the parents. I could see my grandpa liking that."

"I guess." She doted on *some* parents. Luke, as one of the favored students, had a much different view of the old bag than Zak did. Old Cora had made his life hell always comparing him to his stronger, more confident brothers. It didn't matter that his grades were among the top in the class—she still managed to make him feel smaller than he already was.

By mutual accord Zak and Luke resumed running. Once he had a good pace going Zak asked, "Do you think your grandmother knew about the affair?"

"What else could she have thought about the life tenancy on the house? Poor Grams. It must have made her so angry."

Yeah. But had she found out after her husband died when she learned the terms of his will…or before? "How did your grandpa die?"

"It was an accident. He and Grandma were rounding up cattle from the foothills in the fall. He'd gone looking for a couple of missing calves. Grandma found him about an hour later… He'd fallen off his horse on a steep mountain ridge. The horse was okay, but he'd gone over. Died instantly."

"Gruesome."

"It shocked the entire family. I was sixteen at the time. I'd just gotten my driver's license. My folks got so paranoid about safety, they wouldn't let me drive alone for another year after that. And when we were out working on the horses, we had to stay in pairs."

Even after all these years, Luke was still so outraged by what he saw as excessive parental caution that his pace went to hell. Zak slowed, waiting for his friend to recover. He could tell it hadn't even occurred to Luke that his grandfather's death might not have been an accident, that his grandmother could have been involved.

They could have been arguing. Maybe she pushed him, never intending him to fall.

It wasn't an impossible scenario.

Archie Ford had been sheriff back then, running a sparse, two-man office. Which meant either he or Butterfield investigated the death.

In the basement at work were boxes of old files. Somewhere in all those musty papers was a copy of the accidental death report. Had Cora Christensen been interviewed at the time? He bet she had some of her own ideas about Jack Stillman's accident.

One way or another he was going to find out.

Chapter Seven

SUNDAY MORNING TIFF woke up to bright sunshine, a pounding headache, and the smell of something burning. She bounded out of bed and raced down the stairs to the kitchen.

Her mother sat at the table with her head nested in her arms. Smoke furled from the oven.

Tiff turned off the oven and grabbed a towel. Inside the oven were a dozen black disks. She pulled out the tray and set it on a trivet.

Disaster averted, she turned to her mother, who hadn't moved or said a word.

"What's wrong?" She put her hands on her mom's shoulders and gave her a small hug.

"I feel so…I can't…I don't know."

The kitchen counter was cluttered with bowls, measuring spoons, open canisters of flour and sugar. Normally her mother was a tidy baker.

"When did you get up?"

Slowly her mother straightened. She looked rough. Pupils dilated, skin puffy. "I'm not sure. It was still dark. I wanted to bake cookies. So many families are going to be coming to get their trees this week. We can't run out of cookies."

Tiff knew for a fact there were at least twelve dozen cookies of assorted kinds in her mother's downstairs freezer. "You've already baked a lot. We won't run out for at least a few weeks. Maybe you should go back to bed for a bit. Have you eaten?"

"I'm not sure. Marsha made me some tea before she left for Hamilton."

Tiff hadn't heard her aunt leave the house. "She goes there a lot, doesn't she?"

"When she isn't working she likes to visit her friends from her nursing days."

Yes. Tiff had heard that explanation before. But when you factored in the two days a week Marsha worked at the clinic—not to mention her yoga classes and book club meetings—that left a lot of alone time for her mother.

Tiff didn't begrudge her aunt her social calendar. But the isolation couldn't be good for her mom.

"Want to go for a walk after breakfast?"

"Maybe later. I should make some more cookies. But I'm so tired..."

"Let me do it. What's your easiest recipe?"

Her mom gave a faint smile. "You could handle the whipped shortbread. The molasses almond cookies are straightforward as well."

An hour later Tiff was dropping dollops of dough onto a cookie sheet, while her mother napped in the family room with *How the Grinch Stole Christmas* playing softly in the background. On the surface it was a perfect holiday moment.

From the window Tiff watched a steady stream of vehicles driving along the lane to the barn. They all left with a bundled tree tied to the roof or in the box of their truck. No doubt they had sampled the free cookies and cocoa. Some, hopefully, had purchased ornaments for their tree in the little gift shop.

As kids she and her brother had loved working in the gift shop. They looked forward to the day when they'd be old enough to lead the horses for the hayrides.

But Casey hadn't lived that long. And the dream had died for her with him.

Once the cookies had baked and cooled, Tiff put a few on a plate for her mother to sample. But Rosemary was fast asleep on the sofa, so she left the plate on the side table. She stacked the rest in a basket, and then slipped on her boots and coat so she could take them to the barn.

At this time of year the workers' jobs changed from bulk harvesting and shipping trees, to dealing with individuals and families who wanted to select their special tree. At Raven Farms the customer could select the tree they wanted. A staff member would cut it down and tie it to their vehicle while they enjoyed a snack around the fire pit. Christmas lights and music contributed to making the experience festive and memorable.

For those wanting to prolong the event, there were hayrides along Christmas Tree Lane, a twenty-minute circuit that allowed guests to enjoy the magic of the forest in the winter. Though the rides were offered continuously during business hours, Tiff thought they were most enjoyable in the evening, when the world was dark, and senses were heightened. Even the air smelled more intense in the night.

"Those cookies for us?"

She hadn't seen Kenny, but suddenly he was right in front of her, balancing an eight-foot baled tree on his left shoulder. In his plaid quilted jacket, jeans and steel-toed boots he looked the part of a Christmas tree farmer so perfectly it was difficult to remember that just a year ago he'd been one of Montana's foremost mountain guides.

"Mom was worried you might run out. But this batch comes with a warning. I made them."

"Is that so? For the sake of customer safety, I better sample one. Hang on a sec." He placed the tree on the roof rack of a small SUV then expertly secured it with several loops of plastic-coated twine. Then he turned to her and pulled off his gloves.

She lifted the wrap off the corner of the basket and let him take his pick. He popped the entire cookie into his mouth.

"So? How is it?"

"Melted in my mouth so fast I couldn't taste it. Better try

another."

She laughed and watched as he grabbed another two. "So business is good?"

"I don't know what it's been like other years, but we're getting run off our feet."

He walked along with her as she headed for the barn, opening the door for her then watching as she placed the basket on the table next to the gingersnaps. No sooner had she removed the wrap than someone was reaching for one of the cookies.

"You going to hang out here with us for a while?" Kenny asked.

She glanced around the room. Robin Wilson was behind the counter, ringing in a sale for a young woman with an infant strapped to her chest. One other customer waited behind her. Not exactly a crazy rush.

"I don't think I'm needed."

"You could come outside and help me cut down trees."

"I doubt if you need my help, either."

"No. But I'm guessing you need to spend a day outside, with the trees. It can be therapeutic."

"I take it I'm not looking my best." She wasn't surprised it was all catching up with her. The sleepless nights, the worry about her mother, her uncertainty about where she belonged and what she was meant to be doing with her life.

"You look great. But also…stressed."

The last time she'd worked "hands-on" at the farm had

been as a kid, with her father. He would place a hand on the trunk of each tree and be silent for a moment before he started the chainsaw.

When she asked why, he'd reminded her trees were living things, that he'd raised them from saplings. No matter how many he harvested in a day he never forgot that.

And she'd promised him she wouldn't either.

"I'll grab a pair of work gloves and some steel-toed boots." Kenny was right, she needed to reconnect with the land and the trees. And it would be a safe way to spend time with Kenny, try to sort out the confusing feelings he brought out in her.

Monday, November 27

MONDAY MORNING ZAK went to work an hour early, prepared to grapple with dusty boxes and molding papers. Thankfully Rose Newman had skills beyond crocheting and in a mere ten minutes he found the accidental death report for Jack Stillman.

The report itself was a disappointment. Only Lacy had been interviewed and her version of events was summarized in two brief paragraphs, corresponding almost exactly to the account he'd heard from Luke on Sunday.

Photos had been taken of Jack's body from the ridge looking down—a distance of about twenty feet—and also close up. From the skewed angle of Jack's head, it looked as though his neck broke on impact. This was confirmed in the coroner's report, signed by Doc Pittman.

Zak closed the file. Not much here beyond what he already knew. He put everything back where he'd found it and then headed up the stairs, passing one of the dentist's patients on her way into the office.

One side of the middle-aged woman's face was swollen. He grimaced in sympathy. "Good luck with that."

He kept climbing to the second floor where he shuffled through his keys until he found the correct one. Inside he dumped his coat and made coffee. Remembering Nadine's request for an extra day of vacation, he made a smaller pot than usual.

Why was he so interested in Jack's death? The people involved were no longer living. The chance that events from that day could have somehow impacted Lacy's own death were slight. Yet he felt compelled to keep digging.

A call to Doc Pittman went straight to messages. He left his name but didn't specify what he was calling about. No sense incriminating himself.

Butterfield showed up at quarter past eight. Heavier, shorter and less verbally gifted than the sheriff, Butterfield spent as little time in his desk as possible. He'd been in his job almost as long as Ford and the two men shared an allergy to paperwork.

Whenever Zak was feeling magnanimous, or simply

bored, he offered to write up his reports for him. After three years he was skilled at deciphering both Butterfield's and the sheriff's scrawls.

Today, though, he didn't offer. He needed to figure out a way to talk to Cora Christensen. Since he had no legal authority he had to make the encounter appear casual and unscripted. Which would require planning.

When Sheriff Ford came in, about ten minutes after Butterfield, Zak eyed the man discreetly, gauging his mood. Scowl, red-tinged eyes, shuffling gait...not good.

"Damned in-laws. Supposed to leave Sunday, but Margo convinced them to stay a few more days." Ford held out his hand for his messages. "Hope there's something in here that's going to require me to work late tonight."

"Just routine calls, Sheriff."

Ford grunted.

Some bosses might have asked about Zak's holiday, but not this one. Ford directed a frown at the half-full coffee machine. "Bring me a cup."

It wasn't a question but Zak answered anyway. "Sure, Sheriff."

This was his opportunity. He filled a mug and took it inside, closing the door enough to muffle sound but not enough to be obvious.

He set the mug down in a clear space. "Say, Sheriff, I was hanging out with Luke Stillman on the weekend. He was talking about his grandfather. Said he died in a ranching accident."

"Fell off a mountain ridge. That was a long time ago." The sheriff scratched out a signature on the report in front of him. Without looking up he added, "What of it?"

"I just wondered how that could happen. I imagine Jack was an experienced horseman."

The sheriff leveled his gaze at Zak. "Even an expert can get thrown off a horse. Possibly a rattler startled it. Or maybe Jack thought he heard the missing calf and dismounted to go looking for it. That ledge was narrow. One misstep was all it would take."

Interesting that Ford remembered the details so clearly. Maybe Lacy's death had got him thinking more than he was letting on.

"No one else was around? You didn't see anything suspicious?"

Ford threw down his pen. "Jesus Christ, Waller, what is this? Jack Stillman died a long time ago."

Instinctively Zak took a step back. Outbursts made him cautious. "Luke had me curious, that's all. Whenever the richest person in the county dies, you have to wonder, right?"

The sheriff's eyes narrowed. Did he get the parallel to Lacy's death? If so, he didn't let on.

"Get out of here, Waller. If you can't find enough real work to keep busy maybe you should take up crochet."

✕

AT NOON ZAK took his shovel out of his truck and headed for Cora's house. The tidy bungalow was just a few blocks away, across from the cemetery. When he saw the snow piled along the walkway to her front door, he smiled.

It only took ten minutes to clear the snow, at which point the old biddy opened her door and reluctantly thanked him.

"No problem, Miss Christensen." He moved closer, looking up the three steps that separated them. As he did this, she angled the door until it was almost closed, but not before he saw the pile of newspapers on the floor, almost three feet high.

Nadine, who'd been inside a few weeks ago, claimed Cora was a hoarder.

He was not surprised. Someone as twisted as Cora had to have mental problems.

"Say, I heard from Luke Stillman that you've inherited Lacy's old house. I guess when you move out there you'll have a lot more snow to shovel."

She frowned and pulled the edges of her sweater tight across her chest. "As if I'm going to move to the ranch. The idea is preposterous."

"Isn't that why Jack left it to you?"

"Why Jack did what he did, is none of your business."

Any sane person would have slammed the door in his

face by now. But Cora Christensen was lonely. She raised her chin proudly. "I used to be an important person in this community. I've taught most of the people who live here. Jack recognized my contribution."

"It was a long time ago, but it must have been a shock to you when he died."

"That fall was no accident. I tried to tell the sheriff…"

Adrenaline zinged through Zak's veins. There'd been no mention of Cora in Ford's report. "What did you want him to know?"

"Lacy did it of course. She pushed Jack off that ridge."

"DID SHE SEE Lacy push Jack?" Tiff asked later that day at the Dew Drop.

Zak shook his head no. He drank some beer, then glanced toward the entrance. Luke was supposed to meet them here.

The impromptu gathering had been organized by Tiff who called him an hour ago.

"I need a sanity break. Plus, we've had turkey four days in a row. I could use a good burger. You free tonight?"

"Sure. How about I call Luke and invite him too?"

"Perfect. That way we can keep the town gossips guessing about the status of our relationship."

"Just try to keep your hands off me this time."

"Oh, Zak, but I want you so bad." Then she laughed, totally spoiling the effect.

The Dew Drop Inn was owned by Keith Dewy, who'd taken it over from his parents when they retired and moved to Arizona. In a town of Montana log buildings and western-themed storefronts, the three-story, Bavarian-styled building was an original.

In the summer dark red-and-white geraniums spilled out of the boxes under the mullioned windows. In the winter Keith's wife Molly replaced the flowers with sprigs of cedar, pine and spruce. The bit of extra effort added a lot to the appeal of the building.

Molly ran the inn—four bedrooms on the second story—while Keith was in charge of the pub on the street level. Their four daughters had all worked at various times for the family business but currently only the youngest, twenty-five-year-old Mari, remained in Lost Trail, and most nights she could be found waiting tables in the bar.

Mari was efficient, quiet and inconspicuous. She dressed sensibly in flat shoes and dark jeans with a white shirt…and flirting for extra tips was not her style. Though he considered himself a regular at the Dew Drop, Zak had never managed to engage Mari in anything but the shortest of conversations. If he so much as asked how she was, she'd be sure to answer as she did today.

"I'm fine. What can I get you?"

"Burger for me," Tiff said.

He hesitated. He'd love a burger too but they never remembered to remove the onions. "Fish and chips, hold the tartar sauce."

Tiff leaned in close and spoke quietly, continuing the conversation they'd begun before Mari's interruption. "So how does Cora know Lacy killed her husband if she didn't witness it?"

"She said Jack told her his wife was a hothead. He said she could fly off the handle at a moment's notice."

"I guess millions of non-homicidal people could claim the same."

"She also said Jack wasn't dead a month before Lacy was redecorating their house and prancing around town in new clothes and fancy western jewelry."

"Prancing?"

"Cora's word, not mine."

"So let me get this straight. We now know why Lacy hated Cora. It's because Cora was having an affair with Jack."

He nodded.

"Did Lacy know about the affair before he died or only after she'd learned the terms of his will?"

"Don't know."

"What about Dewbury Academy? Why did it shut down after Jack's death?"

"I called my mom this afternoon and asked her that. She said Lacy campaigned hard to close it. Once she convinced the majority of parents to bus their kids to Sula, Cora had no choice but to retire."

"Any idea how long Jack and Cora's affair went on?"

"Nope."

"And finally," Tiff said, "is any of this related to Lacy's death?"

"No friggin' idea. All I can say for sure is the list of people who gained from her death is pretty darned long."

"Obviously her family."

"That's right. Sons Eugene and Clayton, their wives Em and Vanessa, and their children Tom, Luke and Nikki. We can add Cora to the list since she inherited a life tenancy in the Lazy S homestead property."

Tiff snapped her fingers. "I almost forgot, I heard something at our Thanksgiving dinner I wanted to tell you about. You know Gwen Lange?"

"The receptionist at the medi-clinic?"

"That's right. She's dating one of the seasonal workers at our farm, Rusty Thurston. Anyway, I noticed she and my aunt were having words at one point. Later Kenny told me they were talking about Lacy Stillman. My aunt accused Gwen of eavesdropping on their conversation. I assume this must have been at the clinic. Didn't you say Lacy had a checkup the day before she died?"

"She did. Did you ask your aunt for more details?"

"Yes, but she denied being upset with Gwen. I think she was trying to protect her."

Zak was going to ask another question when he noticed a

tall woman with long blonde hair step into the bar.

He didn't often see Nadine Black out of uniform. Every nerve in his body appreciated the view. He was going to wave at her to join them and then he noticed she wasn't alone.

A cowboy trailed behind her. With his hat on he was taller than Nadine by at least six inches, a dark-haired man with a scruff of a beard on a narrow face, and a scar at the corner of his right eye.

Dustin Hart.

Zak recognized the bronc rider from videos he'd watched on the Internet. Back when Nadine first started with the sheriff's department, Zak had done a little research. He'd found out Nadine was born and raised in Helena and started barrel riding when she was thirteen. She'd turned professional when she was eighteen and her career had been steadily progressing until the death of her horse, Mane Event, last spring.

He'd watched videos of Nadine's barrel-racing events. She'd been amazing at guiding her horse around the three barrels in the regulation pattern. He also found her public page on Facebook and noticed a cowboy named "Dustin Hart" was liking all her posts. He figured they must have been a couple, and so he'd checked out Dustin's stats and discovered the twenty-eight-year-old already had an impressive list of buckles and trophies to his name.

Nadine had closed down her official Facebook page once

she started the new job in Lost Trail. And she'd never mentioned Dustin, so Zak had assumed she'd left him as well as her rodeo career behind.

Yet here he was.

Zak caught Nadine's eye when she was about ten feet away. He nodded, and she did the same. Then Dustin put a hand on her arm and gestured her to a table on the other side of the room. Nadine hesitated a second before following him.

Zak's gut twisted. At least now he knew why she'd blown him off the other day.

He took a long drink of beer, finishing off the glass. As he was refilling it from the pitcher, Luke arrived, along with his younger cousin Nikki.

"Hey, Tiff, the night is looking up. I didn't know you'd be here." Luke slid into the seat next to Zak. "You know my cousin Nikki, right?"

"Of course. Hi, Nikki." Tiff shifted her chair over to make more room at the table.

Dressed in jeans and a shearling coat, Nikki looked much more comfortable than she had on the day of her grandmother's funeral. She took off her cowboy hat and settled it on an empty chair. "Hope you don't mind us butting in."

"Nothing to butt into," Zak said awkwardly.

"Is that right?" Nikki cocked her head. "I heard the two of you were hot and heavy at my grandma's house on

Wednesday."

Zak drummed his fingers on the table and tried to laugh naturally. He didn't want to have to explain why he'd been in Lacy's bedroom. But he didn't want to feed the rumors, either. "Yeah, well, we thought we'd give Gertie Humphrey something to talk about. But Tiff and I are just friends."

"Sometimes barely that," Tiff added, making everyone laugh.

Mari showed up with the food. She set the plates down quickly then turned to Luke. "I'll bring some extra glasses. Would you like another pitcher of draft? Maybe some food to go with it?"

Luke checked with his cousin, who nodded. "Sure, we'll have another pitcher for the table and burgers for me and Nik."

"Got it." Mari put a hand on the back of Luke's chair and stuck out one hip bone. "By the way, I'm sorry about your grandmother, Luke. I wanted to go to the funeral but I had to work."

"Thanks, I appreciate that. We're going to miss her, that's for sure."

"She was a character. I always enjoyed serving her."

"Bet she didn't leave you much in the way of a tip."

Zak had never seen Mari smile before. Turned out she had a cute set of dimples.

"That's okay. A lot of our older customers are careful with their money."

Luke nodded and after a semi-awkward pause Mari added, "Okay, I'll get your beers and put this order in with the kitchen."

Zak waited until she was out of earshot. "I've never heard her talk so much before. Guess she must really like you."

Luke batted his hand. "She's a good kid. But young, right?"

"She's the same age as me," Nikki said. "Five years isn't that much of a difference." She glanced from her cousin to Zak. Neither of the guys replied. Zak focused on scraping the tartar sauce away from his fish and fries.

"So how are you guys doing?" Tiff changed the subject. "It must be hard losing your grandmother."

"Harder than you can imagine," Nikki said. "The entire family's gone crazy since Grandma died."

As if on cue, Nikki's phone chimed, and she lowered her eyes to check her screen. As she read, her mouth pinched in an expression of annoyance. "My mother. I thought I'd get a break from her while she was at her stupid spa retreat."

"Let me guess." Luke smiled at Mari as she set down the extra glasses and pitcher. "She's pressuring you to agree to sell that land."

"Big time. I've had about ten text messages today. I wish she would chill. She's going to come home from her spa trip even more wound up than when she left."

"My dad is putting the same pressure on me and my mother. And Tom's in a funk because he can't have Grandma's house. He wants to move in with his girlfriend and he feels like the perfect house has been snatched out from under him."

"It's so bizarre," Nikki said. "Why would Miss Christensen want to live out on our ranch anyway? It's so isolated, and the roads can be dangerous in the winter. And it's not as if our family is going to be friendly to her. If Grandpa did have an affair with her and wanted to leave her something, why not money?"

"It's almost like Grandpa did the one thing he knew would piss off Grandma the most," Luke said.

Zak had been thinking the same thing.

Chapter Eight

When Luke and Nikki's burgers arrived, Zak eyed his haddock and coleslaw with regret, trying to ignore his craving for some juicy, triple A, Montana beef. Around him his friends were digging in and the aroma was killing him.

Luke noticed his envious stare. "Why did you order fish, you fool?"

"They never remember to leave off the onions here."

"That's because they're awesome." Luke pulled a caramelized strand out from his burger and sucked it up. "What do you have against them?"

"Memories of liver and onion dinners at home." And his father making him sit at the table, sometimes for hours, until he'd finished every bite.

"Will you be going to South Dakota for Christmas?" Tiff asked.

"Not if I can come up with a good excuse. Hopefully we'll have a blizzard that'll shut down the highways."

"It's going to be a weird Christmas for us with Grandma gone," Nikki said.

"And everyone at each other's throats," Luke added. "But I suppose we'll go through the motions like every other year. Tiff, that reminds me. Mom wants me to pick up the tree this year. Can you set aside a fourteen-foot noble fir?"

"Sure. That's a great choice."

"Could you set one aside for us too?" Nikki asked. "Sixteen foot high if possible. Mom wants it up and ready to decorate when she gets home from her spa trip."

At the word "spa," Nikki rolled her eyes. Then she turned to Zak. "Will you put up a tree?"

"Nah." His memories of the white-and-silver artificial tree from his childhood were not pleasant.

"You should," Nikki insisted. "I can help you decorate it. Mom changes the theme of our tree every few years so we have boxes and boxes of unused ornaments in our basement."

The idea made him uneasy for several reasons. Mostly he did not want to give Nikki the wrong idea. "My cat would only shred it. He doesn't like new things."

"Come on, Zak, Nikki's totally right. You should get a tree this year. A *real* tree." Tiff's eyes had a mischievous gleam. She loved pressing his buttons.

"I'll think about it," he said.

But he wouldn't.

AN HOUR AND two pitchers of beer later, Tiff watched Nikki pull out her car keys.

"You sure you're okay to drive?" Tiff asked.

"I only had one glass." Nikki turned to Zak. "Let me know if you change your mind about that tree."

Tiff watched the Stillmans leave the bar, wondering how they were going to resolve the issues that divided their family. When she turned to Zak to ask him what he thought, she noticed him eyeing Nadine Black and her cowboy friend, who were talking intently at their table in the back corner.

She'd noticed them earlier, but hadn't wanted to interrupt the conversation. "So who's the cowboy with your deputy?"

Blotches of red darkened Zak's cheeks. "She's not my deputy. The cowboy is Dustin Hart. He's a bronc rider in the PRCA."

"What's the story?"

"I'm not sure. I think they used to date before she moved to Lost Trail."

"And now he's back in the picture? Well that sucks."

"If I said I don't really care…?"

"I wouldn't believe you." She gave his hand a sympathetic squeeze, then topped up his beer glass. "Any interest in Nikki Stillman? I have a hunch you'd have more luck with her."

"You think?" The offer to help him put up a Christmas tree hadn't been subtle. But he couldn't see her that way.

"Bring her around to the farm on the weekend. The two of you can take a hay ride through the forest. I hear it's very romantic."

"Stop it. Can we talk about something else?"

She looked him in the eye for a few moments, then gave a slight lift of her shoulders. "Such as?"

"You know that list of questions we were working on before Luke and Nikki showed up?"

"Yes…"

"One person who might have some answers is Sybil."

"Good point. At the potluck after Lacy's celebration of life Sybil mentioned the fact that Lacy hated Cora. It sounded like she knew some of the history between them."

"Yeah. I'd like to ask her about that."

Sybil had answered some questions for them about Riley Concurran last month. The librarian had lived in Lost Trail all her life. People revealed surprising aspects about themselves at the library and Sybil was not only observant, she also had a keen mind and a good memory.

"You should talk to her tomorrow," Tiff said.

"Yes." He pushed aside his plate of half-eaten fish and coleslaw.

"You want to come too?"

"Why not. You've got me curious."

"Okay," he said. "I'll set up a meeting at the library for noon."

×

Tuesday, November 28

NADINE WAS THE only one in the office when Zak showed up for work the next day. He hung his jacket. "Thanks for making coffee."

"Uh-huh." Her gaze didn't waver from her computer screen.

He sat on the edge of his desk, facing her. "So. Last night."

Her eyes flicked upward. "What about it?"

He took a deep breath. "We need to clear the air."

"What's the problem? You went to the bar with your friends and I went with mine."

"Just a few weeks ago I thought we were friends, too. But hey. We spend our days together. If you don't want to be friendly after-hours I get it."

She got up from her chair and took a stance, planting her hands on her hips. "Okay. I've been a jerk. I'm sorry. Stuff's been happening. I'm feeling confused."

Zak felt like she'd tossed a ball of yarn at him. Which end should he pull? "What kind of stuff?"

"A friend from my rodeo days said he found the perfect horse for me. You know, to replace Mane Event."

"That friend is Dustin Hart? The cowboy you were with last night?"

"Yeah. He called me last week, the night we had plans to

meet up at the Dew Drop. I should have texted to let you know I couldn't make it. But we FaceTimed for over an hour. Then it was too late."

"Are you two…together?"

"No." She looked pissed off. "I told you, he called me about a horse. Her name is Making Magic. She's a gorgeous American quarter horse, just five years old. Over the holidays I drove to Bozeman to look at her."

This was so not what he expected. "And…?"

"I fell in love. Dustin thinks I should get back on the rodeo circuit. I'm not so sure. I like this job." She glanced at the closed door to the sheriff's office. "Though some personnel changes would be nice."

"I second that."

"So I don't want to quit. But I also don't want to let Making Magic slip through my fingers. Trouble is, even if I bought her, right now I have no place to keep her."

"You could board her somewhere."

"No way. If I make a commitment to a horse I'm going to be the one who takes care of her, who grooms her and makes sure she gets her exercise. Who knows, this summer I might enter a few of the local rodeos. Just for kicks."

"Sounds like you should be shopping for an acreage, then."

"You think?"

"We could shop together. I'm in the housing market too."

"What are you looking for?"

Before he could answer the phone rang. Caller ID gave him the name Clayton Stillman.

"Lost Trail Sheriff's Office," he said.

"We've got a problem." It was Clayton speaking. "I need to talk to the sheriff right away."

Zak glanced at the time display on his computer. The sheriff wouldn't be in for at least another fifteen minutes. "Why don't you explain the situation to me first? Then I can get the ball rolling."

"I don't want a ball rolling. I want the sheriff, and I want him at our place *now.* Nikki is missing."

Zak lost his breath and his ability to speak for a few seconds. In a small county, sheriff business could become personal. But this was crazy. He'd seen Nikki at the Dew Drop just last night.

"What do you mean by missing? When's the last time you saw her?"

Nadine's head snapped upright at the word "missing." He tried to ignore her, to focus on Clayton's response.

"Nikki told me she was going into town last night. I went to bed around ten and she still wasn't home. She's usually up before me in the morning. But not today. Her truck isn't in her parking spot and her bed doesn't look like it was slept in."

"Have you talked to Em or Eugene or their boys? Maybe she slept over at their house last night."

"Why would she do that?"

"I saw both Nikki and Luke at the Dew Drop last night. They left well before ten o'clock. I'm pretty sure Nikki was driving. She pulled out her keys when it was time to go."

Neither one had had that much to drink. But maybe they'd gone back to Luke's house and had a few more?

"I'll head over to Eugene's right now and check," Clayton said. "Meanwhile, you get Sheriff Ford to give me a call."

Zak didn't bother arguing, though there were plenty of reasons to do so, most importantly that Nikki was an adult and the fact she hadn't made it home last night was hardly a matter for an official investigation.

But there was also the possibility something bad had happened to Nikki. Zak didn't like to think so. But he was definitely going to feel better once he knew for sure she was safe.

"What's going on?" Nadine was holstering her firearm.

He waved at her to hold on a sec. Quickly he tapped out a message to Luke: *Where's Nikki?*

He was about to explain the situation to Nadine when the phone rang again.

Expecting to see the Stillman name, he was surprised when *Miss C. Christensen* popped up on the display. He was tempted not to answer, but in this job he didn't have that luxury.

"Sheriff's office."

"Zak Waller? You send the sheriff out to my house right

this minute, you hear me?"

He'd taken calls from his old school teacher the day after Halloween every year he'd had this job. But he'd never heard from her at any other time.

"What's the problem, Miss Christensen?"

"The problem is I'm being terrorized. That's the problem."

He'd never heard her sound this upset before. Her lecturing tone was tinged with genuine fear. "Are you okay? Should I send an ambulance?"

"I'm fine. It's my house. Again."

He could tell Nadine was frustrated at hearing only one end of the conversation. He tried to block out her distracting hand signals.

"Was it egged?"

"No, it wasn't *egged.* That monster Trevor Larkin and his friend used red paint this time. On my front door! I want their parents to buy me a brand-new door and I want them to promise their miserable children will never set foot near my property again."

"Did you see Trevor painting your house?"

"I don't need to see them to know they did it. They have a track record. And I don't want to have to wait a few days this time before someone comes to see the evidence."

"Okay. I hear you. We'll send someone out right away to take your statement and get some pictures—"

"No pictures! I don't want any pictures. And I don't

want just anybody coming by. I want the sheriff. This time he better put a stop to these kids."

"Sheriff Ford will get back to you eventually. But we'll start—" He clawed back the 'ball rolling' metaphor he'd been about to use and instead said, "Deputy Black will set the wheels in motion with a preliminary statement. Try to stay calm until she gets there. It shouldn't be long."

He was writing down the address as he spoke and by the time he'd finished, Nadine was standing by his desk.

"I liked the sound of the first call better. Do we have a missing person?"

"It's too early to say. Nikki Stillman, the girl with the braid who was at our table last night, didn't go home after she dropped her cousin home. She's probably fine, at a friend's or something. But I have something else that needs your attention."

He handed Nadine Cora's name and address.

"Someone splashed red paint on her front door. She thinks it's the same kids who vandalized her house at Halloween. I'm not so sure though. The kids threw eggs; they didn't do permanent damage."

"Escalating crime in Lost Trail. This is serious stuff."

He liked her sense of humor. You needed a twisted one when you worked for Sheriff Ford. "Cora inherited a life interest in Lacy Stillman's house. There might be a connection."

"Back that up a few steps for me. Is Cora somehow related to the Stillmans?"

"Nope. But I've heard speculation she had a long-term affair with Lacy's husband. When Jack died sixteen years ago, the house went to Lacy. Now that Lacy's gone, it goes to Cora."

"What was the point? Wouldn't it have been more helpful to leave his mistress some cash?"

"Unless Jack's goal wasn't so much to help Cora as to humiliate his wife."

Nadine's eyes widened. "Gotcha. I like the diabolical way your mind works." She took a quick look at the address, then stuffed the piece of paper in her back pocket. "I'll let you know what I find out."

Zak watched her leave with an unaccustomed pang of regret.

Usually he was perfectly content being the dispatcher. Sure he was over-qualified. And tied to his desk. But working behind the scenes he managed to keep on top of everything that was happening in the office, without ever drawing too much attention to himself.

Today though the office was stifling.

He wanted to see what had been painted on that door, and he wanted to be the one to question the Larkin boy about it. He was almost certain the young teenager would be innocent this time.

More important than any of that, though, was Nikki.

He checked in for a message from Luke. Nothing.

It was highly improbable that anything bad had happened to Nikki. There were all sorts of valid reasons an intelligent woman in her mid-twenties might not go home after an evening at the bar. She could have met up with a guy.

Though it had seemed like she was flirting with him last night.

So maybe she'd had late-night plans with a girlfriend.

But why wouldn't she have mentioned anything to Luke? Suggested he take his own vehicle into town to save her making the trip twice?

According to the law, Nikki would have to be missing a lot more than ten hours before an investigation would be launched.

But knowing Nikki, and her family, and their position in the community, the sheriff would want to make an appearance at the Lazy S as soon as possible.

Generally the sheriff disliked getting work calls at home, except in emergencies.

But this was the Stillmans. And election year was around the corner.

So he took a risk and called.

After a brusque hello, the sheriff listened as Zak explained the situation.

"Thanks for letting me know. I'm going to drive straight out there. If I need any help I'll let you know. Otherwise, expect me back in the office when you see me."

"Got it, Sheriff." Zak hung up, leaned back in his chair and looked around.

After all that excitement the office was quiet now, his coffee was cold…and all he could do was sit and wait.

He was beginning to hate his job.

Chapter Nine

THE LIBRARY SEEMED a magical place to Tiff when she was a child, and she still felt a little thrill when she stepped in the front door. A bachelor farmer had donated the two-story house to the town twenty years ago and Sybil—she was the librarian, even back then—had created a comfortable, homey feel in the place.

There were all sorts of interesting nooks, where you might find a huge beanbag chair or an old-fashioned wing chair flanked by a fringed lamp. Sybil always changed things up so you never knew quite what to expect when you turned a corner.

After exchanging her snowy boots for a pair of hand-knitted slippers, Tiff stepped through an arch into the former living room—now displaying books about Montana or written by local authors.

Sybil, wearing a pair of glitzy red-framed eyeglasses, her unruly hair held back by a similarly colored scarf, entered the room a few seconds later.

"Tiff! Nice to see you, honey. Zak's already here. I thought we'd chat in the children's reading nook in the back.

I'm just going to put up the *CLOSED FOR A FEW MINUTES* sign so we won't be interrupted."

"Thanks, Miss T." She made her way to the back room, formerly the kitchen, but now stuffed with books and toys and a reading corner. Zak sat on one of the beanbag chairs, his thin legs crossed awkwardly in front of him.

Tiff plopped down next to him. "This is kind of cool. Brings back lots of memories, doesn't it?"

But from Zak's serious expression, he wasn't remembering the many times they'd sat here as children for Miss T's famous story hour.

"No time for a trip back to Pooh Corner today. Nikki didn't make it home after the bar last night."

"What? Did Luke?"

"Yeah. He finally answered my text messages an hour ago. He says she dropped him at his house and he assumed she was going to her place next. She didn't say anything about other plans. But according to her dad she wasn't home this morning. He didn't hear her last night, either."

"Is her vehicle missing?"

"Yup."

"She sounded pretty pissed off at her family. Maybe she went to a friend's?"

Zak nodded, but didn't answer as Sybil came back into the room. She folded her petite, curvy frame easily into the lotus position, on a cushion equidistant from each of them.

"So, you two. The last time you came to talk to me you

were investigating Riley Concurran's murder. What's going on this time? Has there been another crime in Lost Trail?" She leaned forward and whispered, "*Another murder?*"

"That's what I need to figure out," Zak said. "I have questions about Lacy Stillman's death and I'm hoping you can answer some of them for me."

Sybil straightened abruptly. "Lacy was an old woman who died in her sleep."

"Yes, it seems so. But the day before we went for a beer. She'd just had her checkup. Said she was in perfect health. And yes, I know that's no guarantee when you're old, but consider this." Zak paused before adding, "The very day Lacy died her family was approached with a two-and-a-half-million-dollar offer for some land. Lacy was opposed to the deal, as you can imagine. Now that she's gone it's possible the deal can go through."

"You're saying the timing of her death was opportunistic for the family. But that doesn't mean they had a hand in it. Even if they did—how was it accomplished? Do you have a theory?"

"No," Zak admitted. "And I'm not accusing her family of anything at this point. There is definitely no official investigation going on. I just have questions. As a private citizen."

"When you have questions, Zak, I've noticed the answers generally lead somewhere." Sybil turned her probing gaze from him to Tiff. "And why are you involved? Last time the girl involved was a Raven Farms employee."

"I don't have a connection this time. I think Zak likes to share his theories with me because he can't go to the sheriff."

"Oh, Zak." Sybil held out her hands, palms upward. "That's a problem you're going to need to deal with one day. You can't get away with working behind Ford's back forever."

"Yeah. I hear you. Does that mean you won't help us?"

"Heavens no! Ask me your questions. I'll help if I can."

"The day of Lacy's funeral you mentioned Lacy didn't like Cora Christensen. Since then we've heard several rumors that Cora and Jack had an affair. Is that true?"

"Oh. My. You aren't thinking Cora killed Lacy are you?"

"I'd say that's a pretty unlikely scenario. But if there's bad blood between them that might still be relevant."

"It was certainly relevant sixteen years ago when Lacy campaigned to have Dewbury Academy closed and our children bussed to school in Sula."

"Right. We were wondering about that, too." Tiff leaned forward. "My mom thought the school closed because Miss Christensen wanted to retire."

"Cora's life revolved around her job. She would still be working now if she could. No, that stuff about wanting to retire was the 'official' line but not the truth. Jack and Cora had been carrying on for more than a decade. While Jack was alive Lacy couldn't do anything. But shortly after he died, Lacy campaigned hard to shut down Dewbury Academy."

"I wonder how she convinced the parents to bus their children to Sula?"

"It wasn't difficult. Most of us were sick of the way Cora manipulated children, making some favorites and turning others into outcasts. Cora did this with Eugene and Clayton, always favoring Clayton and making Eugene seem the fool. She pulled the same stunt with Lacy's grandchildren, belittling poor Nikki, just because she was chubby and a bit more socially awkward than the other girls."

This wasn't the first time Tiff had heard these allegations against her old teacher. Zak had complained for years that Christensen hated him. Until recently Tiff hadn't believed him. According to Zak that was because she'd been one of the favored ones. She shot him a conciliatory glance. He responded with an "I told you so" lift of his brows.

"Why didn't Lacy get Cora fired when her own boys were younger?" Zak asked.

"Oh, she wanted to. But Jack protected Cora. And he had a lot of sway in the community. If you're wondering why Lacy didn't leave him, the answer is simple. She was afraid to lose her sons and the ranch."

"So she stayed with a man who was cheating on her?" Tiff couldn't imagine a life like that.

"Afraid so. But Lacy was tough. She kicked Jack out of her bedroom. Where the boys were concerned, she made sure she called the shots. And she made Jack donate about one hundred acres of wetlands to Ducks Unlimited."

"How do you know all this?" Tiff wondered.

"Lacy loved a good romance almost as much as she loved to talk. I knew I was going to spend at least half an hour gabbing every time she dropped into the library. Not that I minded. Lacy donated generously to the library. Besides, I liked her."

"Did Lacy ever talk about Jack's accident?" Zak asked.

"No. It must have been awful to be the one to discover his body. But she never discussed it, not even with me."

Zak glanced at Tiff. She knew what he wanted to ask. She gave a slight nod. They could trust Sybil.

"This may sound crazy—but do you think Lacy was capable of pushing Jack and causing him to fall off that ledge?"

Sybil gave a small snort. "I've wondered the same thing myself. If Jack goaded her, maybe. Then again, she had a strict moral code and she wasn't a violent woman. So I don't know."

"Wow. You think you know someone and then you find out you didn't have a clue." Zak scrambled to his feet. "Thanks a bunch, Sybil. You've filled in some important gaps for me."

Sybil got to her feet gracefully. "Good luck with your investigations, Zak. If possible, please try to find some reason to arrest Cora. That woman has been a blight on this community for too long."

IT WAS FIVE minutes past the official closing at Little Cow Pokes Day Care when Justin ran through the door.

At the craft table Debbie-Ann was sitting with Geneva and Ashley. She glanced up and smiled at him, not looking the least bit annoyed.

"I'm sorry, I'm sorry." He didn't want to be the annoying parent who was always pushing the boundaries of his child's caregivers. Nor did he want Geneva to carry the stigma of always being the last child to get picked up.

But Clayton Stillman had called him a half hour ago with the news that his daughter Nikki was missing, and he wanted advice on what he should do. Apparently Nikki and Luke had gone to the bar last night and no one had seen her since she'd dropped Luke home.

Though Nikki was an adult, she still lived at home with her parents. According to Clayton she always let him and Vanessa know if she wasn't going to be home at night.

Ford had both his deputies out looking for Nikki but so far he was refusing to open an official missing person's file and put out an APB.

Justin had given Clayton the name of a private investigator. Other than that, all he could offer was reassurance. And Clayton needed a lot of reassurance. Vanessa was cutting her spa vacation short to come home. She was not going to be pleased if Nikki was still missing when she got here.

"It's not a problem." Debbie-Ann was an average-looking woman, but her easygoing disposition and generous smile made her seem more attractive than she was. “The girls and I are having fun making snowflakes. Did you ever do this as a child?”

She folded a piece of paper into quarters, then cut notches strategically on the sides. When she unfolded the paper she had a delicate-looking snowflake.

“Look at mine, Daddy.” Geneva held up several of her own snowflakes. “Aren’t they pretty?”

He kissed the top of her head. “Sure are. We can use them to decorate our Christmas tree.” Noticing Ashley watching him with saucer-wide eyes, he moved to her side of the table. “Did you make snowflakes, too?”

Shyly she showed him one, holding the corners gingerly with both hands.

“Gorgeous. What a great job you guys have done. And yes, I do remember making those when I was a kid, but I don’t think mine were anywhere near this pretty.”

He straightened, glanced back at Debbie-Ann. “I’ll gladly pay for the extra half hour, but don’t worry. I don’t plan on making a habit of being late.”

She waved off his offer of extra money. “It’s not a big deal. Everyone is late at one time or another. But since it is almost dinnertime…would you and Geneva like to eat with us? I have a pot roast in my slow cooker.”

Her tone was friendly and there wasn’t even a hint of a flirtatious glint in her eyes. Still, alarm bells rang in his head.

If he wasn’t careful he was going to set up expectations

with this woman…and maybe her daughter, too.

He didn't know much about Debbie-Ann, only that she was in her mid-to-late twenties and a single parent, like him. Ashley's father, for whatever reason, wasn't in the picture.

"Yes, Daddy, please say yes!" Geneva was tugging at his arm, while Ashley fixed wide eyes at him, hopefully.

"I'm sorry. I shouldn't have asked in front of the girls." Debbie-Ann started tidying the craft table. "Sometimes I speak before I think."

"It's a really nice offer. But you shouldn't reward me for being late."

"Maybe you should taste the pot roast before you consider it a reward."

He smiled. And then, without him even saying yes, it seemed to be decided.

"We live right here, in an apartment above the day care," Debbie-Ann explained as she locked the front door.

"The stairs are back here." Ashley ran to show the way, and Geneva followed.

"This used to be my grandmother's house." Debbie-Ann picked up a piece of Lego and tossed it into a plastic tub, without breaking her stride. "She and my grandfather raised me. She died just a year before Ashley was born. I have mixed feelings about that. On the one hand I would have loved for Ashley to know her. But I'm afraid Grams would have been disappointed in me. She wanted me to study dance in college. Maybe become a teacher one day."

They'd reached the narrow stairwell. Though he couldn't see the girls, he could hear them tromping above them. Justin paused to let Debbie-Ann go ahead.

"What happened to your parents?"

"My mom was just fifteen when she got pregnant with me. She's lives in L.A. She's a yoga instructor, I think. Or she was when I last saw her."

"And when was that?"

"At Grandma's funeral. I hate to say it, but I think Mom only came back to Lost Trail to see what she got in the will."

The stairs opened up into a bright room with a denim-blue sectional in one corner and a wooden pedestal table in the other. In the third corner of the space was a small kitchen, then a hallway, which presumably led to bedrooms and a bath.

The aroma of the pot roast was mouth-watering. "Dinner smells pretty awesome. Wish I at least had a bottle of wine to contribute."

"No worries. I have some. Hope your taste isn't too expensive." Debbie-Ann opened the fridge. "I also have a bagged salad in here somewhere."

"Want to see my Troll collection?" Ashley asked his daughter.

Geneva nodded her head vigorously.

"It's in my room." Ashley took Geneva's hand and led her down the hall.

"How old is Ashley?"

"Six." Debbie-Ann had found what she was looking for. She set the bag of sweet kale salad on the table, then pulled a bowl from the cabinet.

Two years older than his daughter. "She's really patient with Geneva."

"Growing up in a day care has made Ashley good at getting along with kids of all ages."

"That's a plus."

"Is it? I hope so. When she was younger she had a hard time sharing me with so many other children. She's gotten used to it now. But I do feel guilty about that sometimes."

"At least she's with you, and not some babysitter."

Debbie-Ann paused in the midst of tossing the salad ingredients into the bowl. "Do you feel guilty about leaving Geneva in day care?"

"I did at first. But with Willow gone, I don't have a choice."

Debbie-Ann handed him a corkscrew and nodded at a bottle of Pinot Noir on the counter. Taking the hint, he went to open it. "Now that I've gotten to know you and Ashley, though, I feel damned lucky to have such a great option for childcare. And just a block from my office."

"I'm happy to have Geneva. She's a great kid. A little quiet, but given all the changes in her life, that's not surprising."

He thought about some of the pictures Geneva had brought home from the day care. Lots of them were stick-figure families, with a mother and father and little girl. The worrisome thing was that often Geneva made a dark, angry scribble over the father.

"I suppose you've noticed Geneva's odd pictures of our family."

"Hm. I've seen pictures she's drawn of herself with her parents. I don't think they're of you."

"Why do you say that?"

"Because I've asked her about them. The pictures are of her and her mother and a man named Paul."

His heart lurched. "That's her biological father."

"She told me he was a bad man."

"Wow." He set down the open bottle. "How do you get her to open up to you that way?"

"It's pretty simple with kids. You just do fun stuff together. And ask questions. Most of them are incredibly open. A lot of my parents would be very embarrassed if they knew some of the stuff their kids tell me."

"Oh." He tried, in vain, to think of something embarrassing Geneva might have said about him.

Debbie-Ann laughed. "Don't worry. Geneva hasn't shared any of your secrets with me." She put the salad bowl on the table, then turned back to look at him. "At least not yet."

DINNER WAS DELICIOUS. Justin made a mental note to order a slow cooker from Amazon later that night. And get Debbie-Ann's pot roast recipe.

As he'd seen her do before, Debbie-Ann involved the girls in cleanup. Once they'd put their dishes in the sink—there was no dishwasher—she gave them the okay to go back into Ashley's room to play.

Justin washed the dishes while Debbie-Ann put away the leftovers. Soon everything was clean except their wineglasses, which Debbie-Ann had just refilled.

"Want to sit and relax for a minute?"

It wasn't even seven yet, so he couldn't plead needing to get Geneva home to bed. Not that he wanted to leave. He was enjoying Debbie-Ann's company. A lot.

He just didn't want her to get the wrong idea.

They sat in the living room and Debbie-Ann turned on the TV, setting the channel to a nature show. "Are you okay with this? I like watching shows where you can still talk." She sat cross-legged on her end of the sofa, cradling her wineglass with both hands.

On the screen a photographer dressed in a thick parka, hat and scarf was filming a moose and her calf in the forest in the middle of winter. It looked like a very uncomfortable enterprise. The baby moose was so ugly it was kind of cute.

"Debbie-Ann, I really like you. I enjoy hanging out with you. I just need to be upfront about my situation. You know I'm still married to Willow?"

Debbie-Ann did not look at all fazed by his awkward ramblings. If anything she seemed a little amused.

"No need to worry. Not that I wouldn't be open to romance if the right man came along. But I never got that vibe from you. Besides you're almost ten years older than me." When she saw the reaction on his face, she quickly added, "I hope that doesn't offend you."

"No. Not at all." He took a sip of wine. Which turned into a gulp. So he wasn't as irresistible as he thought. Reality check.

"I'm sorry. I *have* upset you."

"Nah. Seriously, don't worry about it."

"About Willow. Do you think you'll get back together?"

"I can't see that happening. She's gone back to the guy she was with before we got married. His name is Paul Quinlan."

"Paul. So he's Geneva's father?"

"Biological father. He gave up his legal rights when Willow and I married so I could adopt Geneva."

"Lucky for Geneva. I think you're a pretty awesome father. But why would Willow go back to Paul if he's such an awful guy?"

"You have to know Paul. There's something about him. He's funny, whip-smart and crazy-rich. The three of us were inseparable in college."

Debbie-Ann tilted her head. "You sound like you're in love with Paul, too."

Wow. This woman. Justin couldn't remember the last time he'd talked to someone who had really listened to him. Who truly seemed to get him. "You're right. I was. Even more crazy…I loved Willow as well."

"Complicated."

Justin laughed. "My life became much more pedestrian after we graduated. Paul and Willow took off to travel the world, on Paul's unlimited budget."

"You weren't invited?"

"I was. But I wasn't born for that sort of lifestyle. I knew my father missed me and I'd always planned to return to Lost Trail. So I decided to study law."

"I wonder if I could ask you—"

Before she could finish, Geneva ran into the room, anxious to show him some of Ashley's Trolls.

"Aren't they funny-looking, Daddy?"

"Sure are." He made a mental note to pick up one for her Christmas stocking. "Glad you're having so much fun, but it's getting late. We have to go home now."

To Debbie-Ann, he said, "Next time we have dinner, we're talking about you."

"Next time?"

"I hope I'm not too old to be your friend? Especially since I've just spilled some of my darkest secrets."

She squeezed his arm. "You are the perfect age for a friend. And Ashley and I would love to come for dinner."

"How about Saturday?"

"Terrific." She leaned forward, put a hand on his arm. "You're not the only one with secrets. Saturday I'll tell you some of mine."

Chapter Ten

Wednesday, November 29

SNOW CAME ON Wednesday morning. Chunky flakes that decorated the ends of Tiff's red scarf and the branches of the evergreens lining the path between the house and the barn. Tiff hummed *It's beginning to look a lot like Christmas,* timing her steps so the crunch of her boots in the snow provided percussion to the song.

"Someone sounds happy today."

She looked in the direction of Kenny's voice just in time to avoid the snowball he flung at her.

"Doesn't it feel like a wonderland to you?" She spread her hands wide to indicate…everything. The red-and-white barn, the stately trees, even the wood rail fencing all looked so much nicer with a trimming of snow.

"Yup. The view sure is pretty from here." He was looking at her, smiling, his stance casual and relaxed even as snow accumulated on his wool hat and the shoulders of his plaid jacket.

He looked good here, solid, handsome, a little bit of a wild gleam in his eyes. She had a feeling Kenny could fit in wherever he found himself. He had that easy confidence some men seemed to be born with.

"Did you set aside the trees for the Stillmans?" She'd sent him a text message after she got home from the pub Monday night.

"Fourteen-foot noble fir for Luke Stillman and sixteen-foot for Nikki Stillman. Yup, they're tagged and ready to go. Will they be here to pick them up soon? We're getting crammed for space in the loading area."

He started toward the barn and she fell in beside him. "I'm not sure."

"Oh?"

She'd texted Zak this morning, asking if there'd been word from Nikki. There hadn't. "Something odd is going on at the Lazy S. Nikki's gone missing since our night out."

"That was Monday, right?"

"Yes. They drove in from the ranch together, in Nikki's Jeep. They were at the Dew Drop for about two hours. Nikki drove Luke home, dropped him off at his front door, and no one's seen her since."

"She didn't say anything to Luke about late-night plans?"

"No. He was surprised like everyone else when he heard she hadn't spent the night in her home."

"Is it possible she went for a drive and had an accident?"

"Zak tells me the sheriff's department combed the roads between the Lazy S and town. There's no sign of her truck."

"The family must be worried."

"Nikki may be an adult, but she's in the habit of letting her folks know if she won't be home at night. They're plenty worried."

"And now she's been missing two nights."

"Yeah."

"I hope she turns up soon. Maybe she just needed a breather from her family."

"They've been arguing a lot about whether to sell a tract of land to a developer. So that might be it. I just hope she either comes home soon or lets her family know she's okay."

They walked a few strides in silence, then Kenny asked, "How's your mom doing today?"

"About the same as yesterday. She didn't have a great night."

She'd had more strange dreams and had come to Tiff's room again in the middle of the night. It had taken a lot of talking to get her to calm down and go back to sleep.

"Right now Aunt Marsha is making sure she eats her breakfast." Tiff sighed. "I don't know how she has coped all these years. I've only been home about a month and caring for Mom is starting to wear me down."

"From what I've seen your aunt gets lots of breaks. Days when she isn't working, she usually heads off on her own. Until you came back your mom spent most of her days by herself."

"Yeah, I'm beginning to appreciate that. But I can't begrudge my aunt the time off. She can't spend her entire life looking after my mother."

"You see your aunt as some kind of saint. But she has a good thing going here in lots of respects. She has the run of that big farmhouse. And her living expenses are covered, even her gas and car insurance."

Tiff almost asked how he knew all this until she remembered he'd been doing the farm books before she took over the accounts.

"Covering Aunt Marsha's expenses is still cheaper than paying for home care. Plus she had to give up her own house to come live with Mom and me all those years ago. That's a big sacrifice."

"She grew up here. Maybe she considers this house hers." He shrugged. "Just saying."

They'd reached the barn and Kenny pointed out where he'd set aside the Stillmans' trees.

Seeing them bundled and ready to go gave Tiff an idea. "I'm going to take those trees over to the Lazy S myself. It'll be one less thing for them to worry about."

"Plus you'll be able to nose around and see if there's any news about Nikki."

"There's that."

SEVERAL TIMES TUESDAY night, Zak woke with ideas that had him groping for his cell phone and mumbling reminders to Siri. Each time Watson, who slept at the foot of his bed, had dug his claws into Zak's feet, registering his disapproval over night-time disturbances that weren't of his own making.

Zak was normally a sound sleeper but Nikki's disappearance magnified the unease he felt about Lacy's death. Yesterday he'd broken his own rule and suggested to the sheriff there might be a link. Ford told him to stick to answering the phone and filing papers, stuff he was good at.

Of course Nadine had been in the room, had witnessed his humiliation.

Zak couldn't afford to worry about his own ego though. Finding Nikki was now even more important than figuring out if Lacy had been murdered.

If Nikki decided to go for a drive after she dropped off Luke, and had an accident of some sort, her truck should have been found by now. That hadn't happened.

Which left two other possibilities. One, she'd run off for her own reasons, or, two, someone had taken her—and either used her Jeep to do it, or stashed her Jeep somewhere.

Zak favored the first theory. He could see no logical reason for Nikki to be abducted. Her parents and uncle might be pressuring her to approve that land sale, but he couldn't believe they would try to scare or threaten her into changing her vote. And the odds she'd been abducted by a random rapist or killer were remote.

But what if he was wrong?

Even a small chance that Nikki could come to harm was

too much to risk.

He thought of yet another possibility. What if she'd been abducted, but it wasn't random? Supposing Lacy had been murdered—Nikki might have seen something, heard something, the killer considered dangerous. In the very worst case scenario, Nikki could have been killed herself to tie up this hypothetical loose end.

Zak skipped his morning run and instead used the time to call Luke. His friend answered quickly. "Any news on Nikki?"

"No. Sorry. I just have a few questions for you."

Zak could hear cows mooing in the background as Luke admitted, "I couldn't sleep last night. Damn but I wish that cousin of mine would turn up."

"Could you give me a list of friends we could check with? I know you've probably contacted them already, but it might help if we talked to them as well."

"Nikki prefers the company of animals to most people, but she does have one friend she hangs out with quite a bit. Sophie Johnson, she's an elementary teacher in Sula. I'll send you her contact information if I can find it."

"Thanks. I'll pass that on to the sheriff. I'm sure he'll want to follow up." Zak would make sure that he did.

"Appreciate everything you guys are doing. We've all been searching the ranch, but it's a big place. Me and Dad, Uncle Clayton and Tom are heading out on the horses once chores are done. Nikki's Jeep is all-wheel drive. She could be almost anywhere."

The prospect of searching over eighty thousand acres sure was daunting. "Good luck. Let us know if you find anything."

While he waited for his steel-cut oats to cook, Zak called Sophie. She hadn't talked to Nikki since Lacy's funeral, but she gave him the name of three other friends, and soon Zak had a list of ten people to be questioned.

When he finally arrived at the office, Zak was tired and out of sorts. He usually relied on his morning run to clear his head. This morning it would have to be coffee.

By the time the sheriff showed up, making a beeline to his office with his usual grunt instead of hello, Zak had added addresses and contact numbers for all the names on his list. He took the sheet of paper into the sheriff's office along with some reports that needed signatures.

"I have the list of Nikki's friends." He made it sound like this was something that had been asked for.

The sheriff hesitated a long moment before holding out his hand for the paper. "Guess I should talk to them. See if any of them have any ideas where she is."

The sheriff was already getting to his feet. To forestall him, Zak handed over the reports he'd been carrying in his other hand. "If you could sign these first so I can file them…"

The sheriff grunted, but settled his weight back into his chair and picked up his pen.

He barely glanced at the report Nadine had written about the vandalism at Cora Christensen's house. He slashed out his signature, then set it aside, working his way through the other documents in a similar fashion, finally pushing away the last one as if its very existence was annoying to him.

"I'll be out most of the day with this." He held up the sheet of names. "And Butterfield will be patrolling, widening his search area. Since it's been a few days we can put out an APB on Nikki's vehicle. And you should also arrange for a helicopter search of the area around the ranch, any place she might be able to get to in her truck."

"Yes, Sheriff." He'd already set both into action first thing that morning—the approvals had been among the papers Ford had just signed.

Not long later, Ford was out of the office, leaving only Zak and Nadine. Nadine, scheduled to give a talk at the grade school in Sula an hour from now, was reviewing her talking points.

"There's a woman missing in our county and I have to give a speech to a bunch of snotty-nosed kids. I hate public speaking," she muttered.

"Eight-year-olds are easy. Show them your badge. Let them try on handcuffs. They'll be cool."

At his desk, Zak pulled Nadine's report from the pile the sheriff had just signed. He was halfway through reading it when he had the sense of being watched.

Sure enough, Nadine was leaning back in her chair with

her arms crossed and a partly smug, partly annoyed smile on her face.

"I thought you were supposed to file that. Not read it."

"I was curious."

"I guess I should be glad someone's interested. I bet the sheriff didn't even skim it before he signed it."

Zak shrugged one shoulder, meaning *What do you expect?* Nadine had worked here long enough to know the drill. He glanced back at the photograph of Cora Christensen's door copied in the report. It took a much different mind-set to spray the word "Slut" in dark red paint on someone's door than it did to throw a few eggs at a window.

Reading further in the report, he saw that Nadine agreed with him.

"So you ruled out Trevor Larkin and his friend?" Fourteen-year-old Trevor was not a bad kid, just a little wild. His inadvertent witnessing of a serious crime last Halloween had probably stripped him of some of that.

"Trevor's Monday night is accounted for and his parents back him up. He got home from school at the usual time, did his homework and ate dinner, then his dad drove him to and from hockey practice, which he also helped to coach. Of course, Trevor could have snuck out of the house after his parents were asleep. But he seemed genuinely surprised about the door when I questioned him."

"Kids have been pulling pranks on Miss Christensen for as long as I can remember, but none of them ever dared to call her names, let alone 'slut.'"

"You think this is connected to her affair with Jack Stillman becoming public knowledge?"

Zak swiveled his chair so he faced her. Arms on his legs, he leaned forward and studied her keen blue eyes. She was smart. No hand-holding or gentle guidance needed here.

"Yeah. But that doesn't mean I know who did the painting—or smearing might be a better word. Cora's got a lot of pride. Being publicly labeled a slut would have stung."

"She had a sheet draped over her door when I arrived. And a painter booked to scrap the door later that afternoon."

"Is that right?" Zak had to smile. Cora had guilted him into cleaning the dried egg off her window last month. But clearly she had the resources to solve her own problems when sufficiently motivated.

"Do you think someone from the Stillman family is responsible?"

"They're the obvious suspects. But I can't see any of them stooping this low." As soon as he said this, Zak questioned his assumptions. He and Luke were friends, but they'd never been especially close. He knew the rest of the family even less.

"Here's another question for you." Nadine's eyes were glistening, a hunter with eyes on her prey. "Is it a coincidence Cora's door was vandalized the same night Nikki Stillman disappeared?"

Zak had been wondering if he was the only one who noticed that. “I wouldn’t think so.”

“Me, either.” Nadine checked her watch, then sighed. “Time to face the kids. But when this is over I’m going to head back to the Lazy S and do some looking around.”

“You’ll have to clear that with the sheriff.” On his way out that morning, Zak had seen Ford dump a stack of paperwork onto Nadine’s desk.

Nadine swore. “Right, and fat chance he’ll listen to a word I say.”

She put on her jacket, jammed her talking notes into one of the pockets. “I’m not sure how much longer I can stomach working for that fool.”

He sensed this wasn’t idle talk, and felt a jab of worry. Despite the way she kept him slightly off balance, Nadine was the best thing that had happened to this department. Ever. “You and me both. But there are ways of working around him.”

“Thank God there’s an election coming up next year.”

“You think that’ll make a difference? No one’s ever challenged Archie Ford for this office.”

“Maybe not so far.” Nadine placed both of her hands on his desk and leaned forward until their eyes were less than a foot apart. “But someone should.”

THE SKY WAS sapphire blue, the trees frosted with silver as

Tiff drove toward the Lazy S with two trees strapped to the roof of her SUV. But she no longer had the uplifting "all's right with the world" feeling she'd woken up with.

Far from it.

Nikki had been missing two days now. That was worrisome enough, but Tiff's growing sense of unease had more to do with the situation at home.

Was Kenny right? Was her aunt taking advantage of Tiff's mother's mental instability? Tiff had to admit there was a weird dynamic between the two sisters. She couldn't say exactly why, but something did feel off.

It took a total shift in perspective for her to see her aunt in any sort of bad light, though.

For as long as she could remember, her aunt had been her champion, making it possible for Tiff to go to college, to take a job in Seattle, to have a boyfriend and live a life unencumbered by the baggage of her past. Her aunt had put her own needs second. She'd sold the cute house she'd lived in before Tiff's father died. And put marriage to Dr. Pittman and the possibility of her own children on hold, as well. She'd done these things for the sake of her sister and the niece she adored…

Or, was the truth the complete converse?

Was it possible her aunt actually wanted Tiff out of the way so that she could be the mistress of her family home? As Rosemary's power of attorney, it was Marsha who ran the house and Raven Farms, Marsha who controlled the money,

Marsha who made all the important decisions…

Marsha and Rosemary had grown up together on Raven Farms. Had Marsha resented the fact that the house and land had been left entirely to her younger sister and her husband?

Tiff wished she could simply ask her aunt that question. In the past she'd been able to talk to Aunt Marsha about anything. Lately though that wasn't the case. When she'd asked her about Gwen, then about Dr. Pittman's late night visit, Marsha had acted annoyed and avoided answering.

The relationship between them was changing. Tiff wished she understood why.

All was quiet when Tiff approached the main gate to the Lazy S. She slowed to a crawl at the cattle guard, not wanting the trees to fall off her roof. Not even a dog greeted her as she pulled up at Eugene and Em's home. No doubt they were looking for Nikki. She knocked at the door to be sure, but no one answered.

So much for finding out what was going on.

She untied the shorter of the two trees and shifted it to her shoulder. She carried it as far as the front porch, then eased it down and propped it against the stairs where it would be easy to carry into the house.

Next she drove to Clayton and Vanessa's place.

Christmas lights had been wrapped around the three pine trees in the front lawn, as well as along the roof-line of the ranch house. When had Clayton found the time to do this—before Nikki's disappearance or after?

As soon as she opened her vehicle's door, she smelled a delicious aroma of apples and cinnamon. Someone was home. And they were baking.

First she untied the tree. This one was taller and more awkward to carry, but she managed to half-carry, half-drag it to the porch. She was about to rest it on the railing when the front door opened.

"Don't put that tree there! It'll scratch the paint." Vanessa Stillman tiptoed out to the porch in bare feet. Her hair was in a ponytail and she was wearing leggings and a fitted tank top. Her skin glowed and she didn't have a spare pound on her tall, small-boned frame.

"Okay." Tiff shifted the weight back to her shoulder, then eased the tree down on the snowbank next to the walkway. "Is this good?"

"Tiffany Masterson. What in the world? Since when does Raven Farms deliver Christmas trees?"

Tiffany brushed her gloved hands together, dislodging a few needles. "We don't usually. But I promised Nikki I would set aside a nice sixteen-foot noble fir for her. She wanted it to be here when you got back from your trip."

Vanessa frowned and then shivered. She glanced at Tiff's vehicle, then beyond it, to the road. She seemed to be weighing options, none of which were good. Finally she nodded her head toward the interior of her home.

"It's too cold to talk out here. Come inside. I assume I need to pay you for the tree?"

Before Tiff could answer, Vanessa disappeared inside and Tiff was forced to follow. She scraped her boots on the outdoor mat, then stepped into the foyer and closed the door.

There was no sign of Vanessa in the grand entrance, or the living room opening off of it.

The place looked like a magazine spread. Every detail was perfect—there was even a fire snapping and crackling in the river rock fireplace built into the bank of windows opposite.

The scent of smoky hickory mingled nicely with the baking aromas she'd noticed earlier.

"Take off your boots and come through to the kitchen."

Tiff did as asked, curious to see if the rest of the house would match up to this. The floor felt warm in her socked feet. Heated tile flooring. Nice. No wonder Vanessa was in bare feet.

The kitchen was huge, with modern, flat-faced cabinets and impressive gray concrete countertops. The cooktop was built into an island that also had seating for six. Vanessa waved her toward one of the stools, just as a timer went off.

Vanessa whisked a muffin tray out of the oven.

Presumably she'd mixed these up this morning, but there wasn't so much as a measuring cup or a dusting of flour to be seen on the counters.

Vanessa turned the muffins into a basket lined with a linen napkin. "Would you like one? They're gluten-free and low-fat."

"No thanks."

Despite the nods to mountain architecture, this house felt more like an upscale hotel than a ranch house. And instead of the distressed mother she'd expected to find, Vanessa was acting like a cross between a Stepford wife and a Martha Stewart clone.

"Any word from Nikki?"

Vanessa's chest expanded on a deep breath. She held the air for a long time, perhaps it was a relaxing technique she'd learned at the fancy Arizona spa. When she finally expelled, some of the lines on her forehead and down the sides of her mouth disappeared.

"No."

"I'm sorry. You must be so worried."

Vanessa swept a tiny crumb from the counter, to her hand, then carried it across the room to the garbage, housed discreetly in a pullout cabinet.

"It would be just like Nikki to pull a stunt like this to make us change our minds about selling some of her grandmother's precious land. Only, it really isn't in her character to defy us so openly." Her gaze moved to the bank of windows facing the mountain view. "Or to worry us this way."

And suddenly Tiff could see it. The bright gleam in Vanessa's eyes, the slight tremor in her hands. She wasn't being the perfect homemaker. She was stress-baking. And no doubt stress-cleaning as well.

"Assuming she was upset about the idea of selling land…do you have any idea where she might go?"

"If it was warmer, I'd guess Nikki drove down some remote forestry road and put up a tent in the woods. But it's too cold for that. Her credit card is linked to the farm, so we've been able to monitor it and she hasn't used it once since she left. So I don't have a clue. Not a single clue."

Her eyes grew shinier. Just as it seemed a tear would escape and roll down her cheek, Vanessa blinked rapidly then bagged a few of the muffins and passed them to Tiff.

"If you're not hungry now, you can eat them later."

Tiff's mother and Vanessa were such different people. Yet they both medicated pain and suffering with baking. Safer than drugs or alcohol, at least.

"Thank you."

Vanessa waved her hand. "It gives me something to do. When Nikki was born I was so happy to have a daughter. I imagined baking cookies together, doing arts and crafts… But Nikki hates anything that keeps her inside. Even as a teenager she never wanted me to paint her nails for her or take her shopping."

Vanessa's shoulders shrank as she said this. Suddenly Tiff saw the loneliness under her sophisticated veneer, and it reminded her of the look she caught on her mother's face sometimes.

"Right from the beginning Nikki was closer to her grandmother than to me."

Daughters disappointing mothers. It seemed to be a theme around Lost Trail. Was it true everywhere? Why did couples even have children, then?

"The sheriff's department is working hard to find Nikki. Hopefully she'll be home soon."

"What if she's left the county? She could be anywhere." Vanessa took a cloth and began polishing the spotless sink. "It's not even much land—only fifty acres. She's such a silly, idealistic girl. That money could make all the difference for our family. And running away won't help her position anyway."

"Why's that?" Tiff pulled the bag of muffins closer. Despite the lack of gluten and fat, they did smell good.

"The purchase offer is only good until December twenty-fourth, so the family has to vote before then. If Nikki's not here to cast her ballot, then the deal is sure to get approved."

Chapter Eleven

TIFF LEFT THE Lazy S determined to prove to her mother—and herself—she was serious about staying in Lost Trail. She needed her mom, and her aunt, to know they could count on her.

First step was building her accountancy business. The bookkeeping at Raven Farms took up twenty percent of her time at most. She needed more clients and she was going to begin by approaching the biggest industry in town.

Luckily, Sparks Construction was owned and operated by a guy she'd gone to school with. Derick Sparks had been a popular athlete back then, while her status as a brainiac had been decidedly lower. A genuine friendship had developed between them though when she'd been asked to tutor Derick so his marks would be high enough for him to stay on the team.

Throughout the years she'd spent in college and working in Seattle they'd stayed in touch, mostly by Facebook. She'd been genuinely thrilled for him when he fell in love with and then married a local girl, Aubrey Jenkins. And even happier when they successfully adopted a baby boy after years of frustrating infertility.

Derick's perfect life had fallen apart in November, though, and Tiff wasn't sure if enough time had passed that he'd gone back to work. The only way to find out for sure was to call. So she did, and Derick answered on the first ring, assuring her he'd be glad to talk to her.

The last time Tiff had gone to see Derick at his office just outside of town limits, he'd been avoiding her. She'd had to brazen her way past the receptionist, Nora Morgan, to get to his office. Today, though, Tiff was here by invitation. Nora was friendly as she waved her through.

Derick's office was in the second-floor loft area created by the building's vaulted ceiling. He hadn't moved into the larger room adjacent that had been his father's. Will Sparks's nameplate was still in place on the closed door, a symbolic token from a loyal son.

Derick's door was open but Tiff still rapped on it to announce her presence. When he stood she thought he looked smaller. Part of it was weight. He'd lost a few pounds. But it was his defeated posture and his dull eyes that most diminished him. He smiled though and seemed pleased to see her.

"You're still in town. Must be a new record."

The teasing stung a bit, especially after witnessing Vanessa's pain and imagining how much it mirrored her mother's.

"I'm here for good this time." If she said it enough times, maybe everyone, including herself, would believe it. "How are you doing?"

"Honestly? Crappy. I'm living with Mom for the time being. She's just back from a mini-vacation with Vanessa Stillman. The break was good for her, but she's pretty down, too."

"It'll take time." Tiff felt like a fraud as she trotted out the phrase that had been said to her so many times, with the best of intentions. Time did heal raw pain, but some losses could never be overcome.

"Christmas is going to be brutal. It should have been such a happy time."

He would be missing his baby's first Christmas, not to mention missing out on spending the holiday with his wife. "Are you allowed to see your family at all?"

"No contact for a year." He folded his hands on his desk and stared at them a few seconds. Then he sighed and met her gaze. "So what's up with you?"

"I've decided to start an accounting business here in Lost Trail. I know you have your own bookkeeper, but if you ever need any higher-level accounting services, I'd be glad to help. At the firm in Seattle I had a lot of experience preparing tax returns and financial statements for small to mid-sized businesses like Sparks Construction."

She gave a wry smile. "That was quite a spiel. Sorry, I didn't mean to come off like a door-to-door salesman."

"Hey, it's good. I bet we could use some expert advice on taxes. Especially this year."

His smile disappeared again and the weight of all that had happened to him recently seemed to settle back on his shoulders.

"Are you and Aubrey legally separated?"

"She—she wants to finalize the agreement before Christmas."

He'd turned away from her to face the window. She heard him swallow as he struggled to keep his composure. Tiff wanted to put a hand on his shoulder and ask if he'd like to talk. But she guessed he would prefer her to keep focused on business.

"Derick, the way you structure the financial aspects will have tax consequences for you. I'd be happy to explain them."

"That's probably a good idea."

"If you emailed me the draft agreement I could give you my comments. Then if you find my input helpful, we could talk about some bigger projects with your company."

"That sounds fair."

There was an awkward pause. She didn't dare ask about his son, Brody, and whether Aubrey kept him up to date with his life. Small talk didn't feel appropriate either.

"Why don't I give you time to send that email, then we can meet again and work out exactly how I can help you and your company?"

He nodded gratefully.

"You should meet Zak and me at the Dew Drop for dinner one night. We're there once a week, at least."

He dropped his gaze. "Thanks. Yeah, I'll do that."

His body language was saying the exact opposite.

She wanted to say more, that she understood his motives for being complicit in the illegal adoption and that she still thought he was a good person. But he needed to hear those words not from her, but from his wife.

✕

ZAK WAS EATING an early lunch at his desk when Nadine returned from her school visit. She went straight to the coffeepot.

"God but I need caffeine."

"You don't have any visible bruises. I take it the kids went easy on you?"

She added cream to her coffee, then went to her work station and perched on the side of her desk. "You were right. The kids were fun. But talk about *energy*."

"Were the handcuffs a hit?"

"Oh, yeah. But what really got them going was when they found out I used to be a rodeo cowgirl."

"Cowgirl trumps deputy?"

"If you're eight years old, apparently it does."

He wasn't surprised. Her barrel-racing past impressed him, too. "Did you show them any of the YouTube videos of your competitions?"

Her eyebrows went up. "How do you know about those?"

He munched on his sandwich.

"You've *watched* them, haven't you?"

"When the sheriff hires a new deputy, of course I'm going to check the person out. The videos *are* pretty amazing."

"I still can't handle watching them. Not yet." She drank some coffee, blew out a sigh, and went to her chair behind her desk. "It took a lot of effort to relive those days with the kids. I focused on the good parts, and avoided the harder stuff."

They'd talked before about her reasons for quitting the rodeo. The death of her horse, Mane Event, had hit her hard.

"Still thinking about buying Making Magic?"

"There's a ten-acre place for sale about ten miles south. It's in my price range. Sort of."

"I know the one. Small barn with four stalls. A corral with a water line. And a creek on the western boundary."

"That's it." She grabbed a spec sheet from her desk and handed it to him. "Would you come look at it with me on the weekend?"

He hesitated. He knew so much about the property because he was interested in it too. But if Nadine bought the place and the horse, then she'd stay in Lost Trail. "Yeah, sure, let's check it out."

✕

THE SECOND CORA Christensen took a chair in his office, Justin could tell she had a plan. Her eyes were sparkling and she had a tight, two-fisted grip on the handle of her purse, holding it like it was a safety bar on a roller coaster ride.

"I want to put Lacy's house on Airbnb."

He was surprised. "You've heard of Airbnb?"

"I'm old, not living under a rock. I've done my research. You can earn a lot more renting a home on Airbnb than with an old-fashioned six-month or yearly lease."

"That depends on the location. Lacy's home is too far from the ski hill to attract families on a ski holiday."

"Lots of people would love to take a holiday on a real, working ranch."

"Yes, but that's assuming the people on the ranch are willing to cater to them. Take them on trail rides, let them try milking a cow and gather eggs from the chickens. That sort of thing. You know the Stillmans won't do any of that."

The Stillmans would be rude, some of them bordering on hostile.

"I don't care."

From the gleam in her eyes, that was the point. To annoy the Stillmans.

"How long is this probate thing going to take? I'm not a young woman. I'd like to start moving forward with my plans as soon as possible. And I was hoping you could help me with the paperwork."

Great. Just the position he wanted to be in, setting up an Airbnb that would annoy the hell out of his biggest clients.

"I'm still working on the formal notice to beneficiaries and creditors. Next I'll have to prepare an inventory and appraise the estate assets. All of this is going to take many months. I suggest you use that time to reconsider your plan. Is the extra money going to be worth the hassle?"

"It doesn't seem like much work to me."

"Someone has to handle the bookings, the transfer of cash and keys. And after each booking someone has to clean the house and do laundry. That's assuming you have nice, respectful guests. You'd need to be prepared for guests who cause damage to—" he checked his natural impulse to say *Lacy* "—*your* house or to the neighboring Stillman properties. Insurance would cover the cost, but there's still the deductible plus the work of lining up tradespeople for the necessary repairs."

"It would be such a shame if irresponsible renters trashed the place." Miss Christensen lowered her gaze, but her twitching mouth gave away her secret. "I suppose I'll just have to take the risk."

She *wanted* Lacy and Jack's home to be trashed. Justin wondered if he would ever stop being shocked by people. He'd known Cora Christensen had a mean streak. But this ugly vindictiveness was tough to stomach.

A movement from the doorway caught his eye. Silently

his father held up a bag from the Snowdrift Café. Justin nodded.

"I'm afraid that's all the time we have right now." He went to help Cora out of her chair. "I'll keep you posted on the progress with probate. As for the Airbnb idea, I suggest you do some serious thinking about whether you want to go that route."

Miss Christensen frowned and seemed about to argue, but when she spotted his father in the doorway, she became all sunny smiles.

"Good day, Clark. You must be so proud of this boy. He's quite the lawyer."

"I've always been proud of Justin," his father said quietly. He set the lunch bag on the table in the corner. "May I walk you out, Cora?"

The hint to leave worked.

"Oh, I'll be fine. I'll take the elevator." She glanced back at Justin. "Call me soon, young man, but don't expect me to change my mind. I won't."

Justin's father closed the door after her, then turned to his son. "I presume I can't ask what that's about?"

"It's minor stuff, I guess. I had no idea that woman could be such a headache. What did Jack Stillman see in her?"

"She was pretty in her day. I know it's hard for you to imagine. Plus Cora can be charming when she wants to be. But let's forget about her. There's something I want your approval on, though I have to admit I've already taken the first step."

Justin had already pulled out his lunch—Janet at the Snowdrift made a terrific Greek wrap—and taken his first bite. The flavors of the marinated chicken, feta, olives and crunchy lettuce were fabulous.

It took a minute for his father's words to sink in. "What step is that?"

"I've contacted *BE THE MATCH* and offered to host a donor drive at the clinic. I want to run it next week. The earlier the better."

Justin chewed his food thoroughly before swallowing. "Are you sure, Dad? It sounds like a lot of work. And the chances of finding a match that way, well…"

"I know. The chances aren't high. But I need to feel like I'm helping in some way. And if the drive doesn't find the right donor for you, maybe it'll help someone else."

Justin was touched by the emotion in his father's eyes. He'd always cared so much. Always put his son's best interests ahead of his own.

"If you're sure, then I'm fine with it. It's one way to spread the news about my cancer without me needing to tell everyone."

"Have you told Geneva yet?"

Justin's mouth went dry. "Not yet. Soon." He'd finished reading the book from the psychologist. He couldn't put it off any longer.

"Keep it simple, Son. She's only four. Now about the

donor drive, I need to pick a day."

Justin picked up his phone and scrolled through his calendar. "I'd like to show up and thank people. Next Thursday is good for me."

His father hesitated. "Um, how about Wednesday? Or even Monday?"

"I've got to go to Missoula for some more tests on Monday. Wednesday is fine, though."

✕

"DOES MY RIGHT knee look swollen to you?" Zak looked down at his long, thin limbs. He'd rolled up his pant legs and was standing in the center of the room facing Nadine. The two of them were alone in the office. "I think it's swollen."

Nadine refused to play along. "I have no interest in examining your skinny legs, Zak Waller. If your knee is swollen you should consult a doctor."

Zak smiled, satisfied. He unrolled his pants and then grabbed his coat. "Good suggestion. I'm going to run over to the clinic right now before they close for the night. Are you okay to watch the phones until six and then lock up the place for me?" He didn't think Ford or Butterfield would be making an appearance this late in the afternoon.

Nadine narrowed her eyes at him. "You just set me up, didn't you?"

"Don't know what you're talking about. See you tomorrow morning, Deputy." He waved on his way out the door.

Outside the frosty air got his blood moving. It was already dark—the sun set around four-thirty at this time of year. He paused to admire the colorful Christmas lights sparkling against the layers of fresh snow on the ponderosa pine outside the sheriff's office.

Then he began to move, his boots crunching on the hard-packed snow as he headed north on First Street. One of Sparks Construction's white trucks drove by on the freshly plowed road. Zak thought he recognized Derick behind the wheel. They exchanged a wave of hello, and then Zak turned right onto Tumbleweed Road.

About a half dozen vehicles were angle parked on Lost Trail's main road. Most of them were at the far end of the road in front of the Dew Drop Inn, but one was near the medi-clinic. Out of habit Zak glanced at the driver's license on his way by.

Local. Not one he recognized.

Inside the waiting room was empty. Gwen Lange looked up from the reception desk and smiled. Her older brother had been friends with his brother Jake—the least obnoxious of his older siblings.

Gwen liked to dye her hair weird colors and experiment with piercings, which made her stand out in their conservative town. Today her hair was purple.

"Hey, Gwen, any chance I could see the doctor today?

I've got some pain in my knee and I think it's a bit swollen."

"He's with his last patient. I'm sure he could squeeze you in. I'll let Farrah know you're here."

"Great. Thanks." Instead of taking a chair, he went up to the counter. When Gwen returned he asked about her family.

"They're all fine. You must miss yours now that they've all left town."

"Not really."

She looked surprised, then she laughed. "Yeah, my brother told me your older brothers could be pretty intense. I love my folks but I'm ready to move out. Rusty's trying to convince me to move in with him."

"How long you guys been seeing each other?"

"Not long at all. Mom thinks Rusty's moving too fast." Gwen tapped the end of her pen against her cheek. "She might be right."

"Yeah, sometimes the old folks actually know what they're talking about." He took a breath. "Speaking of old folks, it was sad about Lacy Stillman dying."

"Wasn't it? She was just at the clinic the day before her heart attack. Honestly, she looked healthier than most of our clients."

"She was quite a character."

"And she was always smiling, wasn't she? Though she got into a pretty intense conversation with Marsha in the examining room."

"What about?"

Gwen frowned. "Marsha accused me of eavesdropping, but the door was ajar and I couldn't help hearing a few words as I walked by. I swear that woman is getting crabbier by the day."

"If you don't mind my asking—what were they talking about?"

Gwen shrugged. "At the time it seemed interesting, but it couldn't have been that exciting because I can't remember now."

She glanced down the hall, as if checking for someone. Then she leaned over the counter and continued, in a quieter tone. "Marsha's been arguing a lot with Doc Pittman lately, too. I wonder if they've been having a secret affair and now one of them wants to break it off."

The sound of a door shutting startled them both. A man in his early forties emerged from the hallway, Farrah Saddler right behind him.

"We'll see you again in a month, Mr. Benson. Make sure to apply the ointment morning and night." Farrah glanced over at Zak. Dark smudges under her eyes betrayed her fatigue but she smiled kindly. "I can take you now, if you'll come this way."

Zak glanced at his watch. "Man, I didn't realize how late it's getting. My knee isn't too bad. I'll get it checked another time."

Chapter Twelve

Thursday, November 30

ON THURSDAY TIFF'S mother didn't feel well enough to get out of bed.

Tiff put a hand to her mother's forehead. No fever. "Want me to bring up some breakfast?"

Rosemary waved off the offer. "Marsha brought it earlier. She cleared away the dishes before she went to work."

"I'll be working in Dad's study if you want to go for a walk later." Yesterday they'd walked for twenty minutes and her mom had seemed brighter and more alert after.

But you couldn't walk if you were sleeping and her mother's eyes were already fluttering closed.

Downstairs, Tiff sat by the bank of windows on the south-facing wall as she ate her own breakfast. She watched as the first customer of the day drove up to the barn in a cherry-red pickup truck. Ten minutes later one of the employees—she thought it was Bob Jenkins—loaded a long balsam fir into the back of the truck. The customer shook Bob's hand then drove off.

Judging by the amount of traffic it was going to be a

good season for the Christmas tree farm.

She was determined her new accounting business would be a success too. Even if Derick gave her only a bit of work to start, Sparks Construction was an important name to have on her client list. She needed to add a few more names to that list.

Tiff refilled her coffee mug and took it into her father's study. The house had a peaceful, restful feeling today. For once when she sat in her father's chair she didn't think about him, but about the work she needed to do.

Last night, with the help of her aunt and her mother, she'd come up with a list of potential clients. Cold calls were never easy, but at least she knew most of the people. Given her family's standing in the community she figured even if they said no to her, they'd do so nicely.

An hour later Tiff was depressed and deflated. While she hadn't expected instant success, she had hoped for a few leads at least. But so far, every single person she'd talked to had politely explained they had no need of her services.

She pushed away from the desk and went upstairs to check on her mother. Rosemary sat in the armchair overlooking the front yard and driveway. Still dressed in her robe, with slippers on her feet, she seemed to struggle to focus when she turned toward Tiff.

"Feeling any better?"

Tiff wasn't surprised when she shook her head no.

"I wanted to get dressed and head down to the kitchen. I

only made it as far as this chair."

"Want me to help you?" Tiff stepped toward the closet. "What do you feel like wearing?"

"Actually, I'd rather go back to bed."

Tiff checked her mother's temperature with a thermometer this time. "You aren't running a fever. Do you have any aches or pains?"

"No. I'm just so tired." Rosemary leaned on her daughter's arm as she raised herself from the chair and then hobbled to the bed.

Tiffany refilled her water glass, then left her to rest.

In the kitchen she brewed some fresh coffee and grabbed a couple of shortbread cookies. Several trucks were parked by the red barn now, as well as a small hatchback. It would be a challenge strapping a tree onto that vehicle. She was tempted to go out and watch, distract herself from her problems.

But she still had more calls to make. The Lost Trail ski hill would be a great client to snag. She didn't know the manager personally but counted on the Masterson name to get the woman to accept her call.

It worked, but after just a few introductory sentences, the manager shut her down politely.

"We don't need any help at this time, but we'll keep you in mind."

Damn.

Tiff went online and checked her Facebook account.

She really should send a reply to Craig. Thanks to the

helpful checkmark Facebook put beside a message once it was opened, Craig had to know she'd read it. But she still wasn't sure what to say to him.

Tiff closed the app and loaded up the accounts for the farm. She wanted to get something productive done today. Maybe she'd calculate the Christmas bonuses and send out the transfers a few weeks early. The guys would be pleased.

One job led to another and soon the sky was growing dark. Shocked that so much time had gone by Tiff went to her mother's room and found it empty. She called out and her mom answered, "I'm in the kitchen."

Still dressed in her robe and slippers, she was peeling potatoes.

"How about beef stew for dinner?"

Pleased at her mother's newfound energy, Tiff agreed. "Can I help? I'll brown the meat."

"Caramelize the onions first. And use the big cast-iron pot. That'll save dirtying a frying pan."

Tiff did as instructed. Her mom was an excellent cook. Once the stew was in the oven, she put together a salad while her mother mixed a batch of biscuits.

At quarter after six they heard the front door open and close. Aunt Marsha coming home from her shift at the clinic. Tiff imagined how wonderful the house must smell to her...aromas of onions and beef, rosemary and thyme, all topped with the buttery goodness of biscuits.

"I'm going to open a bottle of red," Tiff told her mother.

Sometimes her aunt enjoyed a glass after a long day of work, and this meal deserved a good Bordeaux.

Her mother rarely drank, especially when she wasn't feeling great, so Tiff opened the bottle and poured two glasses, ready for when her aunt joined them. Marsha always had a quick shower and changed into lounging clothes after work.

When her aunt appeared fifteen minutes later, looking tired and frazzled, Tiff passed her a glass. "Tough day?"

"One of the worst." Marsha took a long swallow of wine.

"What happened?"

"Clark has decided to hold a stem-cell drive at the clinic next week." After another drink of wine, she added, "Let me back up. The first bad news of the day was finding out Justin has Hodgkin's lymphoma."

"No!" Tiff thought to the last time she'd seen him. It would have been at the wake after Lacy's funeral. He'd been thin and pale, true, but not that different from when she'd seen him and his dad in Seattle last year. "How long has he been sick?"

"Apparently it's been almost two years. Hodgkin's lymphoma is a cancer of the lymphatic system and it's often curable with chemotherapy and radiation. Justin went through both of those without telling anyone, not even his father. By the time Willow and Geneva came to town he thought he'd been cured."

Tiff noticed her mother listening carefully, though she didn't say anything.

Tiff tried to imagine going through all that treatment without anyone in her family knowing. "Is it even possible to keep such a serious illness secret?"

"Justin was strong and he tolerated the treatment quite well. He invented an out-of-town client to explain the days when he had to travel to Missoula. And when his hair began to thin, he shaved his head and pretended it was for charity."

Tiff let that all sink in. "But the cancer came back?"

"It came back. This time his oncologist wants to try a bone-marrow transplant."

"What are the odds of that working?"

"I don't know the specifics of Justin's case. But the average five-year survival rate for males with Hodgkin's lymphoma is around eighty percent."

"So pretty good."

"Well, yes, I suppose so."

"You don't sound very sure about that."

"Clark got permission from his son to contact his doctors. Justin's oncologist isn't as confident in his particular case. I don't know why—perhaps the cancer wasn't caught as quickly as it could have been." Marsha reached for the wine bottle and refilled her glass.

"I'm so sorry to hear this." Tiff gave her aunt's arm a gentle squeeze. "You and Dr. Pittman are so close. You must feel devastated." She was pretty sad, too. Justin was several years older than her, so they'd hung out in different friend groups. But she'd known him all her life and their families were close.

"He has to be okay," Rosemary said faintly. "Think of his little girl, Geneva. Her mother already deserted her. She can't lose Justin, too."

"You're right, Mom. He's a great guy and so many people need him." Tiff swirled the wine in her glass, considering the situation, wondering how she could help. But her aunt had already given her that answer. "When is that donor clinic happening, Aunt Marsha? I want to get tested."

"No." Marsha slapped her hand on the counter for extra emphasis.

It was the last response Tiff expected. "Why do you say that?"

"The chance that you could be an appropriate donor for Justin is almost zero, honey. The odds are so small, but the risks are not. Even worse…once you're in the pool, you could be asked to donate for a complete stranger."

"Would that be so awful? You've always encouraged me to be a blood donor."

"Donating bone marrow is a far different thing. It's much more invasive for the donor and there are risks to you. Besides, Justin has a very good chance of finding a donor in the national registry. Almost all patients do."

"Then why is Clark holding the drive?" Rosemary had slipped on her oven mitts and was holding them crossed at her chest, as if needing a layer of protection for her heart.

Tiff wondered if hearing of Justin's disease was reminding her of all she'd gone through with Casey's heart issues.

"Clark thinks the world revolves around his son. He needs to feel he's doing something to help and hosting the donor clinic was the only thing he could think of. I'm not in favor. People are going to get tested thinking they're helping Justin and then down the road they may be asked to donate for someone they don't even know."

"But they wouldn't be obliged to donate to someone other than Justin would they?" Tiff asked, mentally substituting the world "I" for "they."

"Then why join the pool in the first place? I told Clark he should wait to see if there was an existing match for Justin, before he held the drive. But he wouldn't listen."

Tiff couldn't understand her point of view. This was Justin. Dr. Pittman's son, for God's sake. Even if the odds of success were low, shouldn't they be doing everything possible to help?

But that new, closed expression was on Marsha's face, and Tiff decided to drop the subject.

AFTER DINNER TIFF left her mother and Marsha watching a feel-good Christmas movie on TV. "I'm going to meet some friends at the Dew Drop."

She was hoping for an update on Nikki, plus she wanted to talk to Zak about Justin and the donor drive. She'd texted him after dinner and he'd agreed to meet her at seven-thirty.

Outside it was dark, but the snow was reflecting so much moonlight she easily spotted Kenny heading from his cabin to the barn, Spade loping awkwardly by his side. On impulse she called Kenny's name.

He stopped. Turned her way.

"That you, Tiff?"

"Yeah. I'm headed to town to grab a beer with Zak. Want to join us?"

Kenny didn't need to think long. "Sure. Give me a minute to drop this paperwork off at the barn and put Spade back in the cabin."

"I'll warm up my car." Inside the SUV she turned on the radio and listened to the weather forecast. An arctic cold front was pushing in from the north. Southwest Montana could expect temperatures to drop drastically in the next few days while the skies remained clear and calm.

Tiff thought about Nikki. Hopefully wherever she was, she was protected from the elements.

Weather ended and a Coldplay song was followed by one from John Legend by the time Kenny joined her. He'd substituted his heavy work jacket for a navy pea coat with a gray-and-white-striped scarf knotted casually at his throat.

Tiff shifted into Drive and headed out to the road.

"Tell me about your friend, Zak Waller. What's his story?"

"Anything in particular you're wondering about?"

"I've done some asking around. Did you know it's quite rare for a male to work as a dispatcher in a sheriff's office?"

"So what? If women want the right to traditional male jobs shouldn't it apply in the reverse direction? Used to be you rarely saw a male nurse. Now they're commonplace."

"I'm all for gender equality. That's not my point. When you find a guy choosing a path different from the norm, there's usually a reason. That's all I'm saying."

His point seemed fair. Besides, she too had wondered why a smart, capable guy like Zak wouldn't set his aspirations a little higher. "Zak grew up in a crazy household. One minute his dad might be planning a family trip to Disney, the next he could be throwing one of his kids down the basement stairs."

"You're exaggerating."

"No, I'm not. When we were in grade school Zak showed up one morning with his arm in a cast and bruises on one side of his face. He told the teacher he fell down the stairs himself, but he admitted the truth to me."

"Wasn't anyone in authority at that school suspicious?"

"Social workers were called. They came out and talked to his parents, but nothing changed. Zak's coping technique was to keep quiet and try not to be noticed. He was that way at school, too. If you knew how shy he was back then, you'd be impressed with how well he copes now."

"Poor guy. Now I feel silly for being jealous of him."

The "Welcome to Lost Trail" signpost appeared and she

lowered her speed. Glancing over at him she asked, "You were jealous?"

"I heard he kissed you at Lacy Stillman's wake."

"You got that all wrong. I kissed him."

"Oh, in that case I don't feel jealous at all."

"We were just giving Gertie Humphrey something to talk about."

"Well I'm at your service if the urge hits you again tonight."

He'd made the comment light-heartedly, but Tiff didn't laugh. When it came time to kiss Kenny, she didn't want an audience.

The Dew Drop Inn was before them now and Tiff slid her car into a spot between two trucks. The aroma of barbecued meat, deep-fried chicken wings and French fries lured them inside the pub.

Zak was at their usual table. He'd already ordered a pitcher of beer and two glasses. As soon as he spotted them he held up an arm hoping to attract Mari, but there was no need. As they passed the bar Kenny asked for an extra glass as well as one more pitcher.

"Taking advantage of the fact you have a designated driver tonight?"

"Hell yeah." Kenny stepped ahead to shake Zak's hand. "How's it going?"

"I'll be happier once we find Nikki Stillman, but other than that things are good."

"Hope you don't mind Kenny joining us." Tiff hadn't thought he would but there was no denying a certain stiffness between the two men.

Zak filled both their glasses. "So what's this news you wanted to tell me?"

"It's about Justin Pittman." She glanced at Kenny. "He's the local attorney. Son of Doc Pittman."

Kenny nodded. "Tall, thin guy with super short blond hair? Yeah, I've seen him around town. Looks like a lawyer all right."

"He's sick. Hodgkin's lymphoma." She studied Zak's face for a reaction. "Did you know?"

He shook his head slowly. "Didn't have a clue. That's too bad. He's a decent guy."

Tiff filled them in with the news her aunt had shared. It didn't feel like gossiping to her. She wanted to get the word out about the donor drive. "So next week at the medi-clinic they're going to be taking samples from anyone who's willing to go on a potential donors list."

"Samples of what?" Kenny wanted to know.

"I think they swab your cheek."

"Sounds easy. What if you're a match?" Zak asked, leaning forward a little anxiously.

"There's a whole process that takes months, apparently. In the end what they do is remove your blood through a needle in one arm, pass it through a machine that takes out the blood-forming cells, and then pump the blood back into your other arm."

Zak relaxed. "That sounds doable."

"According to the website for the donor drive, you can feel a bit sick and achy afterward. It takes a least a week to feel normal again."

"If that's the cost of saving someone's life, it's worth it," Kenny said.

"I agree. So we're all going to donate?" Tiff asked.

The guys nodded and just then Mari arrived with the second pitcher. Zak took it out of her hands.

"Next week we donate. Tonight we drink."

Friday, December 1

AFTER MISSING HIS morning run two days in a row, Zak craved an endorphin rush on Friday morning. He jogged into the Lost Creek parking lot at seven o'clock and wasn't surprised to see Luke Stillman waiting in his idling truck.

Running was a great way to deal with stress. And Luke was dealing with a lot of that right now.

Luke cut the ignition and jumped out to the snow-packed ground. "About time, Waller. Let's get at 'er."

Luke shoved a hat over his head, then stuffed his key between the laces of his left track shoe.

"Any word from Nikki?" Zak began jogging again, heading toward the trail that zigzagged up Strawberry Mountain.

He didn't hold out hope for a positive answer. If Nikki had shown up, Zak would have heard.

"None." Luke caught up to him and set the pace a bit faster. "I can't figure her out. My gut tells me she's okay, but you'd think she'd send a message to her folks, at least. They're going crazy."

"The helicopter from Search and Rescue will be going out today." *Huff.* "And Butterfield's organizing a ground search." *Huff.* "Maybe today we'll get lucky."

Zak's lungs burned, his legs felt forty pounds heavier than normal. Hard to believe just two days off could leave him feeling this rough. But when you factored in his lack of sleep and the beers he'd consumed at the Dew Drop last night, it all added up.

They hadn't gone very far when Luke started to talk again. "I need to tell you something I found out yesterday. It's not about Nikki. At least I don't think it is."

"Sure." *Huff.* "Go ahead."

"I picked up the mail yesterday afternoon when everyone else was still out searching. There was a letter for my dad. It was from a bank in Missoula with a confidential stamp. I wasn't thinking straight. I thought maybe they'd tracked Nikki using her credit card and so I opened it right away."

"What was it about?"

"Nothing to do with Nikki, of course. Apparently the bank is calling in a loan—a really big loan—that I didn't even know we had. I'm pretty sure Mom is in the dark too, because just the other night she and Dad were talking finances and she mentioned with cattle prices so low it was lucky they didn't owe any money."

"Maybe that loan is why your father wants to sell those fifty acres to the property developer."

"Yeah. It didn't make sense to me before, but now it does. I wonder if Dad told Tom about the loan and if that's why Tom is backing the deal, too."

"And your uncle...?"

"Clayton's name is in the letter, alongside my dad's, so he must have gone in on the loan. According to the letter, both my dad's and my uncle's shares in the Lazy S were given as collateral."

"That sounds serious."

"Damn right. I wonder if Grandma knew about the loan."

Zak was willing to bet she hadn't. But it was possible Nikki had.

DERICK CALLED TIFF on Friday just before lunch. She was in the barn, in the back office, helping with the paperwork so Kenny could harvest more trees with the rest of the crew. The first weekend of December was upon them and they were about to be slammed with the biggest crowds yet that evening and throughout Saturday and Sunday.

She was tempted to let the call go to messages. But she had a lot riding on Derick's business. He had to feel like he was top priority.

She put a heavy glass ornament on top of the stack of invoices she'd been processing and took the phone with her to the window. *Please let him be calling with work.* She took a deep breath.

"Hey, Derick, how are you?"

There was a slight pause. "I'm okay, Tiff. Wish I was calling with better news though."

Tiff slowly sank until she was crouched on the floor, her back to the hard plank paneling.

He couldn't be saying no to her. He was her friend and she knew she could help him.

"I've been waiting for your email. Is there a problem?"

"I'm afraid I can't hire any of your services right now. There just isn't room in the budget."

"Sometimes getting the right accounting advice can actually *save* you money. I wouldn't want to make any promises. But I have seen it happen."

"Maybe next year. Once things have calmed down around here."

"But it's precisely because of all the upheaval that you need advice, Derick. You want to make sure you structure your separation agreement so that it will be advantageous from a tax point of view. Next year might be too late."

"I'm sorry. It's complicated, but I have to say no."

Tiff stopped herself from saying more. She didn't want to beg for his business.

But only once she'd said goodbye did the reality hit her. She'd thought it would be so easy to start her own business in Lost Trail. Not only had she counted on the goodwill of her family name, she'd also hoped people would respect and trust her, as a person.

But not a single local business owner was willing to give her even a small amount of work.

Chapter Thirteen

Saturday, December 2

FOR DAYS JUSTIN looked forward to Saturday and spending the evening with Debbie-Ann. The anticipation drove home how lonely he'd been. Becoming Geneva's father had filled a massive hole in his life—the desire to be a father and to care for and love someone who needed him. But not since his college days had he enjoyed the company of people he could relax with and be totally himself.

Back then Willow was one of those people. But the Willow who returned to Lost Trail this summer was different. Guarded. Secretive. Her past history with Paul was a wall between them.

It had been such a relief to talk about his college days with Debbie-Ann and to admit the truth about his relationship with Willow. Tonight, though, he wanted to get to know her better. And he also needed to tell her about his illness. Though maybe she'd already heard since news of his cancer was spreading fast thanks to the donor clinic.

Before dinner with Debbie-Ann and her daughter, Justin had a day to spend with his daughter. He was looking forward to it. For breakfast he made her favorite: pancakes and strawberry-banana smoothies. The deal was they would take Dora for a long walk and after that go to Raven Farms to pick out their Christmas tree.

"I've never had a real tree before," Geneva confided after they had finished eating and were out walking Dora.

He'd given her the bag of dog treats to hold. Every time Dora sat nicely at a crosswalk she was supposed to get a reward.

"Did your mom and Paul have fake ones?"

"No trees. Mommy liked hot places for Christmas. With beaches and the ocean."

"Did you put out a stocking for Santa?"

"No, but Mommy bought me presents. I opened them in the morning before we went to the beach. Then a sitter would come and stay with me so they could go to a fancy restaurant."

Justin cupped his hand over Geneva's head, unable to speak for a moment. Willow and Paul had stripped all the magic from Christmas if all they'd done was buy their daughter a few new toys.

When he trusted his voice he told his daughter that they celebrated Christmas the old-fashioned way in Lost Trail. "You're going to help me pick out a tree today and we'll bring it home and put it up in the house. Tomorrow, after it's thawed, we'll decorate."

"Yay! Can I make some more snowflakes to put on the

tree?"

"You bet." Justin hadn't had a tree since he'd moved away from home, so he didn't own a stand, lights or any ornaments. He hoped he'd be able to pick up all that at the Raven Farms gift shop. Once he had the basics, Geneva's handmade decorations would be the perfect touch.

"Maybe Santa *will* come this year if we have a tree."

"If you hang a stocking by our fireplace on Christmas Eve and set out milk and cookies I promise he will."

"Pinkie swear?"

It was a new phrase she'd picked up at the day care. He suppressed a smile and held out his little finger. "Pinkie swear."

✕

BY THE TIME Debbie-Ann and Ashley showed up, Justin had steaks marinating in a spice rub, homemade mac and cheese baking in the oven, and sliced raw carrots and sweet pepper out on the counter for snacking. The veggies were a last-minute addition, so Debbie-Ann wouldn't judge him.

Geneva, watching at the front window, ran for the door before their guests had a chance to press the doorbell. They came in with a gust of the arctic air and Justin hurried to shut the door behind them.

"It smells good in here!" Ashley sank onto the floor to tug off her boots. Before Justin could put them in the closet,

Dora snatched one and ran triumphantly down the hallway. Geneva and Ashley chased after her, shrieking.

"Dora! Give that back!"

"Sorry," he apologized. "Dora's puppy training is obviously a work in progress."

Debbie-Ann handed him a poinsettia plant. "Don't worry about it. The kids love the excitement." She looked through to the living room. "You've put up your tree! It's beautiful—is it from Raven Farms?"

"Yes, Geneva and I picked it out this afternoon." He put the poinsettia on the top of the table where Dora couldn't reach it, then hung Debbie-Ann's coat and showed her where to put her boots so the pup wouldn't find them. "We went the whole nine yards—did the hayride and had cookies and cocoa at the fire pit. It's great to have a kid so you can do all the stuff you secretly want to do even though you're an adult."

"Like go see kid movies at the theater?"

"Exactly."

Ashley and Geneva came running back into the room with Dora in pursuit.

"We got the boot!" Ashley handed it to her mother so she could put it in the closet.

Justin offered the girls one of his famous smoothies, which Geneva assured her friend "doesn't taste healthy at all." When they were done drinking, they scooted back to Geneva's room so she could show her new friend all her toys.

"So what can I get you?" Justin asked. "Eggnog and rum? Red wine?"

"Oh the eggnog and rum. Definitely." Debbie-Ann made herself comfortable at the island and crunched on a carrot stick.

He could sense her watching as he mixed their drinks. When he turned around she lowered her eyes, but not before he saw her concern.

He passed her a drink. "My symptoms aren't that bad, yet. I feel fine."

"So it's true?" Her voice was warm, full of sympathy.

"I have Hodgkin's lymphoma. Yes."

Debbie-Ann cupped her hand over her mouth, and her eyes teared up. After a few moments she said, "Sorry. Hearing you say that just made it seem so real."

"But you'd already heard?"

"Farrah Saddler brings her little guy to my day care. She told me yesterday about the donor clinic and why they were having it."

"Dad just gave me the heads-up yesterday. Sorry I didn't have time to warn you." He was touched she cared enough to shed a tear.

"How long have you had it?"

"I was first diagnosed almost two years ago, long before Willow and Geneva were in my life." He explained how he'd gone through treatment last fall and winter, and the hopes that the cancer had been beaten.

"And you didn't tell anyone you were sick back then? Not even your father?"

"Least of all my father. He would have been so worried. I hoped to spare him that."

"I've never met anyone who protects his family as much as you do. It's almost like you're the parent."

"It was really brutal for him to lose my mom when they were both so young. A lot of people have told me how much in love they were. Not that I needed to be told. It's obvious from the pictures taken when they were dating and in the early years of their marriage. They're never looking at the camera, always at each other."

"That's so sweet. It's sad your mother died young, but at least they had some happy years. There are people who never find a love like that their entire lives."

The naked vulnerability in her voice made him guess she put herself in that category. "What about Ashley's father? Did you love him that way?"

"No. I was young and foolish when I fell for him. Very, very foolish. Ashley's met him, but he isn't in our lives in any meaningful way."

"I'm sorry."

"Don't be. It's always a mixed blessing when a woman has a baby with a man who turns out to be a jerk. On the one hand you've wasted your love on someone who didn't deserve it. But then you also have this very wonderful child. So how can you regret it?"

He nodded. “Mixed blessings.” He had a few of those in his life too.

The strident buzzing of the oven timer interrupted the conversation and reminded him he was off schedule.

“Heck. The pasta’s ready but I haven’t grilled our steaks, yet.”

Debbie-Ann peeked into the oven. “No problem. I’ll cover this with foil and lower the heat. It should be fine for fifteen minutes or so.”

Justin concentrated on grilling then, making sure the steaks were done to order. Then the kids joined them and they ate their meal, after which they played a few rounds of Candy Land.

It wasn’t until Debbie-Ann and Ashley were about to leave that he returned, discreetly, to one of their earlier topics.

“I have some…appointments tomorrow. In Missoula.” His oncologist had scheduled a bunch of testing. To say he was dreading it was a huge understatement.

She caught his gaze, and nodded seriously. “Okay. Geneva will be fine with me.”

“I hope I won’t be late picking her up…but these things are difficult to predict, time-wise.”

Debbie-Ann put her hand on his arm and squeezed softly. “Don’t worry. If you aren’t back by six I’ll take Geneva upstairs to our apartment.”

Emotion clogged his voice again. It had been a long time

since he'd felt he could totally count on someone. Debbie-Ann's friendship felt like the only lifeline he had.

✕

SINCE HIS RUN with Luke on Friday, Zak couldn't stop thinking about the Stillman brothers' loan. Could Clayton and Eugene have been so desperate to pay off the bank they would have killed their mother? Given the longevity on that side of the family, Lacy might have lived another decade...much too long to solve their financial woes.

But if they had been the architects of Lacy's death, how did they do it? Was it even possible to induce a heart attack without being detected?

Zak had a pretty good relationship with Dr. Pittman. Good enough he felt he could phone him on a Saturday night and count on his discretion.

"Sorry to bother you, Doc. I hope I'm not getting you in the middle of dinner."

"It's no bother. I'm going to Justin's tomorrow night to help them decorate their Christmas tree—this will be my granddaughter's first—" he added proudly. "But I'm just sitting home and reading tonight."

"I've got a question, but it's kind of a delicate matter. You know the sheriff's office isn't investigating Lacy Stillman's death."

"Why would they? Lacy died of natural causes."

"Yes. Would you indulge me in a little hypothetical speculation? Not in any official capacity, of course."

"Get to the point, Zak. Something's obviously bothering you. What is it?"

"Suppose for a moment Lacy's family needed money and wanted to sell some land. What if they were actually desperate for that money and when Lacy refused to sell the land, they decided to spur on the aging process?"

"That's quite the 'what if' scenario. And how, exactly, would they *spur on* her aging?"

"That's why I'm calling you. Is there any drug you could give someone that would cause a heart attack and yet not leave any traces detectable in the bloodstream?"

"What a bizarre idea."

"I know it."

"Hang on while I think a bit."

There was a long pause. Zak heard the sound of a cabinet door opening and then water running. Presumably the doctor was getting a drink of water. Finally he came back on the line.

"There is one way I can think of. An injection of insulin."

"But insulin isn't a poison."

"It can be if you're not diabetic and you get too much in your system."

Zak tried to imagine how that would work. Could the brothers have snuck into their mother's room and injected her while she was asleep? That seemed risky, especially if she didn't die right away. "How quickly would the insulin take effect?"

"Anywhere from ten minutes to six hours depending on the type of insulin."

Zak tried to imagine Eugene and Clayton sitting with their mother after giving her a lethal dose and waiting for her to die. Ten minutes would feel like an eternity.

They'd have to be awfully desperate to do something like that.

Zak apologized to the doctor for wasting his time. "Sometimes I get these weird ideas and can't seem to shake them."

"You're a natural investigator, Zak. If it wasn't for you the Concurran case would never have been solved. I'm convinced of it." He hesitated a moment, then added, "I may be going out on a limb here. But not everybody in town loves Sheriff Ford."

Zak was astounded. It was one thing for Nadine to suggest he run for sheriff. She was probably half-joking anyway.

But Dr. Pittman…

"I'm only the dispatcher."

"Yes. So you keep saying."

✕

Sunday, December 3

JUSTIN SPENT SUNDAY morning making paper snowflakes with Geneva. After lunch he strung the new lights around the Christmas tree. Geneva waited, hopping from one foot from the other. To set the tone, Justin put on a Christmas movie, the old Charlie Brown one, but nothing could distract his daughter from the tree.

"Can I put my snowflakes on now?"

"Just a minute, honey. The lights always go first. At least, that was the rule when I was a little boy." He moved the ladder around the tree, so he could wind some lights around the very top. He should have picked a shorter tree, but Geneva had been so excited at Raven Farms yesterday he'd gotten carried away.

"You were *not* a little boy. You're teasing me."

He laughed. "I'm not. A long time ago I was as little as you are. And Grandpa was my daddy. And he put up the lights on *our* tree."

He had some vague memories of his mother, as well. Handing him ornaments, telling him to hang them on the tree for her. Mostly when he pictured his mother it was in a chair or resting in bed. She'd been very frail after he was born.

Finally he was at the base of the tree. He connected the last strand of lights and then plugged the end piece into the wall. Hundreds of red, blue, green and gold lights sparked to life.

"Oh!" Geneva clapped her hands. "It's so pretty!"

Dora barked and tried to nip the tree.

"Leave it, Dora!" Geneva's stern tone made Justin want to laugh. But he was also impressed, because the puppy listened.

"Snowflake time."

"Yes!" Geneva had already stuck clips onto the snowflakes, so all she had to do was hook them onto the branches. He picked her up so she could reach some of the higher branches, then used the ladder so he could get the upper third of the tree.

"Do we have an angel for the top? The tree at the day care has an angel at the top."

"You're my angel. Do you want me to hang you up there?"

Geneva giggled. It was a sound he was hearing more and more these days. The most joyful sound in the world.

"How long until Grandpa gets here? I want to show him our tree."

"Not for a while, honey." His dad had promised to bring a box of ornaments from the attic to help fill out the tree. And then they'd have lasagna for dinner—Justin had bought a frozen one on his last big grocery shop.

"If we take Dora for a walk, the time will go by faster."

"If we run will it go even faster?"

Oh, God. Kids. Sometimes Justin didn't know whether to laugh or cry. He felt sorry for Willow missing moments like this. But then, she'd made her choice. A package had come by courier from her yesterday afternoon, shipped from Amazon. Inside were two gifts for Geneva. But no note.

Time was running out to explain his cancer to Geneva. With the donor clinic happening next week, the news was all over town. It was possible some of the kids at the day care had already heard their parents talking about it.

He needed to prepare her.

He hoped being outdoors, in the sunshine, would make the news seem less scary.

But it was so cold Justin changed his mind about having his serious chat with Geneva outside. They raced around the block with Dora, then hurried inside for hot cocoa and cookies. While they were at the kitchen table, stirring marshmallows into their drinks, Justin said simply, "The doctor told me I'm sick. I'm going to be sick for a long time."

Geneva looked puzzled. "Why aren't you in bed if you're sick?"

"This is a different type of sickness. It's called Hodgkin's lymphoma."

"What's that?"

"It's a kind of cancer."

The word meant nothing to Geneva.

"Grandpa's a doctor. He can give you some medicine."

"I have to go to a different kind of doctor. A specialist."

"But he can make you better, right?" Geneva was starting

to look worried.

What did you say to a four-year-old? She'd been faced with too many broken promises already in her short life. He didn't want to lie, but he couldn't burden her with complexities, either.

"It's going to take a long time."

"How long?"

"By the time you start kindergarten, I should be better."

"That's a *really* long time." She pushed out her bottom lip, chewed it a moment, then patted his hand. "But that's okay, Daddy. I'll look after you."

Wednesday, December 6

ZAK SET ASIDE the report he was writing when Clayton and Vanessa Stillman stepped into the office shortly after eleven on Wednesday. They both looked anguished and worried and exhausted.

"We need to talk to the sheriff," Clayton said.

Ford opened his door. "I'm here. Been on the phone all morning checking with local law enforcement across Montana. No one's seen Nikki or her truck so far."

Vanessa threw up her arms. "This is crazy. She couldn't just disappear."

Zak felt for her and her husband. He hadn't had a solid night's sleep since Nikki had been reporting missing, either, but it must be absolute hell for the family. With Clayton standing right in front of him, he was sorely tempted to ask about the loan, but Luke had sworn him to secrecy.

"Can you think of anything that might have been bothering Nikki? Something that would prompt her to disappear for a while?"

The couple exchanged a glance that was long enough to make Zak wonder if the bank had sent a second letter to Clayton Stillman's house, a letter Nikki might have intercepted and which could have sent her into a tailspin.

If that was the case though, neither Vanessa nor Clayton was ready to admit it.

"There's nothing," Vanessa said.

"Nikki's life revolves around the ranch and her family," her husband added. "It's completely out of character for her to take off like this. It's been more than a week. Someone must have taken her. Maybe…hurt her."

The grim lines around Vanessa's mouth tightened. Automatically she leaned toward her husband, who clasped his arm protectively around her shoulders.

"There's no evidence of any foul play," Ford was quick to point out. "No sign at all that Nikki has come to any harm."

"I wish I could share your confidence, Sheriff." Vanessa's eyes were filling with tears. "There must be more that you can do."

"Butterfield is supervising the ground search. We've got

the copter out again today and an APB for Nikki and her Jeep. Deputy Black and I are working the phones, checking in with the neighboring counties. We'll hear something soon," Ford predicted.

"God, I hope so," Clayton said. "Phone us tonight, would you? We'd appreciate an update."

"You bet." Ford walked them to the door.

Zak imagined metaphorical sweat gathering on his brow. The Stillmans had a lot of sway in this county, both financial and otherwise. If this didn't end well, with Nikki back at the Lazy S in time for Christmas, Ford's re-election campaign was going to be dead in the water.

"Goddamned kids," Ford said a few moments later. "With all their phones and iPads, you'd think they could take the time to send a few messages to the folks who pay for all their fancy toys."

"Nikki's twenty-five," Zak pointed out. "She's been working on that ranch all her life. I'm sure she pays for her own toys by now."

The sheriff grunted. "Then she's old enough to know better than to take off like this."

Zak agreed. That was the fact that worried him most.

The sheriff fetched a stack of rough notes from his office. "I need you to write these up into reports for me." He tossed the papers onto Zak's desk.

Zak had been about to put on his coat. "I'll get right on that when I finish at the donor drive."

"What?" The sheriff frowned. "You mean the one for Justin Pittman?"

"Yup." He wanted to get in before noon, to beat the rush.

"Jesus. We're overloaded with work and you've got time to give DNA samples?" The sheriff turned to Nadine, who had just stood up as well. "Don't tell me you're doing it, too?"

"This is a matter of life and death," Nadine said. "It's our civic duty."

Other bosses might have commended them. All Ford said was, "This counts as your lunch break."

Zak could live with that.

ON THE MORNING of the donor drive, Marsha asked Tiff for help wrapping her Christmas gifts. She'd bought something for everyone at the medi-clinic, as well as bottles of libations for Kenny and the other farm employees.

"I've already given out the Christmas bonuses." Tiff placed the bottle of bourbon meant for Kenny into a gift bag. Then she stuffed several sheets of tissue paper around it.

"That's fine, but this is more personal." Marsha taped a handwritten label to the box she'd just wrapped.

Tiff couldn't argue with that.

Once they'd finished with the gifts, Marsha pulled out

Christmas cards. "We're behind on these. Usually we send them to our customers right after Thanksgiving."

Tiff felt like groaning. They had hundreds of names on their customer list. "The job would go a lot faster if I printed the addresses from the list onto the envelopes. I'd have to use the laser printer in the barn office."

"Hand-written labels are more personal…but okay. Let me know when you're finished and I'll help stuff the cards."

"I can do that in the office as well. Then I can take them straight to the post office." She'd hit the donor drive at the same time.

"No need. I have some library books of your mother's to return."

"Let me take care of them."

"Oh, no, it will give me a chance to say hello to Sybil. I haven't seen her in ages. Just bring me the cards when you're done. And thank you. This is always such a big job—I really appreciate your help."

"No problem." Tiff suspected her aunt was keeping her busy to make sure she didn't go to Dr. Pittman's donor drive. Marsha had brought up the subject again last night at dinner, stating what a waste of time it was. The population in Lost Trail was statistically insignificant. Even if everyone in the suggested eighteen to forty-four age group participated, the chance was negligible that they'd find a match for Justin.

But Tiff couldn't see it that way. If she had some rare

blood disease, she knew she'd appreciate each and every person who tried to help.

Having known Justin and his father all her life, she simply had to go. Even Kenny, who had no history with the Pittmans, wanted to do his bit.

Once she was in the barn, Tiff texted him.

I'm going into town to the donor drive.

He replied almost instantly. *Hang on, I'll come with you. The other guys went earlier.*

Let's take your truck.

They didn't talk much on the drive into town. Last night she'd gone by his cabin to share a drink and to vent about her inability to get any clients for her accounting business.

"How am I supposed to support myself? I'm too old to keep sponging off my family."

Kenny had listened, but he hadn't offered much in the way of advice. It had been frustrating. Now, as he parked as close as he could to the clinic, she turned to him.

"You didn't say much last night."

He stared straight ahead, his jaw annoyingly firm, his posture rigid. "What did you want me to say?"

"I'd like to know what you think. Did I make a mistake moving back here?"

After a few seconds he turned and gave her a long steady look. "That's something only you can answer."

Then he got out of the car.

Inside the waiting room was jammed and they had to

take a number. Zak and Nadine were on their way out.

"We got here before the rush," Zak said. "Derick and Aubrey were here earlier as well. They missed each other by less than five minutes."

"I wonder what would have happened if they'd seen each other. Do you think Aubrey will ever forgive him?" Tiff asked.

Zak shrugged. "Would you?"

Tiff doubted anyone could answer unless they'd been in the same situation. Derick had been motivated by love, wanting to make his wife happy. But he'd deceived her, and participated in something illegal. So…

"I don't know."

Just then Farrah Saddler called out Tiff's number. The process was remarkably efficient. Within twenty minutes she and Kenny filled in their paperwork, provided their cheek swabs and were leaving the clinic. On the way to the truck, they crossed paths with Debbie-Ann from the day care. She nodded at Tiff.

"Did you just get tested?"

"We both did. And you?"

"I'm on my way in. Sybil's filling in at the day care for me so I can do my part." She waved her hands at all the vehicles parked around the medi-clinic. "Isn't it wonderful how many people are coming to get tested?"

"A lot of people care about Justin. I can't imagine this town without him."

✕

WHEN ZAK RETURNED with Nadine from the donor clinic, the sheriff's office door was closed. His muffled voice was audible in short bursts, suggesting he was on the phone.

Nadine threw her coat onto the rack by the door. "If your stem cells are a match—will you go ahead with the donation?"

"A match for Justin, you mean? Yeah, of course I would." He leafed through the stack of papers the sheriff had dumped on him. By now he was proficient at interpreting Ford's sketchy notes. This wouldn't take long.

"What if you turn out to be a match for someone you don't know?"

"Same answer. How could I say no? When someone needs a stem-cell transplant, we're talking life and death. And matches are rare."

Nadine nodded. "That's what I figured you'd say." Her gaze darted to the sheriff's closed door. "If he hadn't been too old to be tested, do you think he would have done it?"

Given how grudgingly Ford had given his permission for them to take time off to go to the clinic, and given everything else Zak knew about the man, he doubted it. But he decided to be generous and say he wasn't sure.

"Well, I am. Ford wouldn't have bothered. And neither would Butterfield."

She looked like she had more to say, but was interrupted

by the ringing of her phone.

"Sheriff's department, Deputy Black here." She automatically reached for a pen. Within seconds her spine snapped straight and she began scribbling madly.

From her end of the conversation Zak could tell the call was about Nikki. Finally, a break. But by the time she'd hung up, the starch had gone out of Nadine's posture.

She circled something on her pad of paper, then looked up at him. "That was the police department in Great Falls. One of their officers reported seeing a blue Jeep Compass an hour ago being driven by a young woman with brown hair in a braid over her shoulder. The license plate was muddy but at least two of the numbers matched. Unfortunately the officer was driving in the opposite direction on a road with a broad boulevard. By the time he circled around, he lost sight of the truck."

"Damn. That's bad luck. But if it was her, at least we know she's alive and well enough to drive. Though with only two matching numbers…that's not much to go on."

"It's the best we've had so far." Nadine eyed the sheriff's closed door cautiously. "I guess I better tell him."

"Yup. It's the first hopeful sign since she disappeared. He'll want to be the one to call the Stillmans."

Chapter Fourteen

AT HOME THAT night Tiff watched as her aunt silently put together a dinner tray for her mother. Tiff was worried, not only about her mom who'd spent the entire day in bed, but also about her aunt.

For most of Tiff's life Marsha had been her one true ally, her only sane relative, the rock she could count on. Marsha had showered her with the sort of love she might have given to her own child if she'd had one.

Lately though, her aunt seemed tense and easily annoyed. Maybe the role of caregiver was finally getting to be too much.

"Aunt Marsha, when is the last time you took a holiday? A real vacation?"

Her aunt snorted. "Like Vanessa and Jen's spa retreat you mean? No thanks."

"What about a few weeks on the beach in Hawaii or Florida? Does that appeal?"

"A beach isn't everyone's idea of a good time."

"Well how about a few weeks in New York? Or maybe a European tour?"

Her aunt swung around. “Are you trying to get rid of me?”

“That’s—not what I meant at all.” Tiff didn’t understand this confrontational attitude. “I’m trying to be considerate. You’ve been looking after Mom and the farm for so many years. If anyone deserves a holiday, it’s you.”

“I was perfectly happy with the status quo. Then you decide to come home. You question my administration of your mother’s medications, you go behind my back to talk to Dr. Pittman, you push to get your mother to see specialists. You act like you have all the answers.”

The verbal attack took Tiff’s breath away. She couldn’t speak. Wide-eyed she stared at her aunt as the assault continued.

“I’m a nurse. I’m your mother’s sister. You show no respect for any of this.”

Tiff’s instinct was to apologize, but her aunt kept speaking.

“No one asked you to move home. You took it for granted you’d be wanted. Can’t you see it upsets your mother to have you around?”

“Do you really believe that?” Tiff’s voice came out small, laced with hurt.

“Haven’t you ever wondered why there are no current photographs of you in the house? Time stopped for your mother when Casey and your dad died. Is that healthy? No. But it’s the only way Rosemary manages to go on.”

The words were hurtful, but they rang true.

Tiff sank onto a stool and stared down at her hands. She felt empty, smashed.

When her aunt spoke next, her voice was kinder. "I'm sorry. I didn't want to hurt you. But the truth does hurt sometimes."

It certainly did.

Her aunt picked up the tray of food. "I'm taking this to your mother then I'm going to my book club meeting. We can talk later when you've had a chance to think things through. Whatever you do, though, please don't upset your mother by discussing this with her."

AFTER HER AUNT left the house, Tiff went upstairs to check on her mom. She was asleep on her back, a troubled expression on her pale face. Tiff picked up the framed photos of herself and her brother from the bedside table. What a carefree kid she'd been back then.

This was the Tiffany her mom wanted to remember. Casey and her dad had been frozen in time. Only she had the bad taste to continue living.

Tiff carried the tray of cold food downstairs, cleaned the dishes, then turned out the lights. From the window she looked across the snowy landscape to the guest cabin.

Icicles hung from the snow-laden roof, but a warm light

glowed from the windows and smoke chugged out the chimney. Kenny must be home.

An overpowering urge to see him washed over her.

She went to the mudroom, slipped on her boots and coat. She wouldn't go for long. Just a quick drink with Kenny.

The cold air felt good, like pressing a reset button after a meltdown. She filled her lungs and ran along the path that wound through her mother's gardens.

When she rapped on the cabin door, Kenny didn't answer right away. Maybe she should have sent him a text first. He could be in the shower for all she knew. She knocked again.

"Hey! It's cold out here!"

The door opened. Kenny blocked the entry, dressed in jeans and a T-shirt, his feet bare. He didn't look welcoming.

"I'm kind of busy."

She looked past him, saw no sign of company, only Spade asleep on the rug by the couch.

"I need to talk about something."

Only when she pushed past him did she notice the mobile phone in his hand. A pretty woman's animated face on the screen.

"What's going on, Kenny?" the woman on the phone asked. "Is someone else in the room?"

Tiff took a step backward. "Sorry!" she mouthed to Kenny. She turned to leave, but Kenny shut the door.

"Hey, Kate, I'll catch you later."

"Sure. No problem."

"Thanks." He disconnected the call, then slipped his phone into his jeans' pocket. He was looking at Tiff like she was the most annoying person on the planet, and Tiff wondered if she'd made way too many assumptions where Kenny was concerned.

Like believing his relationship with Kate was long over. He'd told her they'd broken up a few months after the accident where he'd trashed his knee. Kate was going to pursue her Olympic aspirations for the Canadian ski team, while Kenny was looking to settle down.

All this time she'd figured the reason he hadn't kissed her was because he was waiting for a sign from her.

But maybe he hadn't kissed her because he was still into Kate.

"That was your fiancée on the phone." She sounded stupid, stating the obvious.

"*Ex*-fiancée."

Maybe. But how many guys stayed in touch with their ex-fiancées unless there was a possibility of patching up the relationship?

"Bad timing on my part. I'll go."

"You will not. I've already ended the call. The least you can do is have a drink with me."

He went to the kitchenette, grabbed the glasses he used for mixing drinks.

She veered toward the sofa, crouching to give Spade a belly rub. She knew little of Kenny's past life as a back-country ski guide. He'd told her he didn't miss it, but she wasn't sure she believed him. Once he had the operation to repair his damaged knee, maybe he'd find a way to go back.

A paperback thriller was open, face down on the arm of the sofa. On the floor was a pair of discarded work socks. She imagined Kenny sprawled on the sofa reading. It made an appealing picture.

"Drink's ready."

She headed toward Kenny, meeting him in the middle of the room. He passed her a glass and suddenly Tiff's senses were in overdrive.

The heat from the fire, the soft lighting from the corner reading lamp, the scent of ginger and rum and most of all the strong male in front of her. He radiated an essence that was part mountain man, part protector, and she wanted to throw herself at him, feel the bliss of being wanted and cared for.

Afraid all of this was shining in her eyes, she lowered them to her glass, held her breath and took a drink.

It would be stupid to fling herself into his arms as a balm to that hurtful conversation with her aunt. But she still wanted to.

"Sorry I interrupted your call with Kate."

"No biggie. She calls me now and then to vent about her training."

"I see."

"What sent you running here tonight?"

"I had a talk with Aunt Marsha tonight. Actually, more like a dress-down."

"*She* lectured *you*?"

Tiff blinked back tears. Her aunt had said they would talk later, but clearly there was only one solution. "I need to move back to Seattle."

It was difficult to decide how Kenny reacted to that statement. Maybe his nostrils flared. Maybe his jaw tightened. Or maybe he did neither and she was desperately hoping *someone* would be sad to see her leave.

She took another drink. Went to perch on the hearth. "I came home hoping to help. Instead I've made my aunt's and mother's lives more difficult."

"You came here because you had nowhere else to turn," Kenny reminded her harshly. "You had no job, you'd betrayed your boyfriend and spent all your money. Or, that's the story you told me."

"That's true. And now I've licked my wounds and it's time to go back."

"Is it?"

She looked at him helplessly. "Why do you question everything I say? It's a very annoying habit."

"The message in your eyes doesn't match your words. That's why. You think you have everything figured out, but you don't. Starting with your aunt's motives. She doesn't have your best interests at heart."

"That's not fair. You don't really know her."

"Possibly," Kenny said. "Or maybe it's *you* who doesn't really know *her*."

Thursday, December 7

ZAK GOT A text message from Luke early on Thursday morning. He and his uncle Clayton were driving to Great Falls to look for Nikki. Their plan was to check all the local motels since she had to be sleeping somewhere. It was too damn cold to sleep in her truck.

As a shot in the dark it wasn't a bad one, even though Nikki could have left Great Falls by now. So Zak didn't try to talk them out of the trip. If Nikki was his cousin, he'd be doing the same thing. Yes, law enforcement was on the alert. But they didn't have the same vested interest as the family.

It was a dull day in the office. No new tips came in about Nikki. Nadine spent most of the day on patrol while Butterfield continued to head the search and rescue efforts at the Lazy S. After lunch the sheriff was called out to handle some drunk and rowdy teenagers on the ski hill.

Zak chafed at being the one left behind. There were things he could be doing. Interviewing the Stillman brothers, trying to get them to disclose that loan. Following up with Gwen on whether she recalled any details of the conversation between Lacy and Marsha. Questioning Cora Christensen on her whereabouts the day Lacy died.

If he was the sheriff, or even a deputy, there were so many lines of investigation he'd be following. As the lowly dispatcher though, his hands were tied. He could only pursue his lines of inquiry as a private citizen, on his own time.

Half an hour before closing time, Nadine showed up with a broad grin and a stack of papers in hand. "I've put in an offer on the acreage."

"Seriously? Congrats!" They'd gone to see it on the weekend. He'd made a list of pros and cons about the property, even though it wasn't necessary. He could tell by the gleam in Nadine's eyes that she'd fallen in love with the place.

He didn't blame her. The house, built to take advantage of the view of the Bitterroots, was small but in good repair. Likewise the barn and corral were in working order. The place was move-in ready.

"I hope the sellers accept," Nadine said. "Because I've also purchased Making Magic."

Saturday, December 9

ZAK RAN BY himself on Saturday. Nadine was finalizing the deal for her acreage and Luke was still in Great Falls. It took fifteen miles but he finally outran the stresses of the job. With a clear head, he went home to shower, then settled in his favorite armchair with a cup of coffee and a spiral-ring notebook.

He always thought better when he wrote things down. The technique had worked for the Concurran case and he hoped it would do the same for Lacy's possible homicide and Nikki's disappearance.

He had a strong hunch the two were connected. But first he wanted to focus on Nikki.

Was that Nikki's vehicle in Great Falls?

He circled the question, then drew two lines. One to the word *yes* and one to the word *no.*

If it hadn't been Nikki's Jeep it was a dead end.

If it had been her car, more questions needed to be asked. Most importantly, why was she in Great Falls? Was she still there? And why had she gone in secret?

According to her parents, Nikki had no relatives in the city. They weren't aware of any friends Nikki might have in the vicinity, either.

As far as they knew, Nikki did not use dating websites, though without access to her phone no one could be sure of this. So one possibility had to be she went to meet a guy.

Zak tried to think of other options.

From all accounts Nikki wasn't a complicated person. She loved the ranch and animals. She'd been very close to her grandmother. She wasn't nearly as close to her own parents, a fact that disappointed her mother. She didn't have many friends, and didn't spend a lot of time with the few she had.

She got along well with her cousins, especially Luke.

Zak wrote down another question: *Did she know about the loan and that the bank was calling it in?*

Again he circled the question and drew two lines. If the answer was no, then he had another question…was someone trying to keep her from finding out about the loan?

If the answer was yes…what then?

Zak thought a long time. He was about to close his notebook in frustration when an idea occurred to him. It was far-fetched, but possible.

If Luke was around, he would have given him a call and asked for his help. As it was, he'd have to take the next step himself.

Zak drove out to the Stillmans' ranch. The only vehicle in sight was Lacy's vintage pickup. That was a good thing. He drove along the lane to Lacy's old farmhouse and parked. A raven perched on one of the pine trees to his right gave him a disdainful look, let out a rusty "caw, caw," then swooped past his head to a tree further down the line.

The sky was dull gray, the air almost too cold to breathe. There was beauty to a blue-sky winter day and a peaceful grace when it snowed, but days like this gave winter a bad name.

Zak went to the porch, tried the front door. Locked.

He looked around. There were two old creamery cans on

either side of the door. In the summer they probably held flowers. Now they just contained dirt. He lifted one. Nothing. He lifted the other. A key.

After that it was easy to let himself in and take a quick look around.

Within seconds he had his answer.

He'd guessed correctly. He now had a working theory why Nikki was in Great Falls. He went to the barns next and ran his hand over the dark red siding. Yes. It all made sense.

Monday, December 11

AS HE DROVE north on Highway 93 toward Missoula, Justin had no idea that for the rest of his life he was going to remember this day as the one that divided his *before* from his *after.* His life to date had not been without heartache. But his core values, his self-concept, his world order…these had been firmly in place since the day he was born.

All that was about to change.

His oncologist's office had called him at ten o'clock that morning to request an urgent visit. Justin immediately canceled his appointments, then rushed to the day care to speak to Debbie-Ann. He tried to conceal his worry, but she knew him too well now.

"I wish I could go with you. You shouldn't be facing this alone."

"I'll be fine. I'm just not sure what time I'll get back. If I'm late picking up Geneva—"

"Don't give that a second thought. She'll be fine with us, and I'm happy to have her. Today and any other day." She gave him a hug. "I mean it."

The memory of that hug was with him as he approached the hospital and parked at the cancer treatment center. He walked the now familiar corridors with worry percolating from his stomach, up his throat. He was aware of his body, of the strength he felt in his limbs, of his clear eyesight and good hearing.

Aside from that swelling, aside from the tiredness, he still felt healthy.

When would he lose this? And how quickly?

He headed toward the answers, toward a receptionist who offered him water, which he declined, then a seat, which he perched on the edge of. He avoided looking at the others in the room. He didn't want to speculate on their stories, their illnesses, their prognoses.

He had his hands full with his own right now.

The fifteen minutes before his appointment felt like an epoch. Too anxious to do something useful, like deal with email, he clasped his hands together, leaned forward, and examined the patterns in the tiled flooring.

When his name was called, he thought he might barf.

But he stood. He said something inane about the weather.

He was directed to an examining room where a nurse took his blood pressure, asked how he was feeling, and made some notes for the doctor. After she left he desperately searched the walls for a distraction. A poster on the health benefits of meditation was perfect. He had it memorized when Dr. Zimmermann finally came in.

The doctor was smiling as he shook Justin's hand. It was not a tight smile. It wasn't a smile with secrets. Justin felt the burden of his worry begin to unravel. Maybe this wouldn't be as bad as he'd thought.

He took a deep, belly breath. Rested his damp palms on his thighs and felt the sweat absorb into the cotton of his chinos.

"We rushed the testing of the samples from your father's donor drive," Dr. Zimmermann said. "And I'm glad we did because I have encouraging news."

Justin stared through Zimmermann's prescription lenses, into the dark pupils of the doctor's eyes. Encouraging news, he noted. Not necessarily good. He couldn't find his voice and wouldn't have known what to say if he had. He just waited for the rest to come.

"Why didn't you tell me you had a sibling?" Dr. Zimmermann finally said. "The test results show a perfect match."

Chapter Fifteen

JUSTIN JAMMED HIS foot on the accelerator, speeding down the highway as dozens of jumbled thoughts and questions banged around in his head. What the hell?

He'd just been given the best possible news for his health.

But he couldn't celebrate, or even feel relieved. Not when the solution to his nightmare came from a source that he could not understand or even truly believe existed.

The science was irrefutable, Dr. Zimmermann said.

Justin was an educated man, yet this was damned hard to accept.

Once he reached town limits, his plan to drive straight to the medi-clinic and demand to talk to his father suddenly seemed premature.

He drove to his father's house instead, let himself in with the key, then pulled down the ladder to the attic. His father was a neat and tidy man. Anything that wasn't part of his regular routine was either donated to charity or relegated to a labeled box in the attic.

Vaguely Justin remembered the existence of a baby book

and photo albums of his youth. He found them, in a box labeled *Justin's Childhood.*

The lighting was dim in the attic, so Justin lugged the box down the stairs and set it on the kitchen table. He hesitated a moment, fixated on the label, and the fine, looping scroll. He'd seen this handwriting before, on the recipe cards his father kept in a box on the kitchen counter.

This was his mother's handwriting. As soon as he had the thought, Justin felt a gut-deep, stabbing pain. He couldn't assume anything anymore. The handwriting belonged to Franny Pittman, his father's wife. That was all he knew for certain.

He pulled off the lid.

A plush brown bear stared up at him with small button eyes. "Hello, Mr. Ted." Justin set him gently on the table. Next was a pair of tiny, scuffed leather shoes, no doubt the pair he'd learned to walk in. There was a hand-knitted, baby-blue sweater, a fireman's hat he remembered insisting on wearing to his first day in kindergarten.

Further down were two albums. One, a baby book. The other a photograph album containing pictures up to his sixth birthday, shortly before Franny's death.

She'd been a careful historian of her baby's life, recording his weight and height at various intervals, listing his first spoken words—*mama, up, pop*—and recording all his milestones with captioned photographs.

Justin rolls over.

Justin's first smile.

Justin completes his first puzzle.

He'd seen all these before, many times. Sometimes on Franny's birthday his father would pull down the box and take a trip down memory lane. Partly he did it so Justin would have a sense of his mother and how much she'd loved him.

But mostly he'd done it for himself. Justin had never seen his father smile at any living person the way he smiled at the photos of his dead wife.

Today Justin's main interest was the photo taken of himself at birth. He was in his mother's arms, and she was in bed, clearly exhausted, but smiling. The caption read, *Welcome to the world Justin Pittman!*

Carefully Justin pulled the photo out of the plastic enclosure. On the counter he laid out pictures from birth to his sixth birthday party, examining them for continuity. There was no doubt this was the same child, growing older, reaching a stage where even a stranger would agree the child was him: Justin Pittman.

It seemed irrefutable that Franny had been his mother.

Which raised the next question—what had happened to Franny's second child, the one whose stem cells were the perfect match for his? Zimmerman had assured him that such an ideal match was only possible for people who shared the same mother *and* father.

Justin went back into the attic. He searched the box labeled *Franny* containing photos from his parents' courtship, his mother's high school certificate, wedding photos, and so forth. He found a box labeled *old papers* and went through it page by page. But all he found was prior-year tax returns and yellowing bank statements.

After two hours he was confident that if there was evidence of a second child born to Franny and Clark Pittman, it wasn't in this house.

Unless it was in his father's room…?

Justin went as far as the door. He put his hand on the brass handle, but couldn't bring himself to turn it. Searching the attic was fair game. He'd grown up here, and considered he had the right. But going through his father's private space. That was entirely different.

But he lied to you. All bets are off.

Justin stood there for several minutes, battling his conscience. And then he heard the front door open.

"Justin, are you here? I saw your car out front."

His father was home. Now he would get his answers.

IF SHE WAS going to move back to Seattle, she ought to get in touch with Craig, Tiff decided. She typed several versions of a response to his message, but nothing sounded right. What she had to say was too complicated. She needed to hear his voice.

So she called, but when she was directed straight to Craig's voicemail, she was unprepared to leave a message. "Um, this is Tiff. I saw your messages on Facebook. Sorry it's taken a while to get in touch. I, um… It's been busy here. You know, Christmas trees and all. Can you call me back? I'd like to—I mean it would be good to talk. Thanks."

Argh! She disconnected, feeling like a fool.

Would he return her call? Did she even want him to? God, she had no idea. All she knew was that she couldn't go back to Seattle without letting him know.

There was so much she needed to do. Find a job. An apartment.

Tiff pressed the heels of her hands to her eyes. She rarely got headaches, but thinking about January was bringing one on. She tried to distract herself by wrapping the gifts she'd purchased in Missoula on the weekend.

She'd hoped to bring her mother along on the shopping excursion. But when it came time to get in the car, her mother had come up with a list of reasons she couldn't leave the house.

Marsha had tried to convince her to go, as well. "It'll be fun. You haven't gone shopping in ages."

But Tiff's mother hadn't changed her mind.

More proof that Tiff's presence wasn't helpful, wasn't even wanted.

Tiff gave the ribbon on the final gift a twist, then tied the strands tightly around a miniature candy cane. Pretty. She stacked her gifts in her arms and carried them to the family room where she arranged them under the tree, within the circle created by Casey's train track. There were already gifts here for her, two from her aunt and two from her mother.

"What a pretty scene."

Tiff turned, surprised at seeing her mother. She was dressed in lounging pajamas and slippers, her hair tied up in a messy bun.

"I didn't hear you come in the room, Mom."

"Remember the year you and Casey insisted on spending the night by the Christmas tree in your sleeping bags?"

"Yeah." Yet more proof that her aunt was right about her mother being happier living in the past. Gently Tiff said, "We drank cocoa and ate cookies. You didn't make us brush our teeth again after." She and her mom exchanged a smile.

Her mother took a step closer. "Your aunt told me you're moving back to Seattle."

In a flash Tiff's nostalgia turned to guilt. "Sorry, Mom. I meant to talk to you about this sooner."

"That's okay. You'll be happier in Seattle. In the long run." Her mom's gaze lowered to her hands, which she was twisting compulsively.

"Nothing's set in stone, Mom. If you need me—"

"I'll be fine. Lately I haven't had my usual energy. But after the holidays are over, I'm sure I'll bounce back to normal."

The unspoken message was clear. *Once Tiff was gone her*

mother would feel better. Tiff pushed back her sadness, blinked away her tears.

"We still have Christmas to look forward to," her mother said. "Which reminds me. A romantic holiday movie is about to start and Marsha put a pizza in the oven. Doesn't that sound nice?"

✕

CRAIG RETURNED TIFF'S call about an hour later. Tiff excused herself from the family room, so she wouldn't disrupt the movie. Out in the hall she pressed her back against the wall and sank to the floor. "Thanks for calling back."

"No problem. I just got off work. How are you doing?"

His familiar tenor voice was like a warm blanket on a cold day. He'd been a good boyfriend. He'd deserved so much better than what she'd put him through. But she couldn't apologize again without opening a door she was certain they both wanted to leave closed.

"Okay. Dealing with family drama."

"That doesn't sound good."

"No. But it's only for a short time. I'm coming back to Seattle in January."

"Yeah, that's great."

Something about his answer felt off. "You already knew?"

"Sure. Your aunt told me. Oh hell. I wasn't supposed to say that."

"Hang on. You talked to my aunt?"

"A few weeks ago."

"How did you… Did you call the farm on our landline?"

"I didn't call her. She called me."

What the hell…? How was this even possible? "But—how did she reach you?"

"Through Facebook. She sent me a message and asked if she could call. At the time I said okay because, to be honest, she made it sound like you were in a really bad place."

"And she told you I was moving?"

"Back to Seattle, yeah. She said you were having a hard time getting over me."

Tiff could hear in his voice that he wanted this to be true. "Did she say anything else?"

"That you felt too guilty to contact me and if I was open to renewing our relationship the first move would have to come from me."

"And so you sent that message. Given what I did…that was really sweet of you."

"I was kind of a jerk at the end, too. I never gave you the chance to explain. So if you need to talk. For closure or anything. I'm willing. That's all I wanted to say."

"I appreciate that. A lot. I'm just—wow, I can't believe my aunt actually reached out to you."

"I wasn't supposed to tell you that part."

"She wanted you to pretend getting in touch with me was all your idea?"

"Yeah. Sorry. Don't get mad at her for interfering okay? She sounded genuinely worried about you."

"Right." Tiff took a deep breath. She needed to get rid of Craig. Needed to think. "One day I would like to try and explain why I did what I did. I think it would help with closure, for both of us. Can I call you again after Christmas?"

"I guess so..."

He sounded uncertain, as if he hadn't expected their conversation to end this way. Poor guy.

"Thanks, Craig. And merry Christmas."

Tiff glanced down the hall toward the family room. She could tell by the music that they'd reached a tense moment in the story. The confusion she'd felt during the call was lifting. Anger took its place.

Even if her aunt's behavior was motivated by genuine concern, there was no excuse for Marsha to contact Craig and manipulate him into reaching out to Tiff. Tiff couldn't remember ever telling her mother or her aunt that she was having trouble getting over Craig. So why would Marsha tell Craig that?

Only one reason made sense...Marsha was apparently so determined to convince Tiff to leave that she was willing to manipulate innocent people, go behind Tiff's back and tell outright lies.

Kenny's words about her aunt from the other night came

back to Tiff. *She doesn't have your best interests at heart.*

And then an even uglier suspicion popped into Tiff's mind. Before she could lose her nerve, she called Derick, who answered right away.

"Hey. What's up?"

"I need you to be honest with me. Why did you turn down my business proposal? Did someone warn you off?" Tiff's pulse throbbed in her throat. Her hands were shaking. She couldn't believe she'd put such a ridiculous idea into words and she waited for Derick to shoot her down.

It took Derick a few seconds to answer. "I wasn't supposed to tell you, but your aunt Marsha called me. She said you were only staying in Lost Trail out of a sense of duty. If everyone in Lost Trail refused to give you work you'd be free to move back to Seattle with a clear conscience."

And there it was. Confirmation that Kenny had been correct about her aunt, while she had been totally wrong.

"What if she hadn't called you?"

"I *wanted* to hire you. Hell, I still do. But I know what it's like to feel trapped by family obligations. I wouldn't want that to happen to you."

"I'm sure my aunt meant well." Maybe. Not likely. "But she's wrong about me. I don't want to live in Seattle. If you're serious about needing my services, I'm totally up for it. You won't be sorry. How about we talk after Christmas?"

"Good idea."

"Thanks, Derick." Tiff turned off her phone. She wondered how many more "helpful" calls her aunt had placed to the business owners around town. She wasn't going to do any more checking, though. It was time to talk to her aunt.

✕

JUSTIN RECOGNIZED FEAR in his father's eyes. He felt it too. And somehow he knew…whatever happened in the next hour, the relationship between the two of them would never be the same.

"You've lied to me. I have a sister. Tiff Masterson is my sister."

His father seemed to shrink a few inches. For once Justin felt no compassion for him. His father's reaction was telling him there was no simple solution to this, no clever answer he hadn't managed to think of on his own that would explain everything and make it all normal and good.

"You didn't learn that in my bedroom."

"I had an appointment with Dr. Zimmermann this morning. He had the results of the donor drive expedited."

His father bowed his head and nodded. "Come to the living room. Let's sit down and I'll explain."

As they walked past the kitchen, Justin's father noticed the open box on the table. He touched the edge of one of the photos Justin had lined up to prove to himself he'd been the baby Franny was holding in her arms in her delivery bed.

"You were a beautiful baby. Such a happy little boy."

Stop it! Cut the loving father act already!

Justin wanted to shout, to demand, to accuse. But he didn't.

His role of perfect son was so engrained Justin couldn't lose it, not even as dark rage possessed him, swamping out all the love he'd had for this man.

In the living room Justin tried to sit, but couldn't. His nerves were too jumpy. He paced to the front window and back, while the man who claimed to be his father fussed at cleaning his glasses with a cotton handkerchief.

Who used a cotton handkerchief these days? It was one of those idiosyncrasies that had once made Justin smile. Now he wanted to snarl.

"Is she a match?"

Justin stared at him for several seconds. *This* was where he chose to begin? "Yes."

"Ah." A small smile appeared briefly. "That's so good. Your chances of a successful transplant are so much better with a biological sibling."

"Assuming Tiff agrees to go through with the procedure. By the way, does she have any idea we're…related?"

"No."

Justin jammed his hands into his pockets. Outside the world was growing darker. He thought briefly of Geneva, and her fondness for her grandfather. He closed his eyes for a second. Oh, God, the world could be such a cruel place.

"Why have you lied to me all these years?"

"That is a very good question. At first it was for your mother. After she died, I admit, I acted out of pure selfishness." He hesitated, then added, "And weakness. That's why I arranged for the donor clinic. I let science give you the answer I wasn't strong enough to admit."

Blood pounded in Justin's head as he tried to follow the tangled conversation, to unravel truth from fantasy. "Maybe you think I know more than I do. Can you explain to me how Tiffany Masterson could possibly be my sister? Who is our real mother? Our father?"

Clark Pittman—that was the moment Justin started thinking of him that way, as a man, not a father—looked down at the handkerchief he was twisting in his hands. Then he lifted his head and faced Justin directly.

"You and Tiff have the same birth parents. Irving Masterson and his wife, Rosemary."

Chapter Sixteen

AFTER HER CONVERSATION with Derick, Tiff went to the washroom and stared at her reflection for a long time. Then she returned to the family room.

"That call took a long time," Marsha commented.

"It was several calls actually."

Both her mother and Marsha must have heard the frost in her voice because they turned to look at her. Her mother's expression was confused. Her aunt's, guarded.

"May I speak to you a minute, Aunt Marsha?"

"But we're getting to the good part," Tiff's mom objected. "They've had their big fight, now it's time to come together. Can't you talk after the movie?"

"It has to be now." She waited while Marsha uncrossed her legs and stood up from the sofa. For a second Rosemary looked concerned, then she turned back to the TV screen.

Tiff led her aunt through the kitchen to the dining room. She wanted more than one wall between them and her mother.

"Can you explain why you've been leading a campaign to get me to leave Lost Trail?" As soon as she asked the question, tears welled. She tightened her jaw and blinked away the tears.

"How can you accuse me of such a thing? Tiff, honey, I've always been on your side."

"I once thought so. But contacting my ex-boyfriend behind my back and telling him lies. Coercing all the business owners in Lost Trail not to hire me. How could you do that?"

Her aunt passed her hand over her forehead and down one side of her face. "I went to extreme measures. It's true. I was just so certain you were making a mistake."

"No. You don't care about me. You just want me gone. What I can't work out is why? Isn't this house big enough for the three of us? Why could you possibly object to me moving home and spending more time with my mother?"

"Of course I don't object. You're getting distraught. If you'd only listen to me—" The chiming of her aunt's cell phone cut off her words. Marsha glanced toward the kitchen where her phone sat charging on the counter.

Then she focused back on Tiff. "You and your mother are all the family I have. I'd do anything for you. Yes, I probably went too far. But I was trying to help you."

Part of Tiff longed to believe her aunt. But there was a glint in Marsha's eye she'd never noticed before, and it made her wary.

The phone had gone quiet for a few moments. Now it began ringing again.

"Oh heck," her aunt said. "I'd better get that. Don't go anywhere. We need to settle this tonight." She hurried to the kitchen and snatched up her phone. She took a quick look at the display then pressed the button to talk.

"Clark, this isn't a good time."

He said something to convince her otherwise, because she brought her other hand to the phone and began listening intently.

Tiff watched as lines dug into her aunt's forehead and color swamped her face. Her nostrils flared, and she flashed a glance, a hot, angry glance, at Tiff.

"Enough, Clark. I'll call you right back." Marsha turned off the phone and slipped it into the pocket of her jeans. Anger practically radiated in waves from her aunt as she faced Tiff. Slowly she took one step forward, then another. Raising her hand she pointed a stiff finger at Tiff's heart.

"You went to the donor drive. You gave them a sample of your DNA."

Tiff raised her chin and nodded. "Of course I did. It was the right thing to do."

Her aunt's gaze shifted from one side of the room to the other. She shook her head, and closed her eyes briefly. "That was a big mistake. A big mistake."

"I had to do it. I had a duty."

Marsha focused on Tiff again. "What about your duty to me?" Her mouth twisted with anger. "After all I've done for you and your mother. All these years and I've never asked for anything. Except that. Don't go to the donor drive. A simple request. But you didn't listen. Damn you, Tiff. Damn you to hell and back."

Tiff pressed her back to the dining room wall as her aunt stormed past her. Despite what she'd learned about her aunt today, she was shocked to be spoken to that way.

A moment later she heard the front door open and slam shut. She raced to the window and watched as Marsha drove off into the night.

It had begun to snow again, Tiff noticed inanely. Her emotions bruised, her body suddenly exhausted, she simply stood there, unable to make sense of any of it.

A rustling sound came from behind, and then her mother stepped up, put a hand on her shoulder.

"Are you all right, honey?"

"Something's wrong with Aunt Marsha. She's acting crazy."

Her mother hugged her. "I know the feeling."

IF HE DIDN'T have Geneva to worry about, Justin might have packed his bags and left Lost Trail for good. But he didn't have that luxury.

After his life-altering conversation at the home where he'd grown up, he drove to Debbie-Ann's to get his daughter, hoping he didn't look as depleted as he felt.

One look at him and Debbie-Ann's eyes widened with concern. "Was it bad news?"

He almost nodded yes, until he realized, of course, she was asking about his cancer. "The opposite. They've found a donor."

"That's wonderful—isn't it?"

"It's a long story. I'll tell you some other time." He couldn't wait to be alone. To have some time to absorb all he'd learned. He still couldn't believe the magnitude of the deception. The nerve. The maliciousness.

"Daddy, Daddy!" Geneva came running out of Ashley's bedroom. She threw her arms around him.

A chunk of ice fell off his heart as she squeezed him with her little girl arms. He wasn't her biological father, but she knew that. He'd never lied to her about anything. He promised himself he never would.

TIFF SAT WITH her mother for a long time that evening, as she explained how Marsha had worked behind the scenes to convince her to leave Lost Trail. "Why do you think she wants me gone so badly?"

Rosemary took her hand and squeezed it. "When we were girls Marsha was very jealous of me. She always had to have the biggest slice of apple pie, the best doll, the prettiest dress…"

"Really?" She'd never heard her mother speak unkindly about anyone, let alone her sister.

"Maybe Marsha is jealous that I have such a wonderful daughter. I don't know why else she would try to send you away."

"She told me that it was painful for you to have me around. That I reminded you too much of the past."

"Not true. That is absolutely not true." Rosemary gazed into the distance a moment, then added in a soft voice, "She was just trying to hurt you. And me."

"Could she be that awful? Maybe when you were kids, but now...?"

"I gave up trying to figure my sister out years ago. I've always tried to assume the best, especially since she does so much for me. We'll just have to wait until she comes home to ask her."

"She will come home, won't she?"

"Where else would she go?"

That was a good question and it reminded Tiff of how little they knew about Marsha's life outside their family circle.

"We could try phoning Dr. Pittman."

"Maybe in the morning," her mother suggested. "Though Marsha will probably be back by then."

Tiff made her mother tea, then carried it up to her room for her. As they said good night she noticed how clear her mom's eyes looked in that moment. Maybe tomorrow would be one of her good days.

In her room Tiff read for a while, but thoughts of Kenny kept interrupting. She longed to tell him all that had happened, and get his perspective on what the problem was with Marsha. He'd seen Marsha's dark side before she had. Maybe he had more insights. But the way they'd left things last night, she doubted he would welcome a second unannounced visit from her.

Eventually she fell asleep. At some point in the night she heard her aunt's car, then the motor of the electric garage door opener. *That's strange,* she thought. *Aunt Marsha hardly ever uses the garage. Must be snowing...*

She wanted to get out of bed and talk to her aunt, but she was so warm and cozy, and so emotionally exhausted, she let herself drift and drift until deep sleep sucked her down.

LOUD BANGING INVADED the fog of sleep and Tiff rolled over in bed, covered her head with her arms. Another loud bang. What the heck? Groggy, she tried to open her eyes but she was so exhausted.

Be quiet, I need to sleep. Just as she was sinking back into the most delicious sleep she'd had in years, the pounding started again. And shouting.

Something was wrong. Clawing awake through the strange fatigue weighing her down, she pulled herself to a sitting position. Her head felt four times heavier than normal. She groped for her phone, turned it on so she could see what time it was.

Two in the morning. For God's sake.

For a few seconds all was quiet. Then a loud smash shattered the stillness. It sounded like someone had broken a window.

Tiff jumped to her feet, but her legs wobbled and her head spun. Woozy, she collapsed back onto the bed. The noise. Someone breaking inside. Danger. Her mom. She had to get her mom.

But her body wouldn't move. Was she sick? Hallucinating? What was wrong with her?

"Mom! Can you hear me? I think someone's breaking in. Lock your door!"

She wanted to call 911, but at this time of night the call would be handled by the Missoula call center. Too far away. She dialed Zak instead.

Her friend sounded so alert it was almost as if he'd been awake by the phone.

"What's wrong?"

"Banging…breaking glass." Terror choked the air from her lungs. "Someone's in here!"

"Get your mom and your aunt and run if you can."

"I can't walk! There's…something wrong with me."

She heard footsteps racing around the main floor of the house, a man's voice shouting. And then there was pounding up the stairs. Tiff screamed and dropped her phone as she grabbed for the edge of her nightstand. *Oh, God…oh, God…*

A man appeared in her doorway. It was Kenny. Wild relief made her laugh when she wanted to cry. She tried to run to him but her legs wobbled again. Kenny cursed and ran to catch her before she fell.

"What are you doing in here?"

"It isn't safe. You need to get out of here."

His words came too fast for her to make sense of them. Something about the garage, and doors and windows.

"Can you walk?"

"I-I'm not sure."

"I'll help." He put one arm across her back and supported the majority of her weight. Then he half-carried, half-dragged her down the stairs and pushed her out the door onto the wooden porch floor. "Stay," he barked, as if she was a dog.

Confused, she did exactly that. Not that she had much choice. She was so weak she could hardly crawl to the wicker chair on the porch, and pull down the fuzzy blanket folded over the arm.

She drew the blanket around her shoulders, shivering in the frigid air. Her head ached and she couldn't think straight.

Was the house on fire? Kenny must have seen flames from the guest cottage and come running. He would have found all the exterior doors locked, as per usual. So he'd broken one of the kitchen windows. That explained the crash she'd heard.

Tiff was still putting together pieces of the puzzle when Kenny ran through the front door again, this time carrying her mother. Rosemary was limp in his arms.

"Is she okay?"

"Unconscious." Kenny said between ragged breaths. "I've got to get her to the clinic. I've called Dr. Pittman. He's going to meet us there."

"Is the fire on the other side of the house?"

"Fire?" He stared at her a moment, then shook his head. "Don't move," he repeated. "I'm going to get my truck."

Carefully he set her mother down beside her and then he disappeared into the night.

It was snowing again and Kenny was soon out of sight. Tiffany placed the blanket over her mother's still body. She wished she could run into the house to grab their coats and boots, but Kenny wanted her to stay here, and she wasn't sure she was strong enough to walk anyway.

The cold air helped clear her lungs though. She took several long breaths and felt the fog in her brain begin to lift. Funny she hadn't smelled any smoke. She *still* didn't smell any smoke. Or hear the crackling of fire.

And that's when she remembered her aunt Marsha. She'd gotten home very late and parked her truck in the garage. She was probably in her room right now!

Tiff grabbed the porch railing and pulled herself to her

feet. A little stronger now, she let go of the railing, testing her weight and her balance. And then she headed for the door.

She was almost inside when Kenny called out.

"Tiff! Stop!"

She spun around and almost fainted on the spot. A moment later Kenny's arms were around her.

"Why were you going back in, you fool?" He pressed her tightly to his chest.

"Aunt Marsha's in there. We have to save her, too."

"Tiff, babe, I'm sorry. Your aunt is in her truck in the garage. We can't save her now but we have to get your mom to the clinic." He led her down the stairs, along the path to his truck.

Tiff twisted, trying to see inside the garage. The door was open. She could see the rear end of her aunt's truck. "Why is she still in her truck? I heard her drive home. It was hours ago."

"She's dead, Tiff."

"No!" Tiff slumped back to the ground. "That can't be…no, no, no."

But the look on Kenny's face said it was somehow true.

"How…?"

"Carbon monoxide poisoning." Kenny helped her stand, helped her keep moving.

It wasn't a fire Kenny was trying to protect them from, but noxious gas. "I don't understand."

"Your aunt left her truck running in the garage. She also propped open the door between the garage and the house."

Tiff couldn't follow all these twists and turns. Nothing Kenny was saying made any sense. "Why would she do that?"

"By the time her truck ran out of fuel, all three of you would have been dead."

Chapter Seventeen

"TIFF? GODDAMMIT, TIFF, talk to me!" Zak leaped out of bed and pulled on his jeans. When it was clear Tiff either didn't intend, or wasn't able, to respond, he hit his speed dial number for the sheriff.

"What the hell?" The sheriff's words came out slurred. He was either sleeping or very drunk. Zak hoped it was the former.

"I had a call from Tiff Masterson. She said someone was breaking into their house, and then suddenly she stopped talking. I'm on my way over to Raven Farms right now."

"Jesus, Zak. Hang tight. I'm right behind you."

Zak pushed his truck, squinting through the falling snow, praying that some deer or moose wouldn't pick this of all times to meander across the road. He'd never spot it in time to avoid a collision.

When he pulled into Raven Farms he could see a tall man with a woman draped over his shoulder in a fireman's carry. The man seemed to be heading toward a truck with an open passenger side door. Zak pulled up parallel to the truck and slammed on the brakes. He was out the door while the truck was still rocking.

"What's going on?"

"Need to get her to the clinic." Kenny grunted.

Zak helped him get the woman—it was Rosemary, pale and lifeless—settled into the passenger seat. "What happened?"

"Carbon monoxide poisoning. Tiff has it too, only not as bad. Marsha's in the truck in the garage. Dead." Kenny tucked Rosemary's legs into the floor well, covered her with a blanket and closed the door.

He ran to the driver's side of his truck, then looked over at Zak. "Tiff's on the porch. You take care of her, Waller. Get her to the clinic."

"I will," Zak promised. As the truck screeched off, he turned to the porch. Tiff was sitting on a wicker chair, staring at him. Tears streamed down her face, her eyes were wild with stunned shock. Wearing only pajamas, Tiff visibly shivered and rubbed her arms.

"Zak! Marsha's in the garage. Kenny says she's dead."

Zak hesitated. He'd promised Kenny he'd take Tiff to the clinic, but he couldn't leave without checking on Marsha. "Hang tight. I'm going to see if I can help."

He removed his jacket and placed it over Tiff's shoulders. "Zip up. It's twenty below out here."

Cold enough to freeze a witch's tits, his father would have said. How strange to have his old man's voice in his head at a moment like this.

As he started to run he heard a siren in the distance. Good.

Soon he smelled noxious exhaust fumes. He pulled up his sweater to cover his nose and mouth as he approached the white truck parked inside the garage. Ahead he could see the door to the house was propped open with what looked like a can of paint.

He approached the driver's side of the truck cautiously. "Marsha?"

Through the window he could see her slumped over the steering wheel. In his brain a narrator was reciting a checklist he'd learned in one of his courses. *Stay calm. Secure the area. Get help for victims. Don't disturb evidence if possible.*

He felt remarkably calm as he opened the door and felt for a pulse on her neck.

None.

Thankfully Marsha wasn't wearing her seat belt. He grabbed her under the arms and pulled her dead weight from the vehicle, through the garage and out to the fresh air. The sirens which had been growing louder and louder were suddenly silenced as the sheriff's official SUV pulled up ten yards from where Zak was standing.

"What the hell's going on here?" Ford's coat was open, revealing a misbuttoned shirt and an unbuckled belt.

"Carbon monoxide poisoning. Marsha doesn't have a pulse." As he spoke he arranged Marsha so he could begin compressions. "Get Tiff in the truck, then we'll transfer

Marsha."

Instructions from his first aid course, upgraded just last March, popped helpfully into Zak's brain. He loosened the jacket from Marsha's chest, and searched for the tip of her breastbone. His heart raced, hot adrenaline pumped through his veins, but his thoughts remained clear.

He stacked his hands the way he'd practiced and pressed down. Hard and fast, he aimed for about one hundred compressions per minute.

Dimly aware of the sheriff helping Tiff into the front passenger seat and instructing her to do up her seat belt, Zak kept up the compressions. When Tiff was settled, the sheriff came and helped him carry Marsha into the back seat.

Zak continued the compressions as the sheriff hurried to the driver's seat.

"Where's your mom?" the sheriff asked.

When Tiff didn't answer, Zak said between compressions, "Farm manager has her. Driving her to clinic."

"Huh. I think I passed them on the way here. Almost stopped the guy for speeding. But figured this was more important."

Great deduction, Sherlock.

The truck started moving. Zak lost his balance as Ford pulled a tight three-sixty. Pushing against the side of the door he righted himself. Within seconds he'd regained the rhythm of his compressions even though it was probably too late.

Tiff stopped crying. Every few seconds she sniffed, but other than that she was quiet.

Ford phoned Nadine from the road, instructing her to get to Raven Farms and collect evidence from the garage, in particular Marsha's car. Then he tried to get some details out of Tiff, but she seemed beyond words at this point and after the third unanswered question Ford gave up.

All the while Zak was counting in his head, thirty compressions, two breaths, thirty compressions, two breaths, thirty compressions…

Lights were on at the clinic when they arrived. Kenny rushed out to meet them.

"What the hell took so long?" He opened Tiff's door and led her inside. "Your mom's on oxygen. She's regained consciousness. She's going to be okay."

The same did not hold for Marsha Holmes. Ten minutes later a shaky Doc Pittman gave an official pronouncement of death. The doc looked like he was on the verge of collapse, himself, Zak thought.

It had been a hell of night. Thank God more lives hadn't been lost.

⨯

Tuesday, December 12

ZAK HAD ALWAYS wondered how he'd cope under pressure, when lives were at stake. He was relieved to discover he'd been fine. Better than fine. Last night at the Mastersons, then later in the clinic, he'd been focused and clear-headed. He felt like he was functioning at a higher level than normal—much the way he felt when he was in the middle of a good run.

The minute he got home, everything changed. He started to shake. Then he vomited.

Images flashed through his mind. Kenny lugging Rosemary toward his truck like she was a sack of potatoes. Tiff's shell-shocked face when she told him her aunt was dead. The zombie-like weight of Marsha's body when he dragged her out of that truck.

He put on the TV, found a mindless comedy to distract himself from the horror of the night.

But when he drifted back to sleep he dreamed he was blowing air into Marsha's mouth when suddenly her eyes popped open.

Stop it, she said. *Can't you see I'm dead?*

He awoke in a sweat, Watson curled beside him. He stroked the cat, forgiving him for all his aloof stares and indifferent yawns of the past. When the chips were down, his cat was here for him.

The next morning a run was out of the question. Zak had an extra-long shower and two cups of coffee, but still felt less than human as he made his way to the office. For the first time in his dispatching career he was late—by an entire five minutes.

Nadine had let herself in and started the coffee.

"Last night was intense. I'm still not sure I understand what happened."

"Me either." Before he could ask how she'd made out collecting evidence the sheriff called. "I've got a breakfast meeting and won't be in until around ten."

"Right." No doubt Ford's meeting was with his pillow and comforter.

"We need statements from Kenny and the Mastersons," Zak reminded him.

"Send Black. I know you're only a goddamned dispatcher Waller, but you were there last night. You better go with her."

"So what was it like last night?" Nadine asked on the drive out to the farm. She was behind the wheel, eyes hidden by her aviator sunglasses.

The sun had chosen to come out today and the reflection off the fresh snow was blinding. The temperature had also dropped another five degrees. It was one of those bitter cold days that made Zak's teeth ache.

"It was a nightmare."

Nadine turned to him, lifted her glasses enough so he could see her eyes. "You want to talk about it?"

"Later."

Tiff answered the door seconds after he knocked. From the road he'd texted to warn they were coming. Her eyes were red and watery. She said hello to Nadine, then threw her arms around him.

"You and Kenny. You saved our lives."

"It was Kenny who saved you." Zak looked over her shoulder. "Is he here?"

Tiff nodded. "In the kitchen with Mom. Come on."

She led Zak and Nadine past a framed family portrait to the back of the house. The morning sun was bright in the kitchen, making the events of the previous evening seem all the more surreal.

It was Kenny who poured the coffee and put a plate of cookies on the table. Tiff sat next to her mother and took her hand between both of hers. Rosemary leaned slightly toward her daughter, as if her physical closeness offered comfort. She glanced up at Zak. Shook her head. "I don't believe this."

Tiff squeezed her hand. "Have a cookie, Mom. You haven't had a bite all morning."

"It's a lot to process." Zak hesitated, wondering what you said about the death of someone who had tried to kill you. He decided to keep it simple. "I'm sorry about Marsha."

Both Tiff and her mom acknowledged his condolences with a simple nod.

"What time were you released from the clinic?" Zak asked.

"Just before seven. Kenny drove us home and we've been sitting here drinking coffee and tea ever since. We'll all need a nap soon. We didn't sleep much at the clinic."

"We're here to get statements from each of you about last

night," Nadine said. "If you're not up to it now, we could come back after lunch."

"Mom might need some time but I'd like to get it over with," Tiff said.

"I'm good to talk now," Kenny agreed. "I take it you've already been through the garage?"

"I was here last night," Nadine explained. "I took some prints and photographs." She directed her gaze to Rosemary. "It appears your sister swallowed a bunch of sleeping pills last night as well. I found an empty vial in the console as well as a half-empty bottle of water."

"Any note?" Tiff asked.

Nadine shook her head, then glanced at Zak. He gave a slight nod before explaining. "You and your mother were supposed to die, too, last night. There was no reason for Marsha to leave a note."

"I can't believe this." Rosemary repeated the phrase she'd said earlier, the words heavy with anguish.

"Rosemary, would you like to lie down while we take statements from Kenny and your daughter?" Zak knew she was emotionally fragile. Hearing all the details from last night might be too much.

But Rosemary refused his offer. "I want to stay. I need to hear this." She directed her next question to Nadine. "How do you know Marsha meant for my daughter and me to die as well?"

"I'm sorry," Nadine said. "This must be difficult to hear.

But Marsha deliberately propped open the door between the garage and the house so the fumes would collect in the house. Given how cold it was last night, I'm sure all your windows were closed. With the furnace going full blast, the carbon monoxide would have circulated throughout the entire house. The gas tank was still three-quarters full, so it would have run another four hours at least."

"We wouldn't have lasted that long." Tiff obviously had no doubt about that. "We were both poisoned as it was, though Mom was worse, probably because her room is right over the garage. If not for Kenny..." She shuddered.

"Yes. How did you know there was a problem going on here?" Nadine asked.

"I didn't at first."

Kenny was leaning against the counter, next to the coffeepot. Zak suspected he was too keyed up to sit.

"I was awake when I heard a truck drive up to the farmhouse, around midnight. From my window I could see it was Marsha's truck. She drove into the garage and I thought nothing more of it. I finished the movie I was watching, but I didn't feel tired, so I decided to go for a walk."

"You went for a walk in the middle of the night?" Nadine looked skeptical.

"I'm a night owl. Sometimes when I'm not ready to sleep I go for a drive. Other times I take a walk."

"It's true," Tiff confirmed. "I suffer from insomnia sometimes as well, and I've seen him."

"It was about quarter past one by then. I walked the loop we use for hayrides, probably took me about forty-five minutes. On my way back I still wasn't ready to sleep so I meandered by the farmhouse. The night was cold, but the sky was clear and the stars were amazing."

Zak handed him a piece of paper on which he'd sketched the cabin, the farmhouse, the barn and the hayride loop. "Can you trace the approximate path you took last night?"

"Sure." Kenny took the pen and drew a path from the cabin, to the barn, along the loop, then around the farmhouse. When he reached the side where the garage was he made an "X."

"I was here when I heard a motor running inside the garage. I ran to the garage door and noticed exhaust seeping out from the bottom. I could smell it too. I tried to raise the door, but it wouldn't budge. I saw the lock panel, but didn't know the code so I ran to the front door of the house and banged and shouted, but no one came."

"I heard him, vaguely," Tiff said. "But I was already feeling the effects of the gas. I couldn't make myself wake up enough to get out of bed, let alone down the stairs to let him in."

Kenny wiped his palms on the sides of his jeans, as the stress of the night came back to him.

"Have some coffee," Zak suggested.

Kenny took a drink then continued. "I ran to the back of the house and broke one of the large kitchen windows to get in. Once inside I opened all the doors and windows back there. Then I held my breath and sprinted to the mudroom. The connecting door to the garage was open. That's when I saw Marsha in the truck. Dead."

He took a deep breath of air, perhaps remembering how his lungs must have been burning at that point.

"I hit the button to raise the garage door to let out the fumes, then ran outside to get some air myself. I took a bunch of deep breaths then ran back to the truck and opened the passenger side door so I could turn off the ignition. I checked Marsha's pulse, but I didn't need to. I could tell she was dead. At that point I was most worried about Tiff and her mother so I went back into the house, opening every window as I passed by, as well as the front door.

He paused for another deep breath and a fortifying drink of coffee. "I'd never been on the upper floor before. All the bedroom doors were closed. As it happened, the first door I tried was Tiff's. She responded when I spoke to her, but she was too woozy to walk, so I helped her outside then went back to get her mom."

He glanced at Rosemary. "I tried to rouse Mrs. Masterson and when I couldn't, I called Dr. Pittman. He sounded awful, like he had a bad cold or something, but he agreed to meet us at the clinic. I carried Rosemary outside and that's when you showed up, Zak."

"Do you have any idea why Marsha would have done this? Was she depressed? Did she ever talk about suicide?"

Nadine looked from Rosemary to Tiff.

Both women shook their heads, only Tiff answered.

"Something was bothering her. The last couple of weeks she'd been acting strangely. I discovered she'd been talking to people behind my back, trying to sabotage my efforts to open a business in Lost Trail. When I confronted her, she tried to convince me she'd done all this for my own good."

"She'd talked to me, as well," Rosemary said quietly. "She said I had to encourage you to leave. That I'd be a bad mother if I didn't."

"My aunt and I were arguing yesterday evening when she got a call from Dr. Pittman. In the course of their conversation he must have told her I'd been tested at the stem-cell clinic for Justin. My aunt was livid because she'd specifically asked me not to be tested. Before I could figure out what the big issue was, she ran out of the house and that..." Tiff blinked rapidly and swallowed back a sob. "That was the last time I saw her alive."

"None of it makes sense," Rosemary said quietly.

Nadine leaned over the island. "Kenny said he saw your aunt drive home around midnight. What time did she leave the house?"

"It was about an hour after dinner. I'd say around seven-thirty."

"Any idea where she went?"

Tiff shook her head no. "My aunt spent a lot of time in Hamilton. She said she had friends there, but she didn't like to talk about them." She took a moment to think. "But I suppose she could have been anywhere. I don't think either me or Mom actually knew much about her life outside of this house."

She hesitated, then added, "She's worked for Dr. Pittman a long time. He may know more about my aunt's life than Mom or I do."

Nadine pushed a pad of paper into the center of the island. "We're going to need written statements from all of you. I'll leave you this and come back in a few hours to witness your signatures and collect the statements."

"While we're here we should go through your aunt's bedroom and any other place in the house where she might have kept items of a personal nature," Zak added.

"Yes *we* should," Nadine said, giving him a *what-the-hell* look.

He was over-reaching his role, Zak realized. What surprised him was how naturally it came to him and how much more satisfying it was to be the one on the front-line, asking the questions, seeing things firsthand for a change.

Tiff hesitated, then nodded. "I'll show you her room."

Zak and Nadine followed her up the stairs. Tiff hung back at the door. She seemed to be considering whether to say something. In the end she did, but it was quite innocuous. "Just let yourselves out when you're finished."

Though Zak and Nadine searched thoroughly for half an hour, they didn't find any further evidence in Marsha's tidy bedroom. No clue why she would have wanted to end, not only her own life, but that of her sister's and niece's as well.

✕

TIFF FELT GUILTY for not showing Zak and Nadine the items she'd already removed from Marsha's bedroom. But she needed to do a little research before she exposed her family's dirty laundry to the world.

In the kitchen, she picked up the pad of paper Deputy Black had left behind. "I can't face this right now."

"Me, either." Kenny rubbed his eyes. "We need sleep. I'm going to head to my cabin for an hour or so. You and your mom should try and rest as well."

"An excellent suggestion." Rosemary pushed herself up from the counter. "I'm not sure I can face my bedroom yet, though."

The house had been thoroughly aired, but Tiff knew what she meant. "Let's put on an old movie and nap in the family room. You take the sofa, I'll curl up on the love seat."

The opening credits for *Miracle on 34th Street* hadn't finished by the time Tiff went under. She slept deeply and heavily for over an hour. When she finally opened her eyes, she felt as if she'd been drugged. The feeling was eerily reminiscent of last night's carbon monoxide poisoning.

Leaving her mother asleep on the sofa, she forced herself to move. First she had a glass of water, then she showered.

Once she'd dressed in clean yoga pants and a sweat shirt, she stripped the beds in her and her mother's rooms. She couldn't bring herself to go back into Marsha's room.

Once the washing machine was going, she was ready to face the contents of the shoe box she'd found in her aunt's room. She took out the bubble wrapped medications prescribed for Rosemary Masterson by Dr. Pittman. Marsha had shown her these days ago, when she'd asked about her mother's drugs.

But there were eight more medicine vials in the box, prescribed by two unfamiliar doctors and filled by pharmacies in both Hamilton and Missoula. Tiff googled the drug names typed on the labels.

Some of the medications were for treating anxiety, some for depression, some were sleep aids. On their own, she supposed the drugs would meet their intended purpose. But as a cocktail, well, she had a good idea now why her mother was so tired, listless and confused all the time.

But she was a layman, and she needed her theory confirmed. So she called Dr. Pittman on his cell phone, expecting to hear a message that he would return her call after closing hours at the clinic.

To her surprise, Clark Pittman answered on the first ring.

"Tiffany. I'm glad you called. I've been wondering how your mother is doing?"

"She's resting. We're both still shell-shocked from last

night." It was hard to absorb the fact of her aunt's death. Tiff wondered how you grieved for someone who had tried to kill you. Yet she knew she would eventually mourn the loss of the loving aunt she'd *thought* she'd had.

"I'm so sorry. Marsha was a complicated woman. She had a dark side, but I never imagined she would do something like—" His voice choked on a sob. She heard him swallow. "Sorry. This is terribly difficult."

Tiff had so many questions. But right now she had to stay focused. "I found some medications in my aunt's bedroom. I'd like to talk to you about them. Can I make an appointment to meet you at the clinic later?"

As she waited for his answer—which was a long time coming—she remembered how terrible he'd looked last night. Not simply tired, but like a broken man. Whatever the true nature of his relationship with Marsha, whether it was simply work colleagues, or, as she suspected, a deeper, possibly romantic relationship, her death must have been as hard a blow for him as it had been for herself and her mom.

"If it's all right with you, I'll come to Raven Farms," Dr. Pittman finally said. "And I'd like to bring Justin with me. We have some news that will shed light on your aunt's motives."

Chapter Eighteen

FROM THE HALLWAY outside her bedroom Tiff heard the sound of her mother's shower. A good sign. She went downstairs to heat some soup and make toast. Fifteen minutes later her mother joined her. She looked markedly stronger than she had before her nap and shower.

"Feeling better?"

"Much."

Tiff set the bowls of soup and the plate of toast on the island. She was happy to see her mother pick up a spoon and start eating. She waited until the meal was over to tell the news.

"Dr. Pittman and Justin are coming over later. The doctor says he has something to tell us that will explain why Marsha did what she did last night."

"Oh."

Worry glazed her mother's eyes.

"Should I put them off until tomorrow?"

Her mother lifted her chin. "We need to face this. All of it. Part of me feels absolutely sick to my stomach and part of me feels like crying for a week. But more than anything I have a tremendous sense of relief. And I can't quite figure out why that should be."

✕

SOMETHING FELT OFF to Tiff the moment she opened the front door. Dr. Pittman looked just as terrible as he had last night. As for Justin, she'd never seen his eyes so cold. He was standing with his shoulders broad, his arms behind his back. The moment she said hello, though, the firm line of his mouth softened.

"Tiff. I'm so sorry for what you went through yesterday. What a relief you and your mother are okay."

"We have Kenny to thank for that. And Zak and Dr. Pittman too, of course. Come in. Mom thought we'd be more comfortable in the family room so she's waiting there."

Once all the hellos had been said and their guests were seated, Tiff brought out the shoe box and handed it to the doctor.

"I found this in my aunt's room. There are eight bottles of pills in there. Some of the prescriptions are from a pharmacy in Missoula, others from Hamilton. All of them have my aunt's name on them. But I don't think she was taking them. I suspect she was giving them to my mother. Some she was giving in pill form while I'm guessing others she dissolved in Mom's tea or ground up in her food."

Which explained why her aunt had been so controlling

about her mother's diet and why Tiff's presence in the house had been such a problem for her.

The doctor looked through the collection with trembling hands. "You could be correct. Someone being over-medicated with this cocktail of drugs would suffer similar symptoms to what Rosemary's been going through. Extreme tiredness, confusion and memory loss, among others."

"I'm guessing Marsha varied the dosage, depending on how my mother was behaving and what was going on in their lives. For instance, when I was home she upped the drugs so I would believe that my presence had a bad effect on my mother's mental wellbeing."

"A few days ago your theory would have sounded preposterous," Justin said. "But after yesterday, I'd believe Marsha Holmes capable of anything."

"I just don't understand why she would want to keep Mom drugged." Tiff held up her hands. "I really thought she loved us...honestly I considered her a second mother."

"There's a lot you don't know about your aunt," Dr. Pittman said. "And most of it goes back to before you were born."

Tiff's mother leaned forward, her attention rapt. "Tell us, Clark. Tell us everything."

"It began more than three decades ago, on March twenty-second."

Rosemary's eyes rounded. "Casey's birthday."

"Yes. And—" The doctor's gaze shifted to his own son.

"Mine, also," Justin said.

"That's true," Rosemary murmured. "I'd forgotten you were born the same night. It was the second day of a terrible spring snowstorm. The roads were too dangerous to drive to Hamilton. Irving was out helping a neighbor bring his cattle into shelter when my labor started a week early. I couldn't get hold of Irving, so I asked Marsha to drive me to the clinic."

"I'd been there with Franny for several hours already," Clark said. "We were alone and I'd put up the Closed sign, though of course I didn't turn Rosemary away. I was relieved when I saw Marsha with her. I thought her help would be useful."

"She scrubbed up as soon as we arrived," Rosemary said. "She asked me if I wanted pain relief. Demerol, I think it was. I said no, but she talked me into it."

"Shortly after Rosemary and Marsha arrived, Franny's baby crowned. Marsha helped with the delivery. As soon as we saw the baby we knew something was wrong. The baby was weak, struggling. I put him on oxygen and told Marsha to call the hospital in Missoula and tell them we needed emergency air transport stat for this baby and mom."

"I remember wondering why Marsha left me for so long," Tiff's mother said. "It seemed like hours. When I got the urge to push, I called out for help. Finally Marsha came and she stayed with me until my baby was born."

"She never let you hold him, did she?" Justin asked.

He sounded bitter and Tiff realized he knew where this story was headed. A sudden flash of fear made her want to yell at everyone to stop. But the words were flowing now—there was no way to dam them back inside.

"Marsha told me the doctor needed to examine the baby. The way she said it scared me and I started to cry, but she said I shouldn't worry, just wait and she'd be right back to fill me in. If I hadn't taken that Demerol I would have jumped out of my bed and followed her. Instead I did as I'd been told. It felt like another hour before Marsha returned and told me my son had been born with a heart defect. As soon as the weather cleared enough for a helicopter to get through they'd be sending me and the baby to a pediatric cardiologist in Missoula."

Rosemary closed her eyes. Tiff couldn't remember the last time she'd heard her mother speak for so long. She squeezed her mom's hand, and Rosemary gave her a weak smile.

"And that's what happened," she continued. "At dawn the next morning they sent the helicopter and Casey and I were flown to Missoula. Once the highway had been plowed, Irving drove after us. He was there by noon."

Retelling the story had drained her mother. "Why did you make her relive that?" she asked Dr. Pittman.

"Because there's more to the story." Justin's voice was harsh. He turned to his father. "Tell them the rest."

Doc Pittman bowed his head. He seemed unable to look

anyone in the eyes. "Rosemary, your sister brought your baby into my wife's room. She put him into Franny's arms and told her she had a healthy seven-pound baby boy."

"What?" Tiff bounced off the sofa. Her mother's face went white.

"Once Franny got her hands on that baby, she wouldn't let him go. I asked Marsha to come to the back office with me where I had the sick baby on oxygen in a makeshift incubator. I asked her what the hell she was playing at. It wasn't fair to build up Franny's hopes that way."

"And what did Marsha say?" Rosemary's voice was flat, as if she'd lost the ability to feel anymore.

"I hate to tell you this." The doctor had his hands clasped together so tightly they were both turning white and his gaze was fixed on the carpet. "Marsha said Franny and I should keep the healthy baby. She said Franny was so frail she'd probably never carry another baby to term, but you were healthy. You'd have more children."

"But…that's insane reasoning. Why would she give up her own nephew?" It didn't make sense to Tiff. None of it.

"To hurt me." Rosemary's tone was grim.

The doctor nodded. "Marsha felt Rosemary had already been given so much. The family farm, the family house, and even the man that Marsha loved."

Tiff sucked in a breath. Her aunt Marsha had loved her dad? She looked to her mother for confirmation. Rosemary was nodding.

"I often wondered about that. Marsha introduced me to Irving. She never told me she had feelings for him. But there were times over the years when I'd catch an expression on her face when she was looking at him that made me uneasy."

"She was definitely crazy." Tiff turned to the doctor, someone she'd always thought of as wise and good. "But how could you go along with it?"

"By that point, I felt I didn't have a choice. How could I wrench that baby from Franny's arms? She was so happy. I think secretly she'd been worried there might be something wrong with our child and her delight was just…it was impossible for me to deny her that."

"But what you did was more than wrong. It was illegal."

"I've closed the clinic for good. I'm giving up my license. I've already written a statement for the sheriff, explaining my guilt, and I'm prepared for the consequences of that."

"You going to jail—what will that help?" demanded Justin. "My entire life has been a lie. I was never your son. You kept me from my real parents." He met Tiff's gaze. "And my sister."

The world was spinning, spinning, and everything was changing. Tiff was struggling to keep up, to make sense of it all. But one piece suddenly made sense. "My stem-cell sample. I must have been a match."

"Yes," Justin said. "I went to see my oncologist yesterday and he told me. You're a perfect match for me and that's only possible if we share the same parents. Both mother and father have to be the same."

"That's why Aunt Marsha didn't want me to get tested."

Dr. Pittman nodded. "She knew our ugly secret would be outed. But I no longer cared. All I wanted was for Justin to be cured. So I organized the donor clinic and hoped you would participate."

"What if I hadn't?"

"I would have found another way."

"Why didn't you simply tell the truth?" Rosemary asked.

"If I had the courage for that, I would have done it decades ago."

Chapter Nineteen

ROSEMARY AND TIFF couldn't stop staring at him. Justin understood. It was like all three of them had turned into different people by virtue of their genetic connection.

"You are such a beautiful man," Rosemary said. "I can see so much of Irving in you. It's a wonder I never noticed before."

Justin smiled sadly. "I want to say I wish I'd had a chance to know my real father. But once you start unraveling that mess, it never ends. All of our lives would have been entirely different."

"So much is lost forever," Rosemary said sadly. "I remember how sorry I felt for you when Franny died. Poor boy without a mother now. But you did have a mom. It was me."

She looked at him like she wanted to gather him into her arms. But he was a man, no longer the little boy she was remembering. Maybe one day she would be able to hug him the way a mother hugs a son. But that was going to take a while.

"If I'm your mother, that means I'm also a grandmother."

Geneva. "Yes."

Tiff smiled as well. "And I'm an aunt."

"I hope you'll let us be part of her life," Rosemary said.

"Gladly." Justin's gaze shifted to Clark Pittman. He was refusing to call him father anymore, but in his heart he still felt the connection. It made him angry. This man had cheated him of so much.

"So what happens now?" Tiff asked. "Are we going to make this information public?"

"Yes," Rosemary and Justin spoke simultaneously.

"Won't Clark go to jail, though?" Tiff knew that he ought to. But the man looked so wretched. Living with what he'd done had to be the worst, and most appropriate punishment of all.

"Geneva adores her grandfather and she's already suffered so many losses." Justin didn't add the rest of it, the chance that he might succumb to the cancer and she would lose him too. "I believe Clark should pay for his crimes. But I'm not willing to hurt my daughter to satisfy my need for vengeance. Of course it isn't just my call." He touched Rosemary's shoulder. "I'll go along with whatever you say."

Rosemary stood and left the room. Through the arched opening they could see her studying the family portrait on the wall.

Justin looked uncomfortably from the doctor, to Tiff.

His sister.

Would he ever be able to think of her that way? They

still had to discuss the stem-cell transplant. She'd provided the sample so he hoped she would go through with the transplant. But he couldn't take her acquiescence for granted.

A few minutes later Rosemary returned. She went to stand beside her daughter and linked arms with her.

"This is what we'll say."

Justin straightened. He couldn't remember ever hearing Rosemary sound so authoritative.

"Before she died Marsha confessed to me that she switched the babies without Clark's knowledge. We'll let my sister take the entirety of the blame. After all, it was her idea, and she was the one who physically committed the crime. Besides, Marsha did what she did out of jealousy and hate. Clark's actions were motivated by love for his wife."

BEFORE LEAVING THE Mastersons', Dr. Pittman advised Tiff to take Rosemary to a doctor in Hamilton as soon as possible. "If Marsha's been over-medicating her, your mother might experience painful withdrawal symptoms if she stops everything cold turkey. Take those medications with you and see what the doctor suggests. A gradual weaning should make it easier for her system to adjust."

"Thank you." In that moment Tiff knew that despite what he'd done, she'd never be able to see this man as a villain.

She and her mother stayed up late that night, talking. Wanting desperately to understand why her aunt could have been so vindictive, Tiff questioned her mother about their childhood.

Rosemary told stories of childhood jealousies and temper tantrums. "Marsha was one of those children who hated sharing the spotlight. I would purposefully lose to her in board games so she wouldn't get upset. When we dressed up for parties, I made sure my outfit was never nicer than hers."

"What made her that way?" Casey had never acted that way with her, and she couldn't recall ever feeling jealous of the extra attention he received due to his illness. She'd known her parents loved her as much as Casey. Maybe her grandparents hadn't done the same for Marsha?

"Sometimes people are born a certain way. My relationship with my sister was always rocky but it got worse once we started school. Miss Christensen made a pet out of me, but was always so hard on Marsha. Of course that only made Marsha resent me all the more."

"I never noticed any discord between the two of you."

"After I had Casey, Marsha completely changed toward me. At the time I thought having a nephew to love had softened her and made her more generous toward me and Irving. Now, I know the truth. She was probably rubbing her hands with glee every time poor Casey went through another operation or had another setback. My suffering gave her pleasure."

Tiff shuddered with disgust. "She had me so fooled. I thought she really loved us. But isn't it weird to think that if you'd come home from the hospital with Justin, Casey would never have been part of our family."

"I can't go there. Casey was my son. I could never think of him as anything else."

Wednesday, December 13

THE NEXT MORNING Tiff drove her mother into Hamilton. The doctor was a gentle woman with a lilting Indian accent. She suggested an immediate toxicology screen, with a full physical to follow the next week. After the appointment Tiff was surprised when her mother agreed to go out for lunch. Only a few days had gone by since her aunt had stopped drugging her, but Rosemary already seemed so much better.

Tiff was getting her mother back.

Around four o'clock she got a text from Zak. *Dew Drop at 5?*

The world immediately felt brighter. Good friends and beer and a great burger. *Yes!*

She invited Kenny to come along but he declined.

"All the craziness of the past few days has got me really behind with the paperwork."

"I should stay and help." He'd lost a full day of work after the night he'd saved her and her mother from carbon monoxide poisoning.

"You should not. You need some serious R&R, girl. Go have fun. Next time we go out together it's going to be a proper date."

She smiled. "Is that so?"

"Damn right. You save a girl's life, she has to have dinner with you. It's a rule."

✕

TIFF WAS NERVOUS about leaving her mother alone, but she didn't need to be. It turned out Rosemary had invited Sybil to come for a glass of wine after dinner.

"Don't worry. I won't be having any wine myself, at least not until I know all those vile drugs have cleared my system. Sybil and I have a lot to talk about."

"Are you going to tell her everything?"

"I'm telling her the version we all agreed to."

"Right." Tiff nodded. They were going through with Rosemary's suggestion to protect Doc Pittman, even though the doctor himself didn't believe he deserved it.

Zak was waiting at the Dew Drop when she arrived ten minutes early. She pulled a paper bag from her purse and set it on the table in front of him.

"I have a confession to make. I took these from my aunt's bedroom before you and Nadine did your search."

"What?" He peeked inside the bag. "Why'd you do that?"

"I needed to figure out some answers for myself before Sherlock got on the case." She waved a hand at Mari and gestured that she wanted a beer. Mari nodded and moved briskly to the bar.

Tiff sank into her chair and felt some of the tension leave her neck and shoulders. "Thank God nothing ever changes with you, Zak. I've had way too many surprises lately."

"Things change with me." He gave a second thought. "Well. Things *might* change with me. One day."

"I'm just glad today isn't that day." She smiled and thanked Mari as she set the glass of draft on the table. Tiff took a long, refreshing drink, while Zak studied the labels on the plastic vials in the bag.

"These all have Marsha's name on them. And they come from different pharmacies. Was she drugging your mother?"

"We think so."

"May I ask why?"

"Actually, I'm not totally sure. But I think it has something to do with some babies my aunt swapped more than thirty years ago."

"What the hell?"

"I have a lot to tell you."

Tiff filled him in on the family-approved version of events that had led Justin and Casey to be raised by the "wrong" families. She confessed her mixed feelings about it all. In her heart Casey was her "real" brother. She didn't know if she could ever feel as close to Justin.

"And speaking of Justin, it turns out I'm a perfect match for a stem-cell transplant."

"That's how you figured out about the baby swap?"

She nodded.

"It's an incredible story. Your aunt sure was a dark horse." He went quiet. Frowned. "I wonder if this has anything to do with the conversation Gwen overheard between her and Lacy."

"How could that be?"

"Hang on," Zak said. "I'm going to call Gwen."

✕

ZAK WAS DOWN to the last fry on his plate when Gwen Lange came into the Dew Drop, arm-in-arm with Rusty. Gwen was wearing heavy black boots, floral stockings and a bright red dress. She certainly made a statement.

Tiff smiled and waved hello. Zak stood and pulled out chairs for them.

"What the hell is this about?" Rusty asked.

"Beer's on me." Zak had ordered another pitcher and extra glasses. "I need to talk to Gwen about that conversation she overheard between Marsha and Lacy."

"I wondered if that was what you wanted," Gwen said. "I've been thinking about that today, too." She turned to

Tiff. "Sorry about your aunt."

"Yeah, it must be rough for you and your mom," Rusty added.

Tiff acknowledged their words with a nod. Then she turned to Zak with a silent plea and he knew she wanted him to redirect the discussion.

"You guys have heard about what Marsha did?" Zak asked.

Gwen nodded. "Dr. Pittman called Farrah and me into his office today. Told us the clinic is closing permanently. Then he told us how Marsha confessed to switching babies all those years ago. He feels responsible—that's why he's giving up his practice."

"Which kind of sucks because now my girl is out of a job." Rusty put his arm around Gwen and gave her a squeeze.

"The thing is," Gwen continued, "when he said that I remembered what I'd heard Lacy say to Marsha. At the time it seemed trivial." She turned to Tiff. "But now that I know Justin was really your brother..."

"What did Lacy say?" Tiff prompted, leaned forward in her chair.

"Lacy said the older he got, the more Justin looked like Irving Masterson than his own father."

In that instant Zak knew he'd been right. Lacy hadn't died of natural causes. Maybe Lacy's observation had been innocently meant, but Marsha wasn't willing to take the chance that the older woman had guessed her secret. She told Lacy she was getting a special vitamin K shot to promote her good health. Then injected the slow-acting insulin, instead.

"Gwen, when did you last inventory the drugs on hand at the clinic?"

"Since we're closing permanently, I did that this afternoon."

"Is any slow-acting insulin missing or unaccounted for?"

She drew back from the table and looked at him as if he'd conjured a rabbit from a hat. "How did you know? I thought I was going crazy. I've never had an error in my inventory numbers before."

✕

Thursday, December 14

THE NEXT MORNING Zak sat anxiously at his desk waiting for the sheriff to show up. First Nadine arrived, then Butterfield. They filled their coffee mugs and went to their desks. There were a lot of reports to write up, evidence to file, in the wake of Marsha Holmes's suicide.

His mind was on other matters, though. He'd cut his night at the Dew Drop short after his conversation with Gwen. At home he'd spent hours writing in his notebook and thinking. Once he was clear on what he needed to do he'd tried to figure out a way to make the sheriff feel as if he was the one who had done all the work.

But in the end Zak decided he'd had enough of that. These were his theories and he was going to follow up on them.

Finally, at eight-thirty, Ford arrived. Zak got up from his desk. "I'm going out at nine for a few hours."

Ford looked confused. He took off his coat, hung it on the rack, then poured a coffee. "Is that so? And who'll be watching the phones and doing your job while you're out?"

Zak noticed Butterfield and Nadine had stopped what they were doing to listen. He ignored the question. "I've got an appointment at the Lazy S. I'm going to sit down with the family and explain how Lacy died. I've also got a good theory for where Nikki's gone and what she's doing. I can share that with you now if you'd like."

The sheriff scratched the top of his head. "No one needs to explain how Lacy died. She had a heart attack in her own goddamn bed."

"I don't think so, sir. I know it appeared that way. But I've heard things and seen things that lead me to a different conclusion."

"What, are you a deputy now?"

"These were off-duty observations as a private citizen."

The sheriff shook his head. "It's too early in the morning for these games, Waller. What's your theory about Nikki Stillman?"

It was time to set aside his promise to Luke and tell the entire story.

"I believe the night Nikki went missing, she came home from the bar and found a letter from a bank to her father, warning that a loan of over a million dollars was about to be called. Rather than have her family sell off land to a developer to cover the loan, she took her grandmother's Charlie Russell painting to Great Falls to see what price she could get for it. There's an art gallery there that specializes in the western masters."

"So she's an art thief?"

"Not a thief. I'm betting Lacy left the painting to her in her will. Nikki won't be able to sell the painting until the estate clears probate. But if she can convince her family they have more than a million dollars coming to them, her family won't need to sell those fifty acres to that developer."

The sheriff worked his jaw forward and backward, like a bulldog gnawing on a bone. Zak could tell he didn't want to ask any more questions, but eventually he gave up trying to figure it out on his own. "Why didn't she tell her family what she was up to?"

"She was too angry. The family was squabbling instead of respecting her grandmother's memory."

"Huh." The sheriff shrugged. "Well, we told the family Nikki was in Great Falls. And we were right. You want to go color in the details with the family that's okay with me."

Fine. He'd known Ford would find a way to spin the story so he would look good. Zak went to get his jacket.

The sheriff waited until he was almost out the door before speaking again. "So what's your theory about Lacy?"

Zak glanced at his watch. "I don't have time to explain now, but you're welcome to come to the Lazy S with me while I lay out the entire story."

"I got better things to do with my time than watch you make a fool of yourself. Maybe I'll put out an ad for a dispatcher who actually stays in the office and does their job."

Zak ignored the threat. He'd known the sheriff would refuse his offer. Ford didn't care about Lacy, or the truth. He just didn't want to look bad in front of the Stillmans. If his "crazy" theory turned out to be true, Ford would find some way to take the credit.

He went to the door and pulled it open. The last thing he saw on his way out the door was Nadine. She was grinning and giving him a thumbs-up.

Chapter Twenty

VANESSA STILLMAN OPENED the door to Lacy's house when Zak arrived. Unusually for her, her face was makeup-free and her hair was in a simple ponytail. She was wearing jeans and a blue sweater. Interestingly, the simple outfit only made her natural beauty more apparent.

But for once, he could tell, Vanessa wasn't thinking about her appearance.

"The family's in the living room." She took his coat and waved him inside.

Clayton and Eugene were in the leather armchairs that flanked the fireplace. Luke and Tom sat at either end of a long sofa, and Em was standing by the window, looking out at the snow-covered peaks of the Bitterroot Mountains. Worry and fatigue hung in the room with them.

"Any word from Nikki?" Clayton was the first to ask the question they were all thinking.

"No, but she'll be home soon." He'd called the gallery on his way over and had been told that yes, a Nikki Stillman had been negotiating a transaction with the gallery. They'd reached a conclusion yesterday afternoon, at which time she'd said she had to go as she had a long drive ahead of her.

"Are you sure?" Clayton looked as if he was almost afraid to hope too much.

"Yes. She left Great Falls yesterday. I'm quite confident she was heading here."

"Thank God." Vanessa went to perch on her husband's chair. Clayton took her hand and squeezed it between both of his.

"Any idea what she's been up to?" Luke asked.

"I have a theory," Zak began. "She may have taken Lacy's Charlie Russell to Wrangler's Art Gallery. They specialize in the old western masters."

"I wondered what had happened to Mom's painting."

Eugene looked at the empty space above the mantel, the space Zak had seen as well several days ago when he'd let himself into the house.

"Is it valuable?" Clayton asked.

Zak looked at all the blank faces. Apparently none of them appreciated the quality of the art Lacy had invested in.

"I'm no expert," he said. "But from what I've seen on the Internet, I'd guess well over a million dollars."

The brothers looked at each other with wide eyes. Zak could see the gears working in their brains. He was about to explain further, when the front door opened and a cold draft of air snaked through the room.

Nikki appeared in the arched opening, wearing her parka and Sorel boots. Her expression was a mixture of anger and triumph. She held a piece of paper in the air. "I hope you haven't signed the agreement to sell the land. I've found another way to get the money.

"Nikki!" Her mother ran to her and threw her arms around her. After a few seconds, Nikki returned the embrace.

"We've been so worried. Where were you? Is Zak right—were you trying to sell your grandmother's picture?"

"I'm fine, Mom. I just needed to get away. Grandma's dead and all anyone around here cared about was selling a chunk of the land she loved so much."

A guilty silence settled over the room.

Nikki handed the piece of paper to her father. "I got this appraisal certificate from a gallery in Great Falls. The owner of the gallery was on holiday when I first got there. I had to wait for him to return. But he came back yesterday and he's definitely interested in buying it. I hate to sell the painting Grandma loved so much, but it's better than selling her land."

Her father studied the certificate. "What made you think we needed this much money?"

"I saw the notice from the bank, Dad. I know you owe over a million dollars."

"You owe a million dollars, Clayton?" Em's face was pale. "I hope you didn't use shares in the ranch for collateral."

"My brother and I both owe that money," Eugene confessed. "Clayton and I had to borrow a year ago to cover an operating shortfall and to buy some of the equipment Mom kept insisting we didn't need."

He turned to Nikki. "Your grandma was a woman of her era. She was a fine rancher fifty years ago, but you can't make a living these days without modern equipment. Your dad and I did what needed to be done. And yes, Em, we used our shares in the ranch for collateral. Unfortunately the ranch hasn't generated the revenue we projected the last couple of years."

"I had no idea that painting of Mom's was worth so much money." Clayton looked at his daughter with wonder. "How did you know?"

"Grandma and I used to visit art galleries when we went on road trips. I was with her the day she bought it."

"Why didn't you, at least, send us a text message to let us know where you were and that you were okay?" her mother asked. "We didn't know if you were dead or alive."

Nikki looked stricken. "It didn't occur to me that you would be so worried. I guess I wasn't thinking straight. And I was mad that no one else was sad about Grandma being gone."

"We are sad," her father said gently. "I sure as hell am, anyway. Your grandmother was one-of-a-kind. She was old, but I wasn't ready for her to go. I was sure she'd be around until she was a hundred, at least."

"She might have been," Zak said. He needed to say his piece here, then leave and let the family deal with their private affairs. "I believe Lacy would still be with us if not for something she said to Marsha Holmes during her checkup the day before she died."

Everyone turned to him with puzzled expressions.

"Excuse me while I backtrack a minute." He turned to Nikki. "You've missed some big news while you're away. Marsha Holmes committed suicide four days ago. She'd been protecting a big secret for a long time, and suddenly the truth was out. It was this same secret your grandmother almost exposed three weeks earlier."

"You're talking about the baby swapping?" Em asked.

Zak nodded.

"I heard about it in town yesterday." Em shook her head. "It was so crazy, I couldn't believe it." She turned to Nikki. "Justin Pittman and Casey Masterson were born on the same day in the clinic in Lost Trail over thirty years ago. Marsha was there at the time and she switched the babies. She gave the sickly baby to her sister, and the healthy one to the Pittmans."

Nikki stared in wonder. "Are you saying Justin should have been a Masterson?"

"That's right," Zak confirmed. "To get back to your grandmother...according to Gwen Lange, who's the receptionist at the clinic, Lacy and Marsha spent a lot of time chatting during her appointment. Gwen overheard your grandmother comment on how strange it was that the older Justin got the less he looked like his own father and the more he resembled Irving Masterson."

"She said that?" Em looked shocked. "Do you think she guessed the truth?"

"Maybe she'd become suspicious. Lacy was sharp as a tack, right to the end."

"So you're suggesting Marsha somehow had a hand in her death?" Eugene asked.

"I can't prove any of this," Zak was quick to point out. "And I'm speaking to you as a private citizen, not an employee of the sheriff's department. But I strongly suspect Marsha convinced your grandmother she was giving her a special vitamin K shot that would improve her health, when in actual fact she gave her a dose of slow-acting insulin."

"But that's crazy!" Eugene got up from his chair and began to pace.

"Marsha was a desperate woman. So desperate that once her crime was exposed, almost a month later, she killed herself."

"But what would the insulin have done?" Luke had been listening without comment to this point. Zak was sorry for ambushing his friend this way. But it was only fair that the entire family hear this news together.

"For a non-diabetic person like your grandmother, as the slow-acting insulin was gradually absorbed into her body she would have gone into a hypoglycemic coma, and then eventually died. The process would have taken anywhere from four to six hours. Her appointment was the last one of the day at the clinic, so it was a safe gamble on Marsha's part that Lacy would be at home alone and probably in bed when the full effect hit her."

"The tiredness must have hit her suddenly. That's why she wasn't in her nightgown," Clayton said.

"Yes. The evening of the wake, I took a look in Lacy's bedroom. I found a small bandage in her bed. I had it tested and the speck of blood on it belonged to Lacy. I believe Marsha affixed it after the insulin shot."

If it had still been on her body, maybe Dr. Pittman would have investigated. Then again, maybe not.

"Can you prove any of this?" Tom asked. "Can we have the body exhumed and get an autopsy?"

"Unfortunately no. Since insulin is a natural substance, it wouldn't show up in a toxicology report."

"But you believe this is what happened?" Eugene said.

"I do. I could be wrong. But given the things we're learning about Marsha Holmes, she had motive, opportunity and means to murder Lacy. And she was certainly unscrupulous enough to do it. Then last night, when Gwen Lange told me a vial of slow-acting insulin was missing at the clinic, I figured it couldn't be a coincidence."

There was a long silence as the family digested this.

"I think you're right," Nikki said softly. "Grandma was old, but she wasn't ready to die."

"I loved Lacy like she was my own mother," Em said. "But she did like to stick her nose in other people's business.

If only she'd kept her thoughts about Justin to herself."

Zak stayed a bit longer to answer questions. When it was time to leave, he realized he'd forgotten one thing. "Nikki, the night you took off, did you take one of the leftover cans of barn red paint with you?"

A guilty flush colored her cheeks. "It was childish I know. But like I said, I was so damn mad."

"What's this about?" Vanessa asked. The rest of the family looked puzzled as well.

Zak dismissed the question with a wave of his hand. He wasn't going to rat Nikki out. Not to her family and definitely not to old Cora.

"Thanks for everything Zak. It's good to know the truth. You've got a smart head on your shoulders." Eugene clapped him on the back.

"It's about time you were promoted to deputy don't you think, son?" Clayton asked.

"Hell, why stop there?" Eugene said. "This county could use a shake-up. You should run for sheriff."

TIFF DID A lot of thinking on Thursday. She read the material she'd been given several times and checked the facts with some online research as well. When she had her mind made up she told her mother her decision.

"If it feels right to you, then I support you."

"Thanks, Mom." She called Justin next. "This is going to sound strange, but I'd like to talk to you and I was wondering if you'd meet me at the cemetery?"

"I can be there in thirty minutes."

Tiff put on the warm coat and boots she'd ordered online. "I'll be back in time for dinner," she told her mother, before stepping outside.

The sun had already dipped behind the field of balsam pines in the west. The color of the sky had settled into layers, like a blueberry parfait. Pinkish on the bottom, then a layer of gray, followed by a dark turquoise.

There was absolutely no wind and the world felt peacefully silent. She glanced toward the barn. All was quiet. The workers were home with their families. Kenny would be making his dinner in the cabin.

She drove to town slowly, she had plenty of time. She could still change her mind, it wasn't too late, but she knew she wouldn't.

The cemetery was at the end of Winding Down Way, across from a row of small bungalows that had been built in the nineteen fifties. Cora Christensen lived in the one on the corner, and Tiff had mixed feelings as she looked at the neat little house, curtains drawn tightly on the front windows.

The years when she'd had Miss Christensen as a teacher, she'd really liked her. She'd heard others complain she was teacher's pet, but until recently, she hadn't thought much of it, or considered the potential harm a teacher could inflict by constantly putting one child down, comparing them to another, and finding them wanting.

Miss Christensen wasn't responsible for the way her aunt had turned out. But her style of teaching had added to the hatred and envy Marsha felt for her sister.

Tiff locked her car and removed her flashlight from the glove box. This had been her first stop when she'd come home in October. She'd wanted to spend a quiet moment at the graves of her father and brother, to remember them and grieve for them.

Now she needed to see them again. And she thought Justin did, too.

She'd only gone through the gate when Justin drove up. She waited for him to get out of his car and join her. Like her he was wearing a heavy parka and serious boots. This wasn't weather to play around with.

"Hey, how are you doing?" she asked.

"Everything's still sinking in. It's a lot to process."

They were standing under a streetlamp and she had a clear view of his face. "You have Mom's eyes." As did she. "I never noticed that before."

"I always wondered why I had blue eyes when my father's were hazel and Mom's brown."

"I keep thinking of things too. Like I always thought it was strange Casey was so small when Dad was quite tall—like you. I figured it was because of his heart."

But it had been simple genetics. Both Clark and Franny

were shorter than her parents.

Tiff started walking and Justin fell in beside her. It was cool that he hadn't asked why they were meeting here. After a few minutes, she took a side path. "Dad's grave is over here."

"Do you mind if we stop at Mom—Franny's first?" Justin pointed out a beautiful, white marble grave marker with a heavy shroud of snow. "In the summer there are rose bushes. Dad visits every few weeks to look after them."

"He must have really loved her."

Justin nodded, his gaze fixed on the tombstone. After a few moments of silence he said, "I'm always going to think of her as my mother. Even though she wasn't."

"And Casey will always be my brother."

Justin took a deep breath, then looked at her. "Right. Show me where he's buried? I assume it's near your father?"

"This way." She turned left and walked about twenty yards before she found the familiar double plot. She played her light on the engraved granite so he could read the words. Reached out to touch the inscription: *Irving Masterson, beloved husband and father.*

"Do you have any memories of him when he was alive?" she asked.

"I've been thinking about that a lot. My clearest memory is of him giving us all—you, Casey and me—a ride in the hay wagon. It was just a few days before Christmas. There were so many lights on the trees; it was magical. Afterward we had cocoa around the fire pit. And cookies."

"I remember that, too." She'd gone on so many hayrides with her father and Casey. But just that once with Justin. She couldn't help but think of how much he'd missed out on. "But Dr. Pittman was a good father, too, right?"

Justin hesitated a long while. "He was. In many ways. That's what's hardest for me."

"Because you're angry. But you still love him."

"Exactly."

"I hope the anger goes away eventually. My aunt was a toxic person. She's hurt a lot of people over the years. More than any of us will ever know, I'll bet. Last night Zak told me he thinks she killed Lacy with a dose of insulin because Lacy noticed how much you looked like my dad."

"No. That's—crazy."

"That's the point. My aunt *was* crazy."

"Does Zak have proof?"

"He says it's all circumstantial evidence. But he's pretty confident. I trust Zak. He has good instincts for crime."

"Yeah. That's what my dad thinks, too."

Tiff noticed Justin had called his father 'dad' without even noticing this time. A good sign.

"Let's go," Justin said. "It's insanely cold out here."

"One more thing." She grabbed him by the arm and stopped him from walking away. "About the stem-cell transplant. I want to do it."

He studied her eyes. "I want you to be sure, Tiff. You

don't have to. They might find a donor for me from the national registry."

"But the transplant has a better chance of being successful if it comes from a blood relative."

"That's true, but you shouldn't feel obligated."

"If our positions were reversed, you'd do it for me."

"I'd like to think so. But you can't know that for sure."

"Oh, yes I can...Brother."

Chapter Twenty-One

Sunday, December 24

ON THE MORNING of Christmas Eve Tiff's mother said to her, "Let's go for a drive."

A month ago, Rosemary would never have suggested such a thing. But she'd progressed a lot the past two weeks. Tiff was game. She went to get her purse and her coat.

"Want to drive?" she teased her mom.

Rosemary shuddered. "I can't remember the last time I was behind the wheel of a vehicle. I do want to start driving again, but not in snowy, winter conditions."

It hurt to think how much of her life Rosemary had lost in a druggy haze. So Tiff did her best not to. She didn't want to miss the future by nursing bitterness about the past.

"Where should we go?" she asked, when they were both buckled in.

"Let's drive up to the ski hill. We can have a burger and a beer for lunch."

"Sure." Her mother had been weaned off all her drugs and had been given the all-clear by her new doctor. Anything was possible now, Tiff liked to think. Maybe she'd even talk her mom into skiing again in the New Year.

As she drove down the lane she passed Kenny in his truck. He gave a wave as he headed in the opposite direction. He was going shopping in Missoula today, he'd told her.

The farm was closed for the season, they'd sold almost their entire inventory of trees. The ones that were left would be ground into chips and used as compost or to line pathways.

The county plow had been through that morning, so the roads were clear, at least for now. Flurries were forecast for later that evening, but there shouldn't be enough accumulation to cause problems. Good news for holiday travelers.

Tiff set the radio to a station playing Christmas carols, then turned it off when she caught the refrain for "Silver Bells." That had been one of Aunt Marsha's favorites. She'd hummed it when they were decorating the tree earlier that month.

Back when life had seemed so normal.

Tiff wondered if there would ever come a time when she and her mother could speak of Marsha without feeling overwhelmed with pain and anger. Would they ever be able to remember the good times? But how could they, when so much of their lives had been built on Marsha's deceit?

Once when Tiff had been avoiding a root canal, she'd managed to chew on just one side of her mouth for several months. That's what Marsha was to them now. Something rotten, to be avoided at all costs.

A sign ahead said *LOST TRAIL SKI RESORT, 8 MI.* Tiff followed the arrow, turning right onto a mountain road only just wide enough for two cars to pass. Spruce and pine grew tall on the road to their left, boughs lightly sprinkled with snow that gleamed in the late morning sunshine.

The road fell off sharply to the right, without so much as a concrete curb or wooden posts as a barrier. Tiff drove slowly, and concentrated fully. It wasn't until they were halfway to the ski hill and she saw the white cross that she realized why her mother had wanted to come here.

"Stop the car."

"Mom, I can't. What if another vehicle comes along?"

Her mother pointed ahead. "There's a turnout up there. Should be room for you to pull over."

Tiff examined her mother's face. She looked serious, but calm. "Are you sure?"

Gaze focused on the cross, her mother nodded.

Tiff inched the car forward. Sure enough there was a turnout area thirty yards or so beyond the cross. She tucked her vehicle into the spot and put it into Park.

"Now what?" Tiff asked.

Her mother swallowed, then released her seat belt and got out of the car.

Tiff did not have a good feeling about this, but she followed.

Outside the chickadees and nuthatches were cheerfully passing secret codes to each other, as they flitted from tree to tree. Sunlight fell on her mother as she stood at the far edge of the road. She peered down the mountain ledge where her husband had lost his life.

Sixteen years ago.

Two months after Casey's death.

"I remember," her mother said.

Tiff felt a little girl's fear at those words. Her mother had never talked about the accident before. She'd been in a coma for several days after. When she'd finally regained consciousness she hadn't been the same mother. The change had been put down to a combination of brain injury, shock and grief.

At what point had Marsha started adding her cocktail of drugs to the mix? They would never know for sure, but Tiff suspected it was a long time ago. Those ritual mugs of herbal tea had been part of her mother's routine for as long as Tiff could recall.

"What do you remember, Mom?"

"We'd gone skiing for the day, Marsha, Irv and myself. Irv and I were still mourning and didn't want to go. But Marsha convinced us. She'd said the fresh air and exercise would be good for us."

Tiff nodded. It had been a school day, otherwise she would have gone too.

"I remember ski conditions were excellent that day, not that I cared. I went through the motions of skiing but I didn't go a minute without thinking about Casey. I think Irv enjoyed the skiing though. I hope he did."

That had been her father's last day on earth. Tiff hoped so too.

"We were on our way home and Irv was driving. He was talking about Casey. We'd seen a boy about the same age as Casey when we were leaving the hill and that started Irv thinking."

Tiff shoved her hands into her pockets. The bitter cold didn't seem to affect her mother. She was totally preoccupied with the memories of that long ago day.

"Irv started ranting about the odds of Casey having a heart defect when there was no history of it on either side of the family. And yet Dr. Pittman, whose wife had died because of heart problems, gave birth to a perfectly healthy son on the exact same day."

The world around Tiff disappeared in that instant. All she could see was her mother. "He knew. Dad *knew.* Are you certain you're remembering correctly?"

Rosemary wrapped her arms around her middle and slowly nodded. "I had a glimmer of a memory this morning. Then when I saw this place—it all came back to me. I remember Irv saying that. Then Marsha began arguing with him, she was *yelling.* And then she reached over from the back seat and shook Irving's shoulder *hard.* And that's when it all goes black. We must have run off the road then."

She was trembling now. Tiff moved closer and put her arms around her mom. "Marsha caused the accident."

"Yes."

It would have been easy to discount her mother's story. It had been a long time ago. Why was she only remembering now? But when Tiff thought about all Marsha had done to them, she felt certain her mother was right.

"Marsha was afraid once my brain injury healed I'd remember. That's why she kept me drugged."

Tiff nodded. "The accident never made sense to me. Dad was such a good driver. And he knew these roads so well." The story about him avoiding a deer—Marsha had made that up. And there'd been no one to contradict her.

"Marsha killed him. She stole my child from me and she killed my husband."

Tiff held her mother tighter. What words could she say? There were none.

✕

TIFF DROVE HER mother home. In the kitchen they sat at the island and let it all sink in.

"I'm not sure why that memory came back today of all days," her mother said.

"Maybe your subconscious knew you were finally strong enough to remember."

"Am I? Strong enough?"

"You are, Mom. Want me to make some tea?"

"Marsha always made me tea. I don't want to ever drink it again."

Tiff opened the cabinet where Marsha had stored the herbal teas. Inside almost a dozen assorted boxes were stacked neatly. Chamomile, licorice root, peppermint, and more. She pulled them out and tossed them all into the trash.

Her mother clapped. "Good riddance. I swear I'll never drink a cup of herbal tea again. Now put on a pot of coffee and I'll make us some fried egg sandwiches for lunch."

Tiff started to cry as a huge wave of relief washed over her. Her mother sounded strong, confident.

She sounded like the mother who had called her out for leaving wet towels on the floor. The mother who had scolded her to finish her homework. The mother who had helped her put together a poster for her fourth grade science project.

Tiff had been so afraid her mom would backslide after what she'd remembered today. That she would want to go to bed, that she'd check out, and disappear on her again.

Her real, true mother had been gone for so long. But she was back now.

"What's the matter, honey?" Rosemary brushed a tear from Tiff's cheek.

"I've missed you. So much." She threw her arms around her mother's neck the way she'd done as a child and she let the tears come. Her mother cried too, and then soothed.

"Marsha stole so much from me. From both of us. But we've got each other. We're going to be okay."

✕

AT FIVE O'CLOCK Tiff went to Kenny's with an invitation. "Mom wants to know if you'll join us for dinner. You're welcome to come to church with us after, and then the community potluck at the Lazy S."

"And I thought this was going to be a quiet Christmas." He stepped back. "Come in for a minute."

The cottage had never looked cozier. A crackling fire, Spade sleeping by the hearth, and a tall, spindly tree in one corner, garnished with hundreds of tiny white lights.

"You decorated for Christmas." She clasped her hands together. "I love Charlie Brown trees."

Kenny fingered a branch of the scrawny Douglas fir. "I had to save this one from the wood chipper."

"It's beautiful." Tiff turned from the tree to him. Fate had been kind when it sent this man to Raven Farms. "I haven't properly thanked you for saving my mom and me."

"I don't need more thanks. But there is an outstanding dinner invitation on the table."

He caught her gaze and held it. The cabin seemed to grow warmer with each second. Slowly Tiff walked toward him and he met her halfway.

"When?"

"Are you free New Year's Eve? I thought I'd book a restaurant…and a hotel…in Missoula for the night."

The slow burn between them flared. His eyes were magnets, pulling her closer.

She didn't need to worry about her mother. Sybil would make sure she got to Eugene and Em's annual party. A night of escape and romance would be the perfect end to a most imperfect year.

"I'm in."

TIFF WASN'T OVERLY religious, but the Christmas Eve service that night was a comfort and a tonic. As the choir sang "Silent Night," she could almost feel the pieces of her heart coming together and melding into a whole. There would always be scars, some of them deep and ugly, but she wasn't broken. Not anymore.

When the service was over, Kenny squeezed her hand. She saw compassion and understanding in his eyes when he smiled. Had he felt it too, that wave of benediction washing over them?

During dinner she and her mom had filled him in on the version of events her mother remembered from the day of the car accident.

Tiff had asked Kenny if he thought it possible for a memory to suddenly return, sixteen years after a traumatic event.

He'd said someone who didn't know the facts of the case or the people involved might be skeptical. But he was inclined to believe her mother.

She'd loved him for saying that. She was beginning to think she loved him, period.

✕

LATER IT FELT good to be among friends and neighbors at Lacy's old house. Tiff moved through the crowd with her mother by her side. Rosemary was still a bit uncomfortable in a crowd.

Mulled wine simmered on the stove and every inch of the dining room table was covered with food, from baked ham, to hot potato salad, green beans, salads. Somehow Em made room for her mother's platter of cookies.

"Here you are." Sybil came up to them wearing a vintage Christmas sweater. Her red-and-white eyeglass frames looked like twisted candy canes. "Rosemary, I've been dying for a piece of your shortbread. It won't feel like Christmas until I have some."

"Try this." Rosemary handed her a pretty snowflake-shaped cookie. "I hope you like it. I have a tin in the car, just for you."

"Lucky me."

"We're the lucky ones." Impulsively Tiff gave her a big hug. "You've been such a good friend to Mom all these years."

"I wish I'd figured out what Marsha was up to and put a

stop to it years ago. I never did care for the woman, but I still find it hard to believe she was capable of so much evil."

"I have more to tell you," Rosemary said. "I remembered something about Irv's accident today..."

"Really?"

As the two women moved toward a quiet corner to talk, Tiff looked around for Kenny. She couldn't see him anywhere. Dr. Pittman and Justin must have reached a truce because they were engaged in a lively debate about land management with Clayton and Eugene. Next to them Debbie-Ann and Farrah Saddler were chatting about their plans for Christmas Day.

Tiff slipped through the crowd and moved closer to the Christmas tree. Geneva and Ashley were both asleep on the floor. Someone had drawn a hand-knitted blanket over them. She inched past them to a cushioned seat built into a bay window. It was too dark to see the view outside, but she knew the Bitterroots were out there, stalwart guardians of the west.

"So this is Christmas in Lost Trail." Kenny joined her, handed her a mug of mulled wine.

"Do you like it?"

"It has a crazy appeal, yes." He sipped the wine, then made a face.

"Not a mulled wine fan?"

"I like the *idea.* But not the taste so much."

Nikki spotted them and headed over with a tray of sausage rolls. "Grandma would be so happy if she could see everyone gathered here."

"The house looks beautiful. Who decorated it for Christmas?"

"We all did. We wanted to have one, last family bash here before Miss Christensen turns the place into an Airbnb."

"She wouldn't?" Tiff was appalled.

"That's the rumor. Excuse me, I have to keep passing this around. Aunt Em will be annoyed if these aren't all eaten while they're warm. She spent hours making them today."

Tiff nibbled on the pastry, watching as Kenny finished his in one bite. From the corner of her eye she spotted Zak entering the living room with Nadine Black. "I wonder if they're here together…?"

Kenny followed her gaze. "Hard to say. They seem pretty enthralled with that painting over the fireplace."

"It's a Charlie Russell." When Kenny didn't look impressed she added, "Worth about a million and a half."

Kenny whistled.

Tiff caught Zak's eye and waved for him to join them.

Kenny took a second, longer look at the painting. "It's a nice picture. Better than some of the abstract mash-ups I remember seeing on a field trip we took in grade school. But I can't imagine paying that much for it."

"Fortunately you don't have to." Zak joined them, a plate of sausage rolls in one hand, a beer in the other.

"There's a gallery in Great Falls that's happy to fork over the money."

"I'm with Kenny." Nadine stepped up alongside Zak, also with plate and beer in hand. "I think it's a crazy amount to pay for a painting. You could buy a small ranch for less."

"You interested in a small ranch?" Tiff asked.

"Hell yes."

"She just bought one," Zak said.

"Only ten acres. But it's a start." Nadine looked over-the-moon excited.

Tiff and Kenny both congratulated her, then Tiff grabbed the cuff of Zak's shirt-sleeve.

"Zak. I've been dying to tell you something. My mom remembered something important today."

Zak and Nadine listened raptly as she relayed the drive with her mother to the ski hill, their stop at the commemorative white cross, and her mother's sudden recall of what had happened the day of her father's accident. When she finished, Nadine shook her head grimly and turned to Zak.

"I told you there was something suspicious about that accident."

"Really?" Nadine had been living here less than a year. "The accident happened over sixteen years ago. How did you know about it?"

"I told her," Zak said. "When she first started working with us, I filled her in on some of your family history. Casey's death. Your dad's crash. She wanted me to pull out all the accident reports. She couldn't believe his death was an accident."

"You were right," Tiff said. "It wasn't an accident at all."

"Though maybe it would have been easier for you and your mom if it had been," Nadine said.

"The truth has been buried in Mom's subconscious for a long time. Now that it's out, she can begin to heal."

Tiff glanced over at Justin. He looked so healthy now. But there was a long road ahead of him before he could be cancer-free. She was going to be there to help him with that. Maybe along the way they would capture some of the feelings that a brother and sister should have for one another.

"Marsha had a lot to answer for," Kenny said. "She took the easy way out by killing herself."

"This afternoon Mom and I wrote a letter to her. We thought it would be cathartic to lay out in writing every wrong she'd done to us, every crime, every hurtful thing. Then we burned the letter because we knew that unless we put the bitterness behind us, even in death she would win."

THE CROWD WAS thinning out, it was time to leave. Zak wasn't quite ready, though. He'd been looking everywhere for mistletoe. You'd think a traditional family like the Stillmans would hang some somewhere. He was tired of mysteries and puzzles and death. It was time for mulled wine and presents and kisses.

"What's that?" Nadine pointed to a ball of greenery by the back door. Then she laughed. She knew exactly what it was.

He put his hand to her waist and guided her to the spot. Then he turned to face her.

"Yesterday I told Ford I wanted to be a deputy."

"Seriously?" She punched his shoulder lightly. "Way to go. What did he say?"

"He's going to consider it."

"That's awesome. You and me are going to run this town one day, Waller."

He laughed. He loved her confidence, her boldness, her drive.

"One step at a time," he said. And then he kissed her.

The End

Bitter Root Mystery Series

On the surface Lost Trail, Montana is a picture-perfect western town offering beautiful mountain scenery and a simple way of life revolving around the local ranches as well as a nearby ski resort. But thirty-year old Tiff Masterson and her former school-chum Zak Waller—dispatcher at the local Sheriff's office—know there is darkness in this town, too, an evil with roots that neither of them fully understand.

Book 1: Bitter Roots

Book 2: Bitter Truth

Book 3: Bitter Sweet

Available now at your favorite online retailer!

About the Author

USA Today Bestselling author C. J. Carmichael has written over 50 novels with more than three million copies in print. She has been nominated for the *RT Bookclub's* Career Achievement in Romantic Suspense award, and is a three time nominee for the *Romance Writers of America* RITA Award.

Visit C.J.'s website at CJCarmichael.com.

Thank you for reading

Bitter Truth

If you enjoyed this book, you can find more from all our great authors at TulePublishing.com, or from your favorite online retailer.

Made in the USA
Monee, IL
26 April 2022